RUNAWAY MAN

Also by David Handler

RUNAWAY MAN

A Mystery

DAVID HANDLER

THOMAS DUNNE BOOKS
ST. MARTIN'S MINOTAUR
NEW YORK

A THOMAS DUNNE BOOK FOR MINOTAUR BOOKS.
An imprint of St. Martin's Publishing Group.

RUNAWAY MAN. Copyright © 2013 by David Handler. All rights reserved. Printed in the United States of America. For information, address St. Martin's Press, 175 Fifth Avenue, New York, N.Y. 10010.

www.thomasdunnebooks.com
www.minotaurbooks.com

Library of Congress Cataloging-in-Publication Data

Handler, David, 1952–
    Runaway man : a mystery / David Handler. — First edition.
        pages cm
    "A Thomas Dunne Book."
    ISBN 978-1-250-01162-6 (hardcover)
    ISBN 978-1-250-02047-5 (e-book)
  1. Private investigators—New York—Fiction.   2. Family-owned business enterprises—Fiction.   3. Murder—Investigation—Fiction.   4. New York (N.Y.)—Fiction.   I. Title.
    PS3558.A4637R86 2013
    813'.54—dc23

                                                          2013011922

Minotaur books may be purchased for educational, business, or promotional use. For information on bulk purchases, please contact Macmillan Corporate and Premium Sales Department at 1-800-221-7945 extension 5442 or write specialmarkets@ macmillan.com.

First Edition: August 2013

10   9   8   7   6   5   4   3   2   1

*For David Weir, who never lost his
appreciation for how absurd we are*

RUNAWAY MAN

CHAPTER ONE

I COULDN'T STOP STARING AT MR. CLASSY GUY'S SHOES.
These were no ordinary shoes. They were gleaming cordovan wingtips that were lined with, I swear to you, mink. What's more, they were totally spotless. Even their leather soles were unscuffed. Virtually no sign of pavement wear anywhere on them. How had Mr. Classy Guy and his mink-lined shoes navigated the New York City sidewalks on a slushy, sooty January day without scuffing the soles one bit? Hell, how had he made it inside our second-floor office from his chauffeur-driven Lincoln Town Car parked at the curb outside our not-so-elegant building on our not-so-elegant corner of Broadway and West 103rd Street?

Mind you, the man was spotless all over. Polished, manicured and buffed to a rosy glow. His crinkly salt-and-pepper hair was crisply parted. His rimless spectacles gleamed. He was about sixty. No office drone either. A squash player, was my guess. He looked extremely wiry and fit inside his custom-tailored pinstriped suit. Carried his long, straight blade of a nose up, up in the air. Definitely had an aristocratic air about him. After all, he was Peter Seymour of Bates, Winslow and Seymour, the Park Avenue law firm that handled the private legal affairs of the city's A-list patrician families. The kind who've lived on Fifth Avenue for generations. The kind whose daughters come out at debutante balls. The kind who seldom come in direct personal contact with our sort. Make that never.

Yet here he was, this trusted advisor to the silk stocking district's uber-rich, seated in a straight-backed wooden chair before the boss's battered desk soaking up the full ambiance of Golden Legal Services. An experience that, on this blustery winter afternoon, meant inhaling a rich mix of No. 2 fuel oil from the ancient furnace in the basement, fried onions wafting up from Scotty's twenty-four-hour diner and the bracing aroma of acetone from Pearl's nail salon.

The boss's private office has a homey air. There's a comfortably worn leather sofa. An old Persian rug on the floor. An enormous pre-World War II Wells Fargo safe where we store our firearms, surveillance equipment and good liquor. The outer office is just two desks and some filing cabinets. We don't get many visitors. When clients want to retain us, we go to them. Peter Seymour had insisted on coming to us.

And Mr. Classy Guy was not impressed. His haughty silence told us so. He got up from his chair and strode over to the wraparound windows behind the boss's desk, staring bleakly out at our ragtag little stretch of upper Broadway. The narrow center divider with its spindly trees. The array of less-than-prosperous shops. An icy rain was falling. The forecasters thought it might turn to snow later. Pedestrians were walking extra fast, their heads down, shoulders hunched against the wind.

With a discreet snuffle of disapproval he sat back down in his chair and straightened the crease in his trousers, not that it needed it. We watched him. We waited. He'd declined coffee from Lovely Rita—and hadn't ogled her. Which is highly unusual. Rita is forty-two but still the same eye-popping redhead who'd worked nights as a lap dancer to put herself through the Rutgers computer science program. And she still does wonders filling out a turtleneck sweater and tight slacks. Hell, even gay guys check out Rita.

Not Peter Seymour. He was too busy being huffy. Apparently, he'd gotten trapped inside of our elevator for several minutes. It has a somewhat moody door.

"You should demand that your landlord fix that elevator, Mrs. Golden," he lectured the boss in his rich, burgundy baritone.

She smiled at him warmly. "Call me Abby, will you?" Pretty much everyone does, except for me. I call her Mom. "And it's no use. Our landlord is a cheap so-and-so."

Our landlord being, in fact, she. Mom took over the business and the five-story, circa 1890s building when my dad died of stomach cancer two years ago. It was my dad who'd founded Golden Legal Services. He'd always thought "legal services" sounded more professional than "private investigators." There are two rental apartments up on the third floor. Mom lives in a floor-through apartment on the fourth floor. My own floor-through is on the top floor. On a clear day I can see Amsterdam Avenue.

"I'd still be trapped in that elevator if your upstairs neighbor hadn't coaxed it into operation. An elderly lady? . . ."

Mom nodded. "That would be Mrs. Felcher."

Mrs. Felcher has lived in 3A for thirty-seven years. Mr. Felcher has lived in 3B for the exact same number of years. They're in their eighties and don't speak to each other. Long story.

"Are you aware that she goes out in public in her bathrobe and slippers, Mrs. Golden?"

"Just down to the newsstand to get the paper. And, like I said, it's Abby. If we're going to be in bed together we can use our first names, can't we, Pete?"

"It's Peter," he said stiffly.

"Now we're getting somewhere." Mom showed him her most inviting smile. "How may we help you today, Peter?"

If there's one thing Mom knows, it's how to handle men. Rita isn't the only one-time exotic dancer in the office. The two are gal pals from back when Mom enjoyed the distinction of being the only Jewish pole dancer in New York City. She danced under the name Abraxas in the highest end midtown Manhattan topless clubs. Her dream had been to dance in Broadway musicals, but she had trouble keeping her weight down. Plus her abundant assets were hard to hide. Certainly hard to hide from Meyer Golden, an NYPD homicide detective who took one look at Abraxas and it was love. When he found out Abraxas was actually Abby Kaminsky from Sheepshead Bay it was marriage. My dad started the business after he retired from the job. Mom ran the office and eventually became a licensed PI the same way I did—by amassing three years of experience as an employee and passing the New York State PI exam. She's pushing fifty but still gets honked at whenever she walks down the street. In modern day parlance she's a MILF—and if you don't know what those initials stand for I'm not going to tell you. I'll just say she's a strikingly attractive woman with a sculpted mass of black hair, huge dark eyes and major league curves. Today, she wore a two-piece garbardine suit with a white silk blouse that was artfully unbuttoned, so as to invite Seymour's eyes toward her cleavage.

Instead, his eyes were trained on the wall where my dad's framed commendations were on display. Dad became a genuine hero cop after he caught Briefcase Bob, the subway serial killer who terrorized New York City back in the early nineties. Quite a celebrity, too, after they made a movie about the case. Al Pacino played my dad, who never sought out the limelight. It found him because he was good at his job. He taught me most of what I know about it, and about people. Not a day goes by when I don't miss him. I can't imagine how Mom keeps going. But she does.

Now Seymour was peering at me as I slouched there on the sofa. I'm twenty-five but I look younger. In the world of casting agents I'm what's known as a juvenile type. I'm exactly one-quarter inch shy of five-feet-six, weigh a buck thirty-seven and am exceedingly baby faced. But I'm plenty feisty. You'll just have to take my word for that.

"I understand that you specialize in finding young people who've gone missing," he said to me dubiously.

"You understand right," Mom spoke up. "When it comes to tracking down runaways, there is no one in this city who's better than my Benji. Who are you looking for?"

"We, which is to say Bates, Winslow and Seymour, are endeavoring to settle the estate of one of our clients. An individual of considerable wealth who has passed away."

Mom reached for a yellow legal pad and a pen. "Your client's name?"

"That," he responded, "is not something you need to know."

Mom put down her pen. "So it's going to be like that, is it?"

"This case demands a great deal of discretion. Will that present a problem?"

"I don't know yet, hon. Keep talking. Not that you've said much yet."

Seymour opened his black leather briefcase, removed a manila file folder and set it before him on the desk. "Our late client has bestowed a considerable inheritance on a certain young man. He's a senior at Canterbury College." Canterbury is a small, distinguished liberal arts college in upper Manhattan. Just as hard to get into as the Ivy League. "He's an exemplary young man of twenty-one with a very promising future."

"And do we get to know *his* name?"

"Bruce Weiner."

Mom glanced over at me with a faint smile on her lips. Now we knew why Mr. Classy Guy had shlepped his WASP ass all the way uptown to the offices of Golden Legal Services.

"We're anxious to carry out our client's wishes," he continued. "But we wish to do so without involving the campus police or the NYPD. The private firm that we normally employ is not noted for its delicacy. They're liable to flood the campus with a dozen jarheads in dark glasses. Such a turn of events would not be desirable."

"Who do you usually use?"

"The Leetes Group."

Mom wrinkled her nose. The Leetes Group was the evil empire of the PI business. They'd engulfed and devoured most of the small independent operations like ours over the past decade. Had high-tech offices in practically every major city in America. And zero scruples. They would resort to honey traps, coercion, even outright blackmail. The owner, Jake Leetes, was a former NYPD chief of detectives turned high-profile entrepreneur and cable news talking head. The man was a total pub slut.

"How long has Bruce Weiner been missing?" I asked.

"He's not," Seymour answered curtly. "No missing person report has been filed. He's simply been, let us say, difficult to connect with. We've attempted to contact him at school by phone numerous times over the past two weeks. He hasn't returned our phone calls. Or responded to our letters. We sent him the last one by certified mail. He refused to sign for it. And now his roommate is claiming that Bruce left campus three days ago even though classes are in session. He has no idea where Bruce is. Or, if he does, he won't tell us. Perhaps you'll have better luck."

"What about Bruce's parents?"

"They live up near Scarsdale in a town called Willoughby. The father works on Wall Street, for Farrell and Company. The mother does volunteer work of some sort. Their particulars are in the file."

"Have you spoken to them?"

"Not directly, no. That's where you come in. We'd like you to take over from here. And when you contact them the name of Bates, Winslow and Seymour must never come up. I want to be very clear about that point. Do you understand?"

"Not really," I replied. "But yes."

Gus, our grizzled black office cat, sauntered in and jumped up onto Mom's desk. Since we work directly over a twenty-four-hour diner we have twenty-four-hour mice. Gus keeps the population in check. He walked across her papers toward Seymour, gazing at the lawyer with his urine-colored eyes. Seymour refused to acknowledge his presence there. Gus doesn't like to be ignored—so he leapt from the desk into Seymour's custom-tailored lap, hung out there for a second, then vaulted from the man's groin onto the sofa. Seymour let out a less than classy "oof" before he got busy brushing off his trousers. Gus curled up next to me, immensely pleased with himself.

"What's your client's relationship with Bruce Weiner?" Mom wanted to know. "Are we talking about a grandparent?"

"Our client is not a grandparent," Seymour replied, glaring at Gus.

"Then why has he left this young man something of considerable value?"

"I didn't say our client was a 'he.' And, again, there is no need for you to know that."

"Are his parents aware of this bequest?"

"No, they are not."

"Do they stand to gain from it?"

"Only in the sense that that their son will now be financially independent."

"Do they realize he's missing?" I asked.

"I said he left campus three days ago. I did *not* say he was missing."

Mom puffed out her cheeks with exasperation. "How about we cut the crap, Peter? Do you have reason to believe that something has happened to him?"

"No reason whatsoever. We're simply anxious to clear this matter up quickly and discreetly. As far as we know the young man has not been the victim of a crime. Or had cause to visit the campus health center. Nor has he returned home to Willoughby. He has simply disappeared." Seymour gazed down his long nose at me. "Can you find him?"

"Oh, I can find him. And when I do?"

"Have him contact us so we that can fulfill our legal obligation to our client."

"What if he's not interested?"

"He's always free to donate the money to a worthy cause."

"No, I mean what if he doesn't want to talk to you? Because it sounds to me like he's purposely avoiding you. Any reason why he'd want to do that?"

"None. We're attempting to bestow a considerable fortune on him." Seymour raised his chin at me. "Just find him, all right? Feel free to contact me directly day or night as soon as you have news. This is a priority matter for us. We are highly motivated." He removed a slim envelope from his briefcase and handed it across the desk to Mom. "A down payment for your services. I believe you'll find it quite generous."

Mom opened the envelope and had a look, her eyes widening slightly. "It's quite generous times two."

"You'll receive an equal amount upon successful completion of the assignment—plus a bonus of twenty-five thousand dollars. As I said, this is a priority matter."

She squinted at the check. "What's the Aurora Group?"

"A holding company."

"Meaning, what, we're off the books?"

"Not at all. Aurora's merely an entity that we set up for occasions when we find it necessary to retain outside contractors."

Mom sat back in her chair, took a deep breath and let it out slowly. "Okay, what's really going on here?"

"Just find Bruce Weiner." Peter Seymour's face revealed nothing. The man was impenetrable. He closed his briefcase, fetched his dark gray overcoat from the coat rack and put it on. It looked like cashmere, probably because it was. "I shall take the stairs down," he announced. And with that he was gone.

I headed straight for the window, gazing down at his town car at the curb.

"What are you doing, Bunny?"

"I want to see how he gets out to the car without getting his shoes dirty."

"Simple. He'll change them before he leaves the building."

"How do you know that?"

"Because that's what women do."

Sure enough, Peter Seymour was wearing an old pair of black brogans when he strode across the slushy sidewalk to his car and got in. Must have had them stashed in his briefcase.

"What do you think?" I asked her as the Town Car pulled away.

"I think he's a rat and we're the mice. You?"

"It's a fool's errand of some kind. I just can't figure out *what* kind."

"If we weren't flat broke I'd have told him to take his snippy attitude and get the hell out. Unfortunately, we can't exactly be choosy right now," she confessed as she endorsed Seymour's check. "Rita, we're rich!"

Rita let out a whoop and rushed in, snatching the check from her. "Does this mean I can deposit my last two paychecks?"

"Go for it," Mom said to her.

Rita hurried back out, her wondrous rear end wiggling.

"We wouldn't be so broke if you collected the rent from our tenants," I pointed out. "Pearl is at least three months behind. So is Scotty."

"Times are hard, Bunny. They're suffering."

"How about the Felchers? They're living here rent free."

"It's a sin to dun the elderly."

"Mom, you're a sweet person but as a landlady, you suck."

She brooded in silence for a moment, her lower lip stuck out. "Who knows, maybe Seymour's on the level. Maybe this is exactly what it appears to be—send a nice Jewish boy to find a nice Jewish boy. You've got to like the symmetry, right?"

"Actually, I'm not a big fan of symmetry."

BUT MOM KNOWS BEST.

The part about us being in no position to turn down a lucrative gig, I mean. It's a tough time to be running a small agency. When the economy turns sour people don't hire a private investigator to catch a two-timing spouse in the act. They just cheat on each other in sullen defiance.

An agency can't operate on the cheap. You need state-of-the-art computers, software and surveillance equipment. And you need someone like Rita. Give her ten minutes and she can hack into anybody's most personal records. Mom befriended her way back when Rita was working the clubs as Natural Born—out of respect for not only her boobies, but her flaming red hair. Rita used to babysit me. She was also the object of my earliest, most tumid adolescent yearnings. These days, she's married to Clarence, who used to play outside linebacker for the Jets and is currently serving ten to fifteen at Sing Sing for aggravated assault. Rita spends sixteen hours a day at her desk, consumed by loneliness and raging hormones. But she's true blue to Clarence. Never, ever considers stepping out with another man.

After I graduated from NYU drama school, the folks decided to sell our raised ranch in Mineola and move in over the office. By then I had my own place in the East Village and was trying to scratch out a living as an actor. I caught the show business bug from Mom. Desperately wanted to act. I got two weeks on a soap. A few commercials that went national. Speaking roles on a couple of different *Law & Order* episodes. Given my slight stature and boyish features, they continued to cast me as a high school kid even after I got out of drama school. Until the day they stopped casting me altogether. There isn't much demand for a twenty-five-year-old juvenile type. Make that zero.

So I joined the family business. I have a genuine gift for tailing people. Partly it's my dramatic training. Partly it's what my dad taught me. I can tail anyone through the streets and subways of New York City and they never know I'm there. But my specialty is finding runaways. Thousands of high school and

college-age kids from all over the country disappear into the
Big Apple maw every year. Some are fleeing an abusive home
life. Some are chasing the Broadway or catwalk dream. Some
are just running and have no idea why.

I know all about that. Three weeks before I graduated from
high school I gathered up my life savings of $238, packed an
overnight bag and caught a Greyhound bus for Hollywood.
Didn't tell my folks. Didn't tell anyone. I told myself I wanted
to be a movie star. Mostly, I was just desperate to escape. If I
didn't get away I was positive I'd explode all over the Derek
Jeter posters on my bedroom wall. After ten days out there, I
was shuffling along Hollywood Boulevard with twenty-three
cents in my pocket, starved and homesick. A real nice young
guy named Stan took pity on me and bought me a meal. Stan
even offered me a chance to appear in adult films if I was willing to go down on his extremely large friend Larry. I politely
said I'd rather not. He not-so-politely pointed out that it wasn't
exactly a request. My dad found me in a cheap motel room three
days later, drugged, dehydrated and dazed. When I was cleared
to leave the hospital, we got on a plane for home and the matter
was never discussed again. Except for the occasional nightmare
that awakened me, screaming, my Project Runaway episode
was history.

But I've been there, okay? I know what they're going
through. I know what can happen to them. It's not my job to
choreograph happy endings. I'm a private investigator. It's not
the career that I dreamt of, but given my upbringing I suppose
it was inevitable that I'd end up where I am. Actually, it all
seems pretty normal to me. Mind you, I go to work every day

with two gorgeous women who used to get naked for a living—
one of whom is my mom. So one man's idea of normal is another's oedipal fantasy a trois.

After Peter Seymour drove off, I went up to my book-lined
apartment. Reading is one of my passions. Mostly showbiz mem-
oirs and biographies, the juicier the better. My apartment has
good light, thanks to the wraparound windows. A wood-burning
fireplace. Comfy, overstuffed furniture that I inherited from my
grandmother's apartment in Flatbush. On muggy August after-
noons I swear it still smells like kasha knishes. I built a fire in
the fireplace and put some music on the stereo. Broadway musicals are my other passion. None of that Andrew Lloyd Webber
crap either. Real stuff, like the digitally remastered original cast
recording of *Gypsy* starring the great Miss Ethel Merman.

I stretched out in front of the fire with Seymour's file on the
Weiner family. Bruce's parents, Paul and Laurie, were both
forty-eight years old. Paul was a bond trader with Farrell and
Company, as Seymour had mentioned. Laurie, who'd taught
school before she and Paul started their family, volunteered at the
local elementary school as a teacher's aide. In addition to Bruce,
the Weiners had a daughter, Sara, age seventeen, a senior at Willoughby High School who had applied to Columbia, Tufts, UC
Berkeley and the University of Chicago. Sara was a straight-A
student, a flautist and an all-conference soccer player. Both of
the Weiner kids were athletic. Bruce had been the starting center on the Willoughby High basketball team. He did not play
for the team at Canterbury. He appeared to be a model student.
Had a 3.76 GPA. No record of drug or alcohol-related activity.
No citations from the campus police for excessive partying.

The kid seemed clean. But it also seemed obvious that the Leetes people hadn't put boots on the ground at Canterbury. All they had were the fruits of a computer search. No dirt.

Although they sure had a lot of it on Bruce's parents. Paul Weiner was a Gold Card member of the Gladiator's Club, a high-end online escort service. The man had engaged in twelve assignations in midtown Manhattan hotel rooms over the past eighteen months at a cost of fifteen hundred dollars each. His preference was for Asian women who were young, petite and took excellent care of their feet. He also belonged to an online dating service and had been romantically involved with three different women in the past year. All three were Asian. Four years ago, he'd an affair with an unmarried coworker named Michelle Chen. It had ended when Michelle transferred to the San Diego office. She was presently married and had a small child.

Laurie Weiner had met with two different divorce attorneys in the past six months but had not retained either of them. Instead, she'd embarked on an affair with the married principal of the elementary school where she volunteered. The affair was ongoing. He had rented an apartment in Scarsdale for their trysts, which occurred three times a week between the hours of four and six P.M.

It's like my dad used to say: It's amazing what you find out about people when you find out about people.

There was more. Paul Weiner, who was accustomed to earning a six-figure annual Christmas bonus, hadn't received one last month due to the sucky economy. Their home, which had slid 40 percent in market value since they bought it in 2004, was mortgaged to the rafters. Bruce's tuition and room and board at

Canterbury came to about forty thousand dollars a year. Laurie's eighty-two-year-old mother, an Alzheimer's sufferer, was in an assisted living facility in Armonk that cost even more than that. Between them, Paul and Laurie were presently carrying over sixty thousand dollars in credit card debt. They had a daughter who'd be starting college next year. Almost no savings. They were staring at real trouble.

I set the file aside, wondering once again why Seymour wasn't using the Leetes Group to find Bruce. They had a gazillion operatives on their payroll. If anyone had the resources to track him down it was the Leetes Group. So why us?

It was 6:20 P.M. Paul Weiner probably wouldn't be home yet from the city, but Laurie ought to be rolling in right about now from getting sweaty with her married boyfriend. She answered the phone on the third ring, sounding rushed and harried.

"Good evening, Mrs. Weiner. I'm Benjamin Golden of Golden Legal Services. We've been retained by a law firm to carry out a confidential legal matter concerning your son Bruce."

Her first response was wary silence. Totally normal. I would have reacted the same way. "I . . . don't understand. Is Bruce is in some kind of trouble?"

"Nothing of the sort, ma'am. A certain party has bequeathed something to Bruce. We've been retained to contact you and expedite the inheritance."

"You'd better talk to my husband about it. I can give you his office number."

"Already have it, thanks. And I'd rather discuss it with both of you."

"And *who* did you say you're with?"

I ran through it for her again. This time she was writing it down. "We prefer to handle these matters in person, Mrs. Weiner. I'd like to swing by your home this evening if you don't mind. It won't take long."

Most wives would have put me off with a simple, "I'll have my husband call you." But I had the advantage of knowing that the Weiners weren't getting along. *And* that she'd just been out shtupping her boyfriend and was anxious to jump in the shower before Paul got home.

Which was why she reluctantly said, "I guess that'll be okay. We should be done with dinner by 8:30."

I phoned my own dinner order down to Scotty's. Diego brought it up to me on a covered tray. Room service is one of the perks of being the landlord. Tonight's special was Salisbury steak, mashed potatoes, string beans and tapioca pudding. I watched *Jeopardy* while I ate, washing it down with a glass of milk.

I dressed in my Sincere Young Man ensemble: Oxford button-down shirt, V-neck sweater, Harris Tweed sports jacket, corduroy slacks and the hooded navy blue duffel coat that I got at the Brooks Brothers winter sale for 60 percent off. Then I coaxed the elevator downstairs and took off into the wet, chilly New York night.

We keep our company car in a twenty-four-hour garage around the corner on Amsterdam. Our wheels had been my dad's pride and joy—a somewhat gaudy burgundy 1992 Cadillac Brougham with a white vinyl top and matching burgundy leather interior. He loved that damned boat. Babied the hell out of it. And would have been infuriated that I was taking it out in the slush of a January night. But we can't afford to maintain a car that we don't use.

The evening traffic was heavy and slow. I inched my way up the Henry Hudson to the Cross Bronx, then took that to the Hutchinson River Parkway, an icy rain tap-tap-tapping on my windshield. As I headed into the northern burbs, the rain changed over to snowflakes. And I began to get the feeling that I was not alone. I couldn't make anyone out in my rearview mirror. But I also couldn't shake the feeling that I had a tail.

Willoughby is one exit past Scarsdale. When I arrived there I found myself in an entirely different world. Instead of sooty slush there was a blanket of pure white snow. Instead of the hustle-bustle of today I encountered a sleepy, charming village where time had stopped in about 1936. There was a town green complete with an honest-to-gosh gazebo. A steepled white church. Tidy little shops with parking on the diagonal out front. It was positively eerie. The snow was coming down pretty hard as I made my way through town, past dignified homes set back behind white picket fences. The snowplows were out. Hardly anyone else was.

I still had the feeling I was being followed. I didn't see anyone behind me on the deserted road. But I felt it.

The Weiners lived at the end of Powder Horn Hill Road, a relatively new cul-de-sac of immense center-chimney colonials filled with prosperous, happy people leading prosperous, happy lives—as long as you didn't read their files and know better. As I drew closer to the Weiners' place, I met up with a family of deer standing in the middle of the road. They didn't run away from the Caddy. Just stood there. I had to steer around them.

Paul Weiner answered the doorbell. Bruce's father was a balding, moon-faced man with a pillowy body and soft, round shoulders. He had a cautious, serious air about him. The air of a man you could trust with your money. He wore a cardigan over a plaid flannel shirt, worn khakis and moccasins.

"Good evening, Mr. Weiner, I'm Ben Golden of Golden Legal Services. Thank you for seeing me on such short notice."

"I didn't exactly have a choice," he responded with chilly disapproval. "I just found out you were coming five minutes ago."

Laurie appeared behind him the doorway, wearing designer sweats and sneakers. She was a thin, tepid looking woman with limp brown hair, horsy features and a complexion the color of wet newspaper. It never fails: Whenever I study up on a married couple who are cheats, I always picture the wife as a shmokin' hot cougar and the husband as the spitting image of George Clooney. Reality? The Weiners were painfully plain.

"My wife," he said tightly, "was a bit unclear about what it is you do, son. Are you an intern at a law firm?"

"Actually, I'm a licensed private investigator."

"You've got to be kidding me."

"I am not."

"I suppose you have a license and so forth?"

I took out my wallet and showed it to him.

He looked it over carefully, shaking his head. "And *who* has hired you?"

Peter Seymour had explicitly warned me not to share that information with them. I wanted to know why that was. It's my natural instinct to be curious about such things. "The law firm of Bates, Winslow and Seymour," I replied.

Laurie Weiner drew in her breath, her eyes widening.

Her husband was a cooler customer. He just said, "You may as well come in out of the snow. But I'm warning you—I won't agree to act on Bruce's behalf until I see something in writing *and* review it with my own attorney."

The entry hall smelled of potpourri and teriyaki sauce. There was a cavernous department store showroom of a living room that looked as if it was never, ever used. And a brightly lit den directly across the hall, where the Knicks were playing the Bucks on a sixty-inch flat-screen TV.

As I unbuttoned my coat, a teenaged girl came bounding eagerly down the stairs. Sara Weiner was a small-boned, bright-eyed girl with a long, shiny mane of honey-colored hair.

"Are you a friend of Brucie's?" she asked, gazing at me probingly.

"No, he's not," her father said abruptly. "Mr. Ben Golden is here about a legal matter, Sara. And *you* have a history paper to write."

Sara curled her lip at him and started back upstairs, looking at me curiously over her shoulder. I treated her to my best smile. I got zero back.

Laurie offered me coffee. I accepted. Paul and I went in the den. He flicked off the TV while I checked out the shrine that had been erected in there. A huge glass case was filled with athletic trophies. And one entire wall was lined with framed, laminated newspaper stories and photos.

Paul said, "Bruce's basketball team won the state championship his senior year. Bruce was the starting center and captain. That's my boy, right there. . . ." He pointed to a newspaper photo of a big, dark-haired kid with broad shoulders and a square jaw. A real bruiser. Neither of his parents was particularly large. Nor was his sister. But there must have been some size in the Weiner family tree somewhere. "He's a ferocious rebounder. He wanted to play at the college level but he's only six-foot-three. To play under the basket in college you've got to be at least four inches taller. We talked about him switching to football. They projected Bruce as a tight end. He decided to focus on academics instead. It was a tough adjustment for him. Basketball was his first love. But I told him, hey, sometimes you just have to face up to reality and move on."

"Yes, you do."

"He wants to teach English abroad for a year after he graduates. Has shown no interest in business school, which had been our plan."

"And how do you feel about that?"

"We just want him to be happy," Laurie said as she showed up with my coffee.

I took it from her and sat on the leather sofa. She sat next to me. Paul settled into an oversized recliner.

I sipped my coffee. It was weaker than I like it. "And is he? Happy, I mean."

Paul let out a laugh. "Why wouldn't he be? He's twenty-one years old. He's got his whole great big beautiful life ahead of him." The man's voice was upbeat but there was wistfulness in his eyes. He sounded as if he wanted to live his own life all over again. Perhaps in Asia this time, with a rotating bevy of petite young women who take excellent care of their feet.

"When did you last speak to Bruce?"

Paul shrugged. "Over the weekend, I guess. Why?"

"Bates, Winslow and Seymour have made numerous attempts to contact him at Canterbury. He hasn't responded to any of their phone calls or letters. According to his roommate, Bruce left school three days ago."

The Weiners exchanged a look of surprise.

"Chris told them Bruce took off?" Laurie's voice quavered slightly.

"Yes, ma'am."

Paul stroked his chin thoughtfully. "So that's why they sent you here."

"Yes, sir. My initial thought was that perhaps he'd come home for a few days. Which I gather he hasn't."

"You gather correctly."

"Do you have any idea where he can be reached?"

He peered at me, puzzled. "We're Bruce's parents. Why didn't they just come to us in the first place?"

"Because he's twenty-one. The bequest is in his name."

"Bequest," he repeated. "Somebody's left Bruce money? How much money?"

"I'm not privy to that information."

"Well, do you know who left it to him?"

"I'm afraid not. I've simply been retained to locate Bruce. Do you have any relatives who've passed away recently?"

"My folks are long gone," Paul replied with a shake of his head. "So is Laurie's father. And her mother was still kicking the last time I looked."

"She's kicking all right," Laurie said glumly.

I kept staring at Laurie, trying to imagine her in the throes of passion with her married lover. Or anyone. I couldn't. "How about a family friend or business associate?"

They looked at each other blankly.

"Perhaps an elderly neighbor? Someone who took an interest in Bruce when he was a boy?"

"Maybe old man Kershaw," Paul offered. "He retired to Phoenix a few years back. Bruce used to shovel his driveway for him. The old fellow took a shine to him, remember, Laurie?"

"What I remember is the way he used to stare at Sara when she played in the front yard. That man made my skin crawl."

"Do either of you know why Bruce might have left school?"

"No idea," he said.

"Has he ever taken off before?"

"He and his friends go off on little unscheduled ski trips to Bear Mountain," Laurie said. "He is a kid, after all."

"But a responsible kid," Paul said, getting testy. "He's no partier."

"I didn't say he was," she said, getting testy right back.

"Does he have a girlfriend?"

"No one steady," he said.

"That we know of," she said.

Which Paul didn't like. "Laurie, if he had a girlfriend we'd know."

"Not necessarily," she shot back.

As the two of them bickered I heard a floorboard creak in the hallway. Someone was eavesdropping on our conversation.

Paul heaved a sigh of annoyance. "You know what? There's a simple way to get to the bottom of this." He grabbed his cell phone from the coffee table and speed dialed a number. Waited as it rang, then shook his head at us. "Voice mail." He left Bruce a message: "Hi Beefer, I was just watching the Knicks get killed and thought I'd check in. Talk to you soon." He rang off, scrolled his directory and tried another number. "Hi, Chris, sorry if I'm interrupting anything. It's Paul Weiner . . . I'm fine, son. Just fine. Been trying to get in touch with Bruce and he's not . . . Oh, he is? Uh-huh. . . . Sure, I understand. Glad to hear it. Okay, thanks." Paul rang off, gazing at me with amusement. "Somebody gave you a bum steer, young fellow. His roommate just told me that Bruce has been pulling long hours at the library every night this week. He couldn't answer my call just now because they make the kids turn their cell phones off."

And yet this very same roommate had told Peter Seymour's office he hadn't seen Bruce in three days. Who was Chris Warfield lying to? And why?

"If you hear from him please let me know." I left my business card on the coffee table and stood up. "Excuse me for asking, but have you folks had any prior dealings with Bates, Winslow and Seymour?"

Laurie lowered her eyes, coloring slightly.

Paul looked me right in the eye and said, "Never heard of them." He was a good liar.

It was still snowing lightly. There was a thin coating on the windshield of the Caddy. Nothing the wipers couldn't take care of. I was just about to back out of the driveway when someone came darting out of a door next to the garage, jumped in next to me and dove under the dashboard.

"Just keep going," Sara blurted out, crouching there. "Drive around."

"Drive around where?"

"Park down the block or something. Just *go*, will you?"

I backed out of the driveway and started up the street. As soon as I'd gone around a bend, Sara sat up on the seat next to me, tossing her long, shiny hair. She wore an oversized fleece top, a pair of tights and Ugg boots. She was a cute little thing with big brown eyes, a soft, plump mouth and glowing skin. A real doll. A nervous doll. She was wringing her hands.

"I was listening to what my parents were just telling you in there," she said with great urgency. "And they are, like, totally full of shit, okay? They don't know *anything*."

"And you do?"

"Well, yeah. So does Chris. He was lying his ass off to my dad."

I pulled over to the curb and idled there with the heater cranked up high. We had Powder Horn Hill Lane all to ourselves, unless you count the deer.

Sara was studying me from across the seat with those big brown eyes. "You don't look like a Ben."

"My friends call me Benji."

"I like that much better. Tell me why you're looking for Brucie."

"It's my job. A law firm hired me."

"Some big fancy law firm in the city?"

"Yes."

"That totally figures." She glanced around at the interior of the Caddy. "*This* is your ride?"

"Company car."

"So what do you drive?"

"I don't. I live in the city."

"God, I can't wait to. It bites out here. There's nothing to do, nowhere to go. A lot of my friends are applying to these small, elitist colleges in the New England countryside. Not me. I want to be in a city where shit happens." She pulled a hand-rolled joint out of the pocket of her fleece top. "Does your lighter work?"

"I imagine so."

She pushed it in and waited, gazing at me curiously. "So you're a real dick."

"Excuse me?"

"Isn't that what they call a guy who does what you do?"

"Generally, they call me a private investigator."

The lighter popped up. She yanked it out and lit her joint, toking deeply on it. "Want some?" she asked, opening her window a crack to let the smoke out.

"No, thanks."

"It helps me relax. I'm hardwired to excel—academics, music, sports. I'm a little tightly wound." Sara flashed a smile at me. She had a sweet smile. A set of dimples you could go spelunking in. "Trevor? This guy who I'm sort of boning? He's really into old Bogie movies. That's why I asked you about the dick thing. Trevor likes to wear this old gray fodera just like Sam Spade."

"Fedora."

"It's like a hat? He said it was called a fodera."

"Fedora."

"Are you sure?"

"I couldn't be more sure. What does 'sort of boning' mean?"

"We're fuck buddies but it's not serious."

"You don't consider fucking serious?"

"Not really. Why, do you?"

"Yes, I do."

"That's so sweet." She toked on her joint. "Do you carry a roscoe?"

"No one has used that term for at least seventy years. But, yes, I'm licensed to carry a firearm."

"Have you ever shot anyone?"

"No."

"But you know how to use it?"

"I go shooting regularly at the Westside Pistol Range in Chelsea."

"Are you carrying it with you right now?"

"It's locked in the glove compartment."

"Can I see it?"

"No."

"Well, what kind is it?"

"A Smith and Wesson Chief's Special. It has a short, two-inch barrel. Is easy to conceal. I find it easy to handle, too. I don't have very big hands."

"That's too bad." She arched an eyebrow at me. "I've heard what they say about guys who have small hands."

I let that one slide on by. She was too young to get frisky with. A straight-A student, according to her file. An adorable little hottie, according to me. Too bad she wasn't five years older. Hell, even three. I gazed back out at the deserted road.

Once again I was sensing a shadow out there somewhere. I saw no one. Yet I couldn't shake the feeling. "Sara, you said your parents don't know anything. Did you mean in regards to Bruce's unnamed benefactor?"

"Wait, you're the one who's looking for him, right?"

"Right. . . ."

"And *you* don't know who his benefactor is?"

"Also right."

She smoked her joint some more. "That's fairly weird, isn't it?"

"Yes and no. I'm only told what clients choose to tell me. Do you have an idea who it is?"

"Some giant, sleazoid sneaker company, obviously. They're trying to buy him off. I wonder how much they're offering Brucie. I bet it's a million. A million means nothing to those people."

"Sara, I think we'd better hit rewind," I said, not following one word she was saying. "Tell me about Bruce, will you?"

She leaned her head back against the headrest. The joint was calming her down. "He's a great brother. Just a real sweet guy. Smart, but not one of those ego kings who's always trying to chump you. In high school he was a major, major baller. But not anymore, except for pick-up games. I think that's how he and Charles met."

"And Charles is? . . ."

Sara rolled her eyes at me like a suffering teenager. God's subtle way of reminding me that she was one. "Charles," she said, louder this time. "*The* Charles."

"Do you mean Charles Willingham?"

"Duh."

"Your brother and Charles 'In Charge' Willingham are friends?"

"Benji, they're more than friends. They're lovers."

I looked at her in shock. "Charles Willingham is gay?"

"The two of them mean everything to each other."

"Charles Willingham is gay?"

She glared at me. "Yes, Charles Willingham is gay. And, by the way, so is my brother. Get over it, will you?"

Easier said than done. There had been *no* mention of this particular mother lode in the Leetes Group file. How come? Was it possible they hadn't uncovered it? Or was their report redacted because they didn't want me in the loop? I had no idea. I only knew that our case had just taken a sharp swerve toward weird.

I looked back out at the falling snow, soaking in the enormity of it. Canterbury College was by no means a hotbed for intercollegiate athletics. It didn't even offer athletic scholarships. But for the past two seasons the tiny Division II school had produced one of the top men's basketball teams in the entire country, right up there with powerhouses like North Carolina and Kansas. Canterbury's Athenians had been the Cinderella story of last year's NCAA tournament, toppling the mighty UCLA Bruins and Pitt Panthers on their way to the Elite Eight before they were finally eliminated by Duke in a nationally televised prime time game. *The Canterbury Tale*, the media had dubbed this improbable run of upsets engineered by John Seckla, the team's dynamic young head coach. And it was no fluke. Coach Seckla's Athenians had kept right on winning this season. They were even favored to make it into the Final Four. And the overwhelming reason why was six-foot-five-inch

Charles "In Charge" Willingham, their incandescent All-
American shooting guard. Charles Willingham was a consen-
sus top three pick in the next NBA draft who'd chosen tiny
Canterbury over the traditional hoops schools because he was
also a 4.0 brainiac who planned to go to law school someday.
Charles was the ultimate feel-good story. A black hometown
hero out of Harlem's Martin Luther King housing projects who
never made a false move on or off the court. He was modest in
victory, gracious in defeat, polite, well-spoken and movie star
handsome. The media adored him. Everyone did. Charles Willingham was a once-in-a-generation talent. The black Bill Brad-
ley, old-timers called him.

"Sara, how long have Bruce and Charles been together?"

"More than a year. Brucie hasn't told our folks because they'll
freak."

"About him being gay, you mean?"

She nodded. "Their values are totally outmoded."

"But you're cool with it?"

"Of course. We are who we are. We can't let . . . Oh, *shit*!"
She narrowed her gaze at me. "Did you just scam me?"

"Scam you how?"

"You're not going to go blab this to, like, TMZ or Gawker
are you?"

"Of course not. You can trust me."

"How do I know that?"

"Because I just gave you my word."

She studied me carefully for a moment. "Benji, how old are
you?"

"Twenty-five, why?"

"Because you don't look like someone who'd do this kind of work."

"Looks can be deceiving."

"So that means you're not?"

"Not what?"

"A total bunny."

I smiled at her. "My mom calls me Bunny."

"I would kill for your eyelashes. Are you married?"

"No."

"Do you have a girlfriend?"

"No."

"Are you gay? It's okay if you are."

"I'm not gay."

"Good, I'm glad," she said, showing me those dimples of hers again.

"You were saying something about sneakers? . . ."

"Well, yeah. Charles is going to pull down *huge* endorsement deals this spring after the NBA draft. Sneakers, power drinks, all of that. He is *such* a golden boy. Except he won't be if the public finds out that the great love of his life is a guy named Bruce Weiner. So somebody wants to pay Brucie to go byebye. It's got to be that, don't you think?"

I didn't know. A sneaker manufacturer didn't exactly sound like Bates, Winslow and Seymour's usual sort of clientele. Then again, we were all working a bit harder these days. "Sara, I'm still wondering something. Why did you jump in my car?"

She lowered her eyes. "Because I'm really worried about Brucie. The last time we talked he sounded incredibly down. Which is not a good thing. When nobody offered him a basketball

scholarship he got super depressed and tried t-to hang himself in
the basement. I'm the one who cut him down. The ambulance
guy told me, like, one more minute and he'd have been a goner."
Sara took a ragged breath that was almost but not quite a sob.
"I've left him ten messages on his cell. He hasn't called me back
or answered my e-mails. He didn't tell me where he was going. Or
what's bothering him. Although it has to be about Charles. Having to sneak around and be invisible. It's hard on Brucie. And *so*
hard on Charles. That poor guy is under constant pressure to
make every shot, ace every test, smile for every camera, be
nice to everyone all day long. He's on stage twenty-four/
seven *and* he's been hiding his sexual identity this whole time.
Bruce wishes he'd come out. So do I. Charles would be *such* a
trailblazer—the sports world's first openly gay male superstar.
But he's afraid to. And the whole situation's really getting to
him. He had to be hospitalized overnight a couple of weeks ago."

"I read about it. They said he had food poisoning."

"Benji, it wasn't anything Charles ate. His blood pressure
spiked so high during practice that he passed out. He's carrying
around too much stress. It's not healthy."

"Do his teammates know about Bruce?"

"No way. No one connected with the team knows. Just a few
people who they really trust. Charles trusts his mom, Velma,
who's a nurse at St. Luke's Hospital. She raised Charles all by
herself and is his best friend. She knows. So does Brucie's roommate, Chris. He's good people."

"Who else?"

"Me. I know the real deal. And now so do you."

"Why me, Sara?"

"I'm not stupid, Benji. If that law firm hired you to find him then that means somebody else must know. Which totally bites. But when I saw you at the bottom of the stairs just now, I was positive you were sent here to help him. I have good instincts that way. I'm very empathetic."

"Do you have any idea where Bruce might be?"

"No, but Chris might. Although he'll never tell you. Not if Brucie swore him to secrecy. I'm worried about my brother, Benji. He's all alone somewhere and I'm afraid he might go into another downward spiral a-and . . ." She was fighting back tears. "He just sounded *so* down. He's been that way ever since Christmas vacation."

"You mean because of Charles?"

"Well, yeah. And no."

"Is something else bothering him?"

"Maybe. There was this lady . . ."

"What lady, Sara?"

"Just some really strange lady. She came up to him at the mall when we were shopping for presents together. Asked if she could talk to him for a minute. The two of them walked away from me and started talking. Or she talked. Brucie hardly said a word. She was real freaky-deaky. Wild-eyed, waving her arms around in the air. Plus she was a total mess, you know? Like a homeless person. Had this stringy blond hair that I swear she hadn't washed in weeks. And her clothes were all ratty. Brucie couldn't get away from her fast enough. After she left I said, 'What was *that* about?'"

"And what did he say?"

"Not a word. He got real quiet."

"Do you think he knew her?"

"He definitely knew her."

"How old was this woman?"

"Thirty. Maybe thirty-five. Whoever she was, she upset him. And he wouldn't tell me why."

"Does he usually shut you out that way?"

"We're incredibly close. But, yeah, he can be pretty private sometimes." Her half-smoked joint had gone cold. She stuffed it back in her pocket. "Benji, I'll take the train into the city tomorrow morning instead of going to school. I'm going to help you find him."

"I don't think so, Sara."

"But I have to help him."

"You already have."

"I want to do more. Please? I'll do anything."

"Will you back my play with Chris? I may have to come at him a little sideways."

"Okay, I don't know what that means."

"It means don't narc me out. Go with it. Are you up for that?"

"Totally. I won't let you down."

I took out a pen and two of my business cards. Gave her one card in case she needed to reach me. Had her write her cell number on the other for me.

"You can take me back to the house of horrors now, Benji."

"Can you sneak back inside without your folks knowing?"

"I do it all of the time," she said with a toss of her long, shiny mane. "My parents are *so* clueless. I mean, they actually think they still belong together. How pathetic is that?"

CHAPTER TWO

"NOW LET YOUR LIMBS GO HEAVY," Svet commanded us as she paced back and forth in the basement community room of Congregation B'Nai Jacob. "Allow the *prana* to course through your body on this beautiful winter morning."

Eight of us had shown up at six o'clock on this blustery, not-so-beautiful morning. It was now an hour later and we'd arrived at *savasana,* or corpse pose, our exhausted limbs splayed out on our mats, sweat pouring from us. Russian-born Svet's sunrise yoga class is a grueling workout. But stamina and core strength are important in my line of work. And so I drag myself out of bed before dawn three mornings a week.

"Welcome the day," she implored us, her thick accent and commanding bearing infusing her words with a vaguely martial aura. "You *will* feel peaceful. You *will* embrace your inner strength."

B'nai Jacob is the small neighborhood temple where my dad became a regular after the cancer took hold of him. It's a squat stone building on West 102nd Street, midway between Amsterdam and Columbus, that looks like either an undersized firehouse or an oversized mausoleum. No windows face the street. In the final months of his life my dad took to attending the minyan service that's held in the basement there every morning at 7:20. I went with him. After he died I gave it up.

We closed out our practice by chanting "Om . . ." Then opened our eyes and headed up the stairs to greet the new day.

The minyan regulars were already filing down those stairs, punctual as ever. A minyan requires no rabbi. Just ten congregants who share a desire to pray or reflect. At B'Nai Jacob, it's also a social thing. The regulars coffee klatch for at least an hour. Many are retirees. As they came clomping down the stairs in their dark overcoats and heavy wool scarves, I waited to say hi to them. Morris Kantor and Jerry Granick had both been on the job with my dad. Milt Miller had been his CPA and still handles the books for my mom. Al Posner, a sarcastic old grouch who always smells like pickled herring, was my dad's bookie.

"Hey there, high pockets!" Al Posner has called me that since I was a kid. It's a subtle knock on my height. "I'm glad you're here today. My nephew Herb's girl, Sonya, is dropping off a coffee cake. Real nice kid. She teaches kindergarten over on West End Avenue."

I sighed inwardly. The minyan regulars are always trying to fix me up with their assorted homely daughters, granddaughters and nieces. "Al, I wish I could stick around but I'm on a job today."

"What's so important you can't wait five minutes?"

"Hey, if he's gotta go he's gotta go." Morris Kantor patted me on the back. "Say hi to that beautiful mother of yours, okay?"

I promised I would and started up the stairs with my yoga mat. Too late—Sonya Posner was already descending those same stairs. I knew it was Sonya because she was clutching a coffee cake in a Tupperware container. The high-heeled boots she had on were not ideal for stairs. Or possibly she was just a natural born klutz. But she teetered and lost her balance about halfway down. As the coffee cake went flying, she let out a shriek and took a full-tilt header right at me. I swear she would have broken her neck if I hadn't caught her. Somehow, the two of us tangoed our way down the stairs unharmed. When she loosened her Vulcan death grip on my shoulders I got my first good look at her.

I let out a startled gasp. Sonya was, well, she was drop-dead gorgeous. It wasn't just that she had creamy, perfect skin framed by lustrous black hair that I wanted to run my fingers through right away. Or that she possessed a pair of bruised, overripe red lips with just a hint of an overbite that made her mouth incredibly, erotically kissable. Or that she had a striking aquiline nose and chiseled, terrific cheekbones. She had *the* most arrestingly beautiful pair of pale green eyes I'd ever gazed into in my whole life. All I wanted to do was get lost in them for a good long weekend. Preferably while naked. True, she towered a good four inches over me and was not exactly light as a feather. But *something* happened to me when our eyes met. My pulse raced. My belly fluttered. I even felt a slight sensation of dizziness.

Whatever it was I swear she felt it, too. Because the two of us stood there staring at each other for the longest time before she said, "You're Benji, am I right? Sure, I am. You're the only one here who's under the age of ninety." Okay, there was a small

issue with her voice. It was a bit nasal. A lot nasal. And she yam-
mered in gulpy fits and starts. "Uncle Al? He's told me all about
you. How you're a lawyer. How you own all sorts of buildings
in the neighborhood."

"He may have oversold me a bit." My own voice sounded
strangely rusty.

"I told him for-get-it. No more fix ups. How many smug,
self-important dickheads does a girl have to meet before she's
had enough?" Sonya's gaze fell on the coffee cake container on
the floor. "I spent half the fucking night baking that thing and
now it's roadkill. What am I saying? It probably sucked anyway. I suck at baking. *And* I have to do cupcakes at school with
the kids today. You like cupcakes, Benji? Of course you do.
Who doesn't like cupcakes? Screw it, maybe I can salvage a few
pieces." She picked up the fallen cake and set it on the counter,
then unbuttoned her shearling coat and took it off.

Now all I could do was gape. I'd been right about Sonya's
bone structure. Frail she wasn't. A tad hippy even. But it
wasn't her hips I was staring at. It was her cowl-necked sweater.
Or, more specifically, what was inside of her cowl-necked
sweater. Sonya Posner had herself a serious rack. I'm talking
major league zoomers. She could give even Lovely Rita a run
for her cup size.

"And here they are," Al joked, nudging me with his elbow.
"My niece Sonya."

"No offense, Uncle Al," she snapped. "But that has never been
funny."

Me, I still didn't say a word. I'd gone mute.

"The answer is yes," she informed me matter-of-factly.

"They're a hundred percent real. But enough about me and mine. What's *your* deal? Are you Mister Hit It and Quit It? How many girls have you got on the string right now? Two, three? Plus maybe a few helpless, juicy tenants who are a teensy bit late on their rent, am I right?"

"You couldn't be more wrong."

She nodded knowingly. "That's what I figured. There isn't a straight guy on the planet who has eyelashes like yours."

"No, that's not it either."

"Well, then what is it?"

"I just haven't met the right girl yet."

Now it was her turn to stare at me. "Anybody got a pen?"

You never saw a gang of old men whip out their ballpoints so fast.

She accepted Morris Kantor's Bic, grabbed hold of my left hand and started scribbling all over the back of it. "Here's my cell *and* my land line. Call me. And don't wash that hand or you'll never see me again. Which you'll regret for the rest of your life." Sonya gave my hand a little squeeze, then tilted her head at me, her alluring pale green eyes shining. "You really don't have a girlfriend?"

"I really don't have a girlfriend."

"Wow, maybe this is my lucky day. Would that be a fucking scream or what?"

I DIDN'T REALIZE OUR FURNACE had seized up again until I tried to jump into a nice, hot, steaming shower and discovered that it was a nice, freezing-cold one. If Mom had been an early riser she'd have let me know. But Mom seldom stirs before nine.

And she always waits up for me when I'm out on a case. She'd been watching Letterman when I tapped on her door after I got home from Willoughby. I ran it for her over dishes of rocky road ice cream.

Shivering, I threw my clothes back on and grabbed my toolbox. Our furnace is down in the dimly lit, supremely creepy basement. I took a wrench to the nozzle, which promptly spewed black water into the bucket that I keep down there for such occasions. The nozzle was clogged with gunk again. So was the filter. The lines were gunky. The tank was gunky. The whole system needed to be replaced.

I was doing what I could when the elevator door opened and out marched a scowling Mrs. Felcher, her shock of white hair uncombed, a lit cigarette dangling from her lip. Our deadbeat tenant in 3A smokes four packs a day, is somewhere between the ages of eighty-five and hundred and not exactly easy on the eyes. Picture Albert Einstein as a drag queen. Now picture him in a ratty old bathrobe and fuzzy slippers.

"How are you today, Mrs. Felcher?" I said pleasantly.

"Feh," she snarled.

"And how is Mr. Felcher?"

"Who, *that* two-timing son of a bitch? He'd chase after a fart if he thought he could plow it."

Near as I could tell, there'd been a brief indiscretion back in the Gerald Ford years between Mr. Felcher and a Chock full o'Nuts counter girl. Mrs. Felcher still hadn't forgiven him. She stubbed out her cigarette with her slipper, removed a fresh one from the pocket of her robe and started to light it.

"Would you mind not smoking that right now, ma'am?"

"You people today," she said accusingly. "With your political correctness thing."

"It's not a political correctness thing. It's a kaboom thing. I'm working with fuel oil here."

"My apartment is freezing cold. The furnace isn't on."

"I know this, ma'am. It'll be up and running soon."

"This sort of thing *never* happened when your father was alive. Your father took care of things."

"My father collected the rent every month, too."

She cupped a hand behind her ear. "What's that you said?"

"I said, yes, ma'am."

She got back in the elevator and lit her cigarette, glowering at me in defiance. Mercifully, the door closed and I was left in peace.

I cleaned everything, reassembled it and hit the restart button. The old furnace rumbled and grumbled, but it did fire up and begin to run. I toted the bucket of gunky black water upstairs and dumped it in the gutter with all of the other gunky black water. The lights were on in our second floor office windows. Lovely Rita had arrived.

She was putting the coffee on and, in sharp contrast to Mrs. Felcher, was primped and polished to perfection. Hair and makeup just so. Cream-colored turtleneck and tailored grey flannel slacks hugging her every curve for dear sweet life.

"Hey there, Benji," she exclaimed, a dazzling smile on her face. She never lets her pain show through—even though she's staring at eight long years before no-good Clarence is even eligible for parole.

"Rita, you sure do look like a million bucks today."

"You're sweet. I wish you meant that."

"I do mean it. You're a major babe," I said, sniffing hungrily at the air.

There was a fragrant paper bag on her desk. Fried egg sandwiches from Scotty's. They made them on fresh onion bagels from H & H Bagels.

"I got two of them," she said. "One's for you."

"Rita, I don't know what I'd do without you."

"I do. You'd stumble around, clueless and starved."

Our radiator pipes began to clank. A truly horrible noise, but welcome.

"I ran Bruce Weiner's credit cards for you last night," she reported. "He hasn't used his Visa or MasterCard in the past seventy-two hours. He withdrew two hundred bucks from a Citibank ATM near the Canterbury campus four days ago. That's the last activity of any kind I could find."

"I need to know which residence hall he lives in," I said, munching on my breakfast. "Also his roommate's class schedule. Chris Warfield's his name. If you could scan Chris's ID photo for me that would be great. Also anything you can dig up on his family background." I polished off the last of the bagel, tossing the foil wrapper in the trash. "Me, I'm going to take another crack at a hot shower."

Rita arched an eyebrow at me. "Just one second there, little lamb. You're not getting off that easy."

"You're absolutely right. My turn to pay, sorry."

"That's not it and you know it. You've been holding out on me. What's her name?"

"Whose name?"

"The girl you met."

"Who says I met a girl?"

"I do. You have stars in your eyes."

"I just came from yoga. That's my *prana*."

"Screw your *prana*. That's pure testosterone. You've practically got steam coming out of your nostrils, you little stud bull. Come on, who is she?"

"Honestly, Rita, I don't know what you're talking about."

In response she stuck her pink tongue out at me. Not so long ago, there were Wall Street titans who would have stuffed a C-note in her G-string for that particular privilege. Me, I get it for free. Just one of the many perks of working for Golden Legal Services.

Back upstairs in my apartment, I pulled a beat-up duffel bag out of my bedroom closet and stuffed it with enough T-shirts and sweaters to approximate a couple of weeks' worth of clothing. By now the water was good and hot. I stripped down and got clean. Didn't comb my hair or shave when I climbed out. I was getting into character now—the scruffier the better. I sifted through my vast collection of college sweatshirts. Settled on the one with cropped sleeves, from SUNY Binghamton. Put it on over a long-sleeved thermal T-shirt, along with the oldest pair of jeans I owned. For shoes I went with Timberland hiking boots. For a coat I chose a down jacket from my high school days that was ripped in a couple of spots and repaired with silver duct tape. A wool stocking cap completed the outfit.

Downstairs in the office, Rita was on the phone dunning one of our former clients for money we were owed. The info that I'd requested was waiting for me in a file folder on my desk. I waved good-bye and headed out, my daypack slung over one shoulder, duffel over the other.

The stairs leading down to the 103rd Street subway platform are right there on our corner. An uptown No. 1 train was pulling in with a screech as I was swiping my MetroCard. I hopped aboard, found a seat and inserted my iPod earbuds. A lot of the riders were tucked inside of iPod cocoons—although I was probably the only one listening to the original Broadway cast recording of *Pajama Game* with John Raitt, Janis Paige and Eddie Foy, Jr.

As I rode uptown, duffel between my feet, I studied the file on Chris Warfield. Judging by his student ID photo, Chris was a prototypical slacker type with a mop of curly blond hair, four-day growth of beard and an impish grin. Except you have to be seriously smart to get into Canterbury. Not to mention well-heeled, unless you're able to secure an academic scholarship like Charles Willingham had. Chris's father was the top pediatric neurosurgeon in the city. Owned a co-op on Park Avenue as well as a weekend place on Candlewood Lake in northwestern Connecticut. Chris had attended the ultra-exclusive Dalton School. He was a straight-A student at Canterbury. And he wasn't exactly feasting on gimme courses. Today he had Latin from 8:00–9:00, Greek philosophy from 9:15–10:45 and Roman history from 11:00–12:30. After a lunch break, Chris would be coasting his way through pre-Revolutionary American economic history.

By now my train had rattled its way beneath Harlem to Washington Heights. At 168th Street I changed to the A train and kept on riding up, up, up toward the remote northernmost tip of Manhattan. The population really thins out up there. On the west side, facing the Hudson, there's Fort Tryon Park and not much else. Once you get above Dyckman Street you're in the Inwood section, home to The Cloisters. At the narrow northernmost tip of Manhattan, where the island is separated from the Bronx by a narrow waterway known as the Spuyten Duyvil Creek, there's windswept Inwood Hill Park with its panoramic views of the New Jersey Palisades. You'll find Baker Field up there. That's where the Columbia Lions try to play competitive Ivy League football. And you'll find Canterbury College. In fact, the very last stop on the A train, 207th Street, is commonly known as the Canterbury stop.

When I emerged from the subway tunnel there, I didn't feel as if I was in New York City anymore. And I for sure didn't feel as if I was in the twenty-first century. Canterbury was built of brownstone in the late 1800s in a style known as Collegiate Gothic. If you didn't know it was a college campus you'd swear it was a monastery of some kind. Maybe it was the gargoyles that helped put that over. Or the bell tower. Or those high stone walls.

A pair of twenty-foot wrought iron gates provided access to the walled campus yard. Outside of the gates, 207th Street was lined with campus pubs and take-out food places. Not a whole lot of them. Canterbury had fewer than two thousand students and the only graduate degree programs they offered were academic ones. This was a place where serious scholars passed what they knew on to future serious scholars. It was not a place where you expected to find the most celebrated college basketball player in the whole country.

It was past eleven o'clock by the time I got there. Chris would be soaking up Roman history in Chichester Hall. An Asian kid with round glasses directed me across the quad to a stone building next to the bell tower. I set my duffel on an ice-encrusted bench there and sat atop it, my nose buried in *Scarlett O'Hara's Younger Sister: My Lively Life In and Out of Hollywood* by the late actress Evelyn Keyes who, I swear, shtupped everyone in Tinseltown *except* Scarlett O'Hara. When Chris's class was over, the door to Chichester Hall opened and students came pouring out. Chris was walking with a slender, gorgeous Middle Eastern girl. He wasn't a particularly big guy. Not much taller than I. He wore a vintage tweed topcoat over a fisherman's knit sweater, chalk-striped suit trousers and lumberjack boots.

"Hey, it's Chris, am I right?" I slung my duffel over my shoulder and started toward him, grinning. "The Beefer told me—just look for the guy with blond hair who's walking with the best-looking girl on campus."

"Yeah, I'm Chris," he acknowledged, affably enough. The girl just looked right through me. "And you are? . . ."

"His cousin Benji? Benji Golden? He said to look him up when I got to town." I'd eased into a slightly more adolescent upspeak. "I've texted him, like, six times in the past two days but I haven't heard back. I stopped by your residence hall, Hudson, but nobody seems to know where he is. I thought *you* might know."

Chris stood there nodding his head. "Sure, sure."

"I must be going," the girl said to him coolly.

They exchanged a hug before she walked away. He watched

her go, beaming, before he turned back to me. "So you're
Bruce's cousin?"

"*Benji*. The Beefer hasn't mentioned me?"

"He may have, bro. Just doesn't ring a bell. Where do you
go?"

"Binghamton? I'm studying film up there. Or I was. Just
decided to take this semester off. Or I should say *they* decided
on account of I still owe them my tuition money from last year.
Thought I'd Kerouac around before I head back to the West
Coast. My folks live out there. Sherman Oaks? Believe, I am in
no hurry to go back. The Beefer said I could crash on your
residence hall sofa for a couple of nights."

"I wish I could help you but I don't know anything about it."

"Well, this sucks. Do you know where he is?"

"Bruce . . . isn't here right now. He's left campus."

"No way! *I'm* the designated family fuckup. What's going
down?"

"It's kind of complicated." Chris ran a hand through his un-
ruly blond curls. "Have you eaten lunch yet?"

He led me out the main gate to a bustling pizzeria called
Rico's. The legend of Charles Willingham lived large in there.
Every inch of wall space was lined with framed *New York Daily
News* and *New York Post* back page headlines crowing about
Charles In Charge and the magical Canterbury Tale. An au-
thentic replica of his green No. 11 jersey was hanging behind
the cash register along with several autographed photos of
Charles standing behind that very counter with his big arms
wrapped around the owner and his wife.

We ordered meatball heroes and Cokes at the counter and

grabbed ourselves a table. Then Chris excused himself and headed for the men's room, pulling his cell phone from his coat pocket. No doubt reaching out to Sara, who would be on her lunch break at school, if my timing was right.

Our sandwiches were ready when he returned. Chris insisted on paying for them, took off his coat and flopped down across from me. "Sara says you're her favorite cousin in the whole family. The coolest of the cool."

"That's my Sara." I bit into my hero, which was huge and tasty. "Were you checking up on me or something?"

"Had to, bro," he said apologetically.

I lowered my voice. "You mean because of Charles?"

He looked at me in surprise. "You know about Charles?"

"Totally."

Chris chomped on his hero, shaking his head. "I don't get this. I've roomed with Bruce for two years. How come he's never mentioned you?"

"He compartmentalizes his life. But I don't have to tell you that, do I?"

"He's a private guy," he acknowledged. "Still hasn't told his parents that he's gay. He's pretty positive they won't be able to deal."

"But you're okay with it, right?"

"Of course. I have lots of gay friends."

"He's been e-mailing me about Charles for months. I'm kind of his sounding board."

"Why is that?"

"Take a wild guess."

Chris swallowed some of his Coke, studying me. "You're gay, too."

"Doink." I munched on my hero, not rushing the guy. That was one of the first things my dad taught me: Never seem anxious. "So where did he go? And do *not* tell me home to Willoughby because Sara would have said so."

"I can't say, Benji. It's nothing personal. He asked me not to tell anyone."

"Sure, I understand. You made a promise. I can respect that." I ate some more of my hero and sipped my Coke. "Your parents have a place on Candlewood Lake, don't they?"

"Yeah, they do."

"Pretty quiet up there this time of year, I'm guessing."

"Real quiet," he said, his eyes avoiding mine.

"Damn, Chris, don't ever play high stakes poker. You'll lose your shirt, your pants. . . ."

He ducked his head. "You're right. I totally suck at the lying thing."

"You did okay on the phone last night with my uncle."

"How'd you know about that?"

"Sara told me."

Chris ran a hand through his mop of hair. "I loaned Bruce my keys to the guest cottage. But no one's supposed to know, okay?"

"Not even Sara?"

"Not even Sara. He's turned off his cell. The landline's off the hook. He just really wants some alone time to get his head straight. Charles is playing Syracuse tonight. After tomorrow

morning's shoot-around he'll be joining Bruce up there. The
team has a mandatory three-day lay off for the Gauntlet."

"For the what?"

"It's a Canterbury tradition. Began as a sadistic pop quiz in
some Greek history professor's class back in the twenties. Over
the years it's been ritualized into this campus-wide round of nut
crunchers. They're next week, and they get weighed almost as
heavily as finals, so no basketball practice or any other activities. You just hit the books. Charles and Bruce will be hitting
them together up at the lake."

"That should be nice for them. To get away, I mean."

"Maybe not so much," Chris said darkly. "Bruce is thinking
seriously about breaking up with him."

"No way! Why would he want to do that?"

"Because he loves the guy so much. Charles lives under a
microscope, bro. And now some fancy law firm is trying to
contact Bruce about a quote-unquote bequest. He's been duck-
ing them. He thinks it means someone's found out about them.
Bruce doesn't know who. Or how. But he's truly terrified."

I let this slide on by. That's another thing my dad taught me:
Never show too much interest in what you're interested in.
"How did the two of them meet? The Beefer's never been real
clear about that."

"There aren't a lot of ballers on campus. Hell, Bruce probably could have made the team if he'd wanted to. It's not like
Charles's teammates are lottery picks. Just good suburban high
school players like Bruce was. But Bruce gave it up cold turkey
when he came here. His thinking was that if he didn't have the

skills to play at some basketball factory, then it was time to move on. A bit extreme if you ask me, but Bruce is all about moral absolutes." Chris paused to wave hi to a pair of girls walking by. "The game's still in his blood though. He shoots hoops to unwind. Charles spotted him draining jumpers by himself in the gym one night. The two of them got into it one-on-one. For real, to hear Bruce tell it. Charles putting his shoulder into him. Bruce giving it to him right back. By the time it was over they both had bloody noses. And Charles was asking him to be his sparring partner."

"His what?"

"Bruce is burly. Hard to budge inside of the paint."

"I know this."

"Well, there's an acute shortage of practice players on the team who have the heft, and the nerve, to shove Charles around. He was looking to toughen himself up. The guy's incredibly dedicated. Bruce agreed to help and they started playing one-on-one regularly. Then going out for beers together. And then it turned into something more."

"Where do they usually? . . ."

"At his mom's place in the projects. Velma's totally cool with it. She accepts Charles for who he is. And she likes Bruce a lot. The neighborhood guys think Bruce is one of his teammates and let him be. Charles is a deity there. It doesn't occur to *anyone* that he might be gay. He's just so perfect."

"Being gay doesn't mean you're *im*perfect."

"Sorry, that didn't come out right. I just meant he's this all-American hero, you know?"

"And all-American heroes aren't queer—as far as we know."
I dabbed at my mouth with a paper napkin. "You said some law
firm is putting the screws to the Beefer?"

"Trying to. He thinks someone wants him to stay far away
from Charles."

"Like who?"

"My best guess? Our very own Canterbury College."

I shook my head at him. "Don't follow you."

"They took a huge financial hit when the stock market
tanked. The endowment fund is still down something like 40
percent. Alumni contributions are way off, too. There was a
story about it in our online newspaper just last week. The
school's had to scale back course offerings, lay off non-tenured
faculty, defer scheduled building maintenance. Tough times,
okay? And then along comes Charles in Charge. As much as
the board of trustees sneers at athletics here at hallowed Canterbury, they're making a fucking fortune off of the guy. Before
he arrived we played our home games at Stuyvesant Field
House, which seats maybe two thousand and was never even
half full. Thanks to Charles we're now filling Madison Square
Garden *and* a lot of our games are televised. If you make it into
the Final Four you're talking *millions* in TV revenue. Face it,
bro, Canterbury needs Charles. And they intend to milk him
for all he's worth until the day he graduates. A gay sex scandal?
Really not part of their plan."

"So you think this law firm's fronting for the board of
trustees?"

Chris nodded. "Something like that."

His theory rang truer to me than Sara's did. A distinguished college like Canterbury was exactly the sort of twenty-four-carat client that Bates, Winslow and Seymour was accustomed to dealing with.

Chris glanced at his watch. "I have to run to class, but I can't throw Sara's favorite cousin out in the snow. If you want to crash in the suite tonight you're more than welcome."

"That's incredibly nice of you, Chris, but I think I'll catch a train out to Willoughby. Stay with my aunt and uncle for a few days."

He eyed me curiously. "You get along with them?"

"Well enough. Why are you asking?"

"Because Bruce can't stand his parents. Especially his father. We're talking extreme loathing here. He once told me that his single greatest ambition in life is to grow up to be someone who his father thoroughly disapproves of."

"That sounds fairly damning."

Chris let out a laugh. "You think?"

"YOUR NEW GIRLFRIEND STOPPED BY," Rita informed me dryly as I came in the office door.

"New girlfriend?" I frowned at her. "What new girlfriend?"

At the sound of our voices, Mom popped out of her office, her eyes twinkling at me.

"She left you *those*," Rita explained, nodding toward my desk.

Waiting there for me on a paper plate were two slightly squished chocolate cupcakes. On one of them *Call* was scrawled in white icing. On the other *Me*.

Mom and Rita both gazed at me expectantly, anxious for the lowdown.

"That must have been Sonya. Did she say her name was Sonya?"

"I believe she did say her name was Sonya," Mom confirmed.

"You see, Abby? I told you he met someone. He has that special glow. Look at him—he's glowing right now."

"I can see it, Rita. Our little boy's all grown up."

"Would you two kindly give it up? I barely even met the girl."

"And yet," Mom said, "she's bringing you cupcakes that she made with her own little hands. Who is this Sonya?"

"The daughter of Al Posner's nephew."

Mom shuddered. "I can't stand that man. He's a total lech. Plus he smells just like—"

"Pickled herring, I know. Look, she stopped by B'Nai Jacob this morning with a coffee cake for the gang. We chatted for exactly one minute. She's a kindergarten teacher. She and her kids were making cupcakes today."

"Hence the cupcakes," Rita said.

"You don't generally see such a rack on a kindergarten teacher," Mom said.

Rita nodded in agreement. "Not unless you're watching on-line porn. She must have had a boob job. Those girls of hers are *torpedoes*."

"Maybe she just had chicken filets stuffed inside of her bra," Mom said.

"No way," Rita argued. "I could clearly make out her nipples."

"They're doing wonderfully inventive things with filets now."

"It so happens that Sonya's tits are real," I interjected.

Mom blinked at me. "And just exactly how do you know that?"

"She told me so."

"She told him so, Rita." Mom was vastly amused. "And, God knows, a young lady would never lie about such a thing to a young man who she's just met at temple."

"Sonya also asked me to give you a message. . . ." Rita squinted down at her notepad. "She wanted to make sure you hadn't 'washed your hand.' Exactly where *was* your hand?"

"Sonya wrote her phone numbers on it. She wants me to call her."

"Hence the subtle message on the cupcakes," Rita said. "Are you planning to?"

"I really don't know." Although I'd definitely transferred her numbers from my paw to my smartphone and laptop. "What did you think of her?"

"Pushy and nosy," Rita sniffed. "A regular little ferret, showing up here at your workplace asking a million questions about you. And what is up with that voice?"

"What kind of questions?"

"Where do you live? Do you have a girlfriend? What exactly do we do here at Golden Legal Services?"

"She's under the impression that I'm a lawyer."

"Not a problem, Bunny," Mom assured me. "We were purposely vague. And if you ask me she's very nice. Not to mention a total knockout—even if she is related to Al Posner. I think you should call her."

Rita clearly didn't. Her disdainful silence told me so.

I said, "I've found Bruce Weiner, in case anyone's interested.

He's staying at the Warfields' weekend place on Candlewood Lake."

"Excellent," Mom said brightly "I'll call Seymour and tell him."

"Not so fast, Mom. Before we throw Bruce to the wolves I'd like to take a run up there and make sure he's okay."

She frowned at me. "Why wouldn't he be?"

"Sara told me he tried to hang himself in high school. And Chris said he's very upset about his relationship with Charles. The guy's not answering his phone. For all we know he may have swallowed a bottle of pills."

"We were hired to find him, period. I'll pass your concerns along to Seymour."

"Sara did me a huge solid, Mom. And she's worried."

"Which I can understand. But Sara's not our client. Seymour is. And you'll be running a huge risk if you drive up there. He might rabbit on us."

"I'll make sure he doesn't."

"How, by tying him to a chair?"

"By telling him that Sara sent me. I promised her everything would be okay. I have to make sure it is. It's the right thing to do."

Mom let out a sigh. "Sometimes I wish we hadn't raised you so well. Fine, go ahead. But call me the second you make contact so I can tell Seymour. I want to button this up tonight."

"Sure thing, boss."

"And don't call me boss."

Rita printed me out the most direct route to the Warfield place on Candlewood Lake. I stuffed it in my daypack and took

off. Left my duffel on the office floor right where it lay. Didn't
bother to change out of my SUNY–Binghamton outfit. Just got
the Brougham out of the garage and took off. It was nearly 4:00
P.M. I was hoping to beat the evening rush hour traffic out of
town. Thought I had beaten it, too, until I got onto the Cross
Bronx and ran into a bumper-to-bumper crawlfest.

I was sitting there at a standstill when my cell rang. It was
Sara.

"I was just going to call you, cuz. Thanks for backing my
play with Chris."

"No big, cuz. What's up?"

"Bruce went to Chris's house on Candlewood Lake. Charles
is planning to join him there tomorrow."

"God, that sounds *so* romantic. But why isn't Brucie answering his phone?"

"That I don't know. I can fill you in later. I'm heading up
there as we speak to check it out."

"Benji, where are you at this very second?"

"In da Bronx, why?"

"You can pick me up on your way, dat's why. I'm coming
with you."

"That's a big no, Sara. I can't take you along."

"Why the hell not?"

"Just for starters, Candlewood Lake's in Connecticut. It's
against the law for me to transport you across state lines unless
you're accompanied by a parent or legal guardian."

"The age of consent is seventeen in New York. In Connecticut it's sixteen. Try again, liar mouth."

"Okay, it's like this: I'm a licensed private investigator. I'm going there on official investigative business. And you're *not* coming with me, understood?"

"Jeez, Benji, you don't have to go all butthead on me."

"Sorry, you left me no choice."

"This is my big brother we're talking about. Will you call me when you get there?"

"Count on it."

After I rang off I reached for my iPod and inched my way along in the gathering darkness to the original Broadway cast recording of *South Pacific* with Mary Martin and Ezio Pinza. Took the Hutch to 684, which led me into the northern exurbs of Armonk, Mount Kisco and Croton Falls. By the time I was closing in on Brewster, I was getting bleary-eyed. I needed to stretch my legs, too. Pulled off at a big highway rest station there and went inside for a cup of what they alleged to be fresh-brewed gourmet blend coffee. I milled around the fast food court and sipped it, eyes wide open. I'd had a bad feeling ever since I'd left Manhattan. The same feeling I'd had last night in Willoughby. I sensed I was being tailed. Not that I'd spotted anyone. But I still felt a tickle on the back of my neck. And I've learned to respect that tickle.

I got back on the road. At Brewster I picked up Interstate 84, which took me over the state line into Connecticut—where I understand the age of consent is sixteen. I got off the highway at Danbury and relied on Rita's coordinates to navigate me through the narrow, twisting back roads to Candlewood Lake. The roadsides were banked high with plowed snow. It was desolate and pitch black out. I put my high beams on and kept them on. Absolutely no one else was out on the road. For sure not on my tail.

I couldn't see the lake as I made my way around it. All I saw out there was blackness. Almost all of the lake houses were dark. City folk used them as summer places mostly. During the winter hardly anyone was around, particularly in the middle of the week. Just an occasional light revealed the million-dollar waterfront homes that were nestled there.

A quaint wooden sign at the edge of the driveway marked the Warfield place on Candlewood Lake Road. It was a circular driveway that was plowed regularly. The snow banks were piled at least three feet high. But it hadn't been plowed since yesterday. Two or three inches of fresh snow blanketed the driveway. A black Honda CR-V with New York plates was parked there under that same blanket of snow. It was Bruce's black Honda CR-V, according to the plate numbers. Apparently, he hadn't gone out today. I pulled in behind his car and got out.

Lights were blazing inside of the Warfield house, which was a nice old shingled cottage that looked as if it had been added on to about six times. A glass-walled great room looked out over the frozen lake. Floodlights gleamed off of the pure white snow cover that sloped down to their dock. The snug guest cottage that Chris had lent Bruce was next to the dock. Footsteps in the snow led down to it. Lights were on inside. Wood smoke came from its stone chimney. It smelled good in the frigid country still of night.

I tromped my way down there. The cottage's front door was half open. I could hear the television blaring inside. Bruce was watching the Canterbury-Syracuse game. Syracuse was ahead 42-38 with less than a minute to go in the first half.

"Bruce, my name's Benji Golden!" I called out. "Sara asked me to stop by!"

He didn't answer me. I heard no response. Just the ball game on the TV.

I glanced around, wondering if he'd gone up to the main house for firewood or whatever. I called out his name again. Again I heard nothing. I pushed the cottage door farther open—or tried to. It wouldn't budge. I pushed harder. Stuck my head through the open doorway to find out why.

I found out why.

Bruce lay on the floor just inside the doorway in the fetal position with his eyes wide open. He'd been shot three times— twice in the chest, once in the forehead. The entry wounds were just like the ones I'd found once in a fifteen-year-old runaway from Raleigh named Jennie Faries. The weapon that made those wounds had been her pimp's Glock 9-mm semi-automatic handgun.

He was still warm. Still bleeding out onto the hooked rug. It had *just* happened. Within the past ten minutes someone had pulled in, shot Bruce Weiner dead and taken off. Quickly, I looked around the cottage. It had only one room with a loft bed. A tiny bath. French doors out to a deck, bolted from the inside. There was no sign that anyone had forced open the front door. Bruce had invited his killer in. It didn't appear to be a robbery gone bad. The flat-screen TV had been left behind. So had the Rolex on Bruce's left wrist. Yet his laptop was missing. No

way he'd be cramming for the Gauntlet without it. And I didn't
see his cell phone anywhere either.

I went back outside with a sick feeling in my stomach and
headed up the path to the circular drive, stepping carefully now
so as not to disturb any crime scene evidence. I fetched my
flashlight from the glove compartment of the Brougham and
flicked it on. Followed my tire tracks back to the road, searching for any other tire tracks that might be there in the fresh
snow. Bingo. Someone else had pulled in over by the main
house, parked and gotten out. I could see footprints in the snow.
One set. A lone gunman. His shoe prints led from the car down
to the guest house and then back again. The prints weren't any
bigger than my own. Possibly even a bit smaller. The guy was
no behemoth, whoever he was. I followed his tire tracks back
toward the road. He'd made a sharp left when he pulled out of
the driveway, meaning he'd headed north from there toward
absolutely *nowhere*. There was only one possible reason for him
to head north—so he wouldn't bump into me.

He'd *known* I was heading there. I was the one who'd led
him to Bruce. I'd been his bird dog. That explained the tickle.

But how had he shadowed me?

I returned to the Caddy, climbed in ass backwards and shined
the flashlight on the wiring underneath the dashboard, studying it inch by inch until I found it—a flat square plastic disc held
in place with adhesive putty. I yanked the damned thing out of
there. It was a voice-activated three-watt UHF transmitter. A
bugging device capable of sending a radio signal roughly a mile
for every watt of power. Which meant he could have been three

miles behind me on the Cross Bronx and still heard every word
I'd said to Sara on the phone. It was sophisticated equipment.
Ran about a thousand bucks. Plus you'd need a receiver, too,
and those didn't come cheap. He must have planted it in the
Brougham while it was tucked away in the garage. But that still
didn't explain how he'd known which way I was heading when
I left the city. Because I *didn't* have a tail. I got out and knelt
under the car with the flashlight until I located it. A web-based
GPS tracker was attached to the rear axle with magnets. The
bastard had been following me by laptop. This was no goon.
This was a pro who knew his trade.

I stood there in the snow, boiling with rage. We'd been set up,
used, chumped, punked—whatever you want to call it. Golden
Legal Services had been hired to locate Bruce Weiner so he
could be taken out by a hit man. *Why?* Was his love affair with
Charles Willingham *so* toxic that this harmless college kid had
to be gunned down? *Who?* Was Peter Seymour behind this?
Had the patrician law firm of Bates, Winslow and Seymour
given the scruples-free Leetes Group the green light to murder
Bruce? As I stood there, my hand clenched around the bugging
devices, I asked myself what would have happened if I hadn't
stopped for that cup of coffee in Brewster. What if I'd gotten
here ten minutes sooner? What if I'd been inside of that cottage
with Bruce when the killer showed up? And, God, what if I'd
let Sara come with me?

I smashed both devices under my heel, went out to the road
and flung them deep into the woods. Then I pulled my cell out
of my coat pocket. For all I knew they were bugging my calls.
But I needed to use it. Besides, the damage was done.

"Did you make it up there okay?" Mom asked me when I got through to her on the office line.

"I made it."

"Did you find Bruce?"

"I found Bruce."

"You sound strange, Bunny. What's the matter?"

I told her. How I'd found Bruce dead. How I'd led his killer right to him.

"Why, that no-good WASP shithead!" she erupted when she was done listening. "I am going to get him on the other line right now. Hang on, Bunny. I'll put him on speaker."

The lawyer's number rang twice before I heard his burgundy baritone intone: "This is Peter Seymour."

And heard mom say: "It's Abby Golden. We found the Weiner boy up at Candlewood Lake."

"You people move fast, Mrs. Golden. I'm impressed. I was just sitting down to dinner. Could we continue this after I've?—"

"He's dead. Somebody shot him."

Seymour fell silent. "Dear God. . . ."

"But you already knew that, didn't you?"

"Whatever do you mean by that, Mrs. Golden?"

"I demand to know who your client is."

"That's privileged information. You know that."

"Here's what I know," she shot back. "You won't get away with this. We won't take the fall for you. My mother didn't raise no patsies. And Benji's mother sure as hell didn't."

"Madam, I assure you that I have—"

"Don't 'madam' me, you *momser*. You played us. Benji found the bugs in our car."

"Has he spoken to the Connecticut State Police yet?"

"Why are you asking me that?"

"Because I'd appreciate it if he kept our firm's name out of this—as a professional courtesy."

"Not a chance. We're telling them chapter and verse."

"I wouldn't advise that, Mrs. Golden."

"Guess what? I don't take advice from lying snakes. I didn't like you from the second you walked in this office. I just liked that nice, fat check from your so-called Aurora Group. I should have smelled it for what it was—blood money."

"Does that mean you're returning it?"

"Hell, no. We earned every penny of it. *And* the twenty-five thou bonus you promised us. I'm expecting a certified check for the full amount on my desk by ten o'clock tomorrow morning. If it's not here, I'm suing your ass. And don't *ever* call us again, hear me?"

"Loud and clear, Mrs. Golden. Are we done now?"

"We're done. What are you having for dinner?"

"Steak au poivre."

"I hope you choke on it." She hung up on him. "Bunny, are you still there?"

"Still here," I said, standing there in the frigid snow.

"Have you phoned it in?"

"Not yet."

"Make the call. I'll get there as soon as I can."

CHAPTER THREE

"LET'S GET ONE THING STRAIGHT RIGHT AWAY, tough guy. I don't like anybody trying to tell me how to run my investigation."

"I don't blame you one bit, Lieutenant. I wouldn't either."

"And *don't* get smart with me. I don't like anybody trying to get smart with me." Which already made two things Detective Lieutenant Marco Battalino really didn't like, and we were just throwing our warm-up tosses.

"Absolutely. Whatever you say."

We were seated at a table in a windowless interview room in the charm-free Troop L Barracks up in Litchfield. I was there to provide the lieutenant and his sergeant with my detailed witness statement. I was not, as of yet, considered a suspect or person of interest. I'd been allowed to accompany them there from Candlewood Lake in my own car. The door to the interview room was open. We were drinking coffee together. Battalino was sprawled comfortably in his chair with one foot plopped on the table. It was all quite cordial—except for the way he kept pointing out that I, a New York City private investigator, was a source of annoyance to him. Not a major source of annoyance. More of a petty one along the lines of, say, jock itch.

Battalino was a squat, baleful fireplug in his early thirties. He had a twenty-inch neck, curly black hair that grew unusually low on his forehead, a furry black strip of monobrow, furry ears, furry knuckles. The man was just really furry. As I looked at his brogan-clad foot on the table I realized how happy I was that this wasn't open-toe sandal season. He was dressed in a shiny black suit, white shirt and muted tie. On his shoulder he wore a good-sized chip.

His sergeant was a young black man named Gallagher who was taller than Battalino, better looking, a better dresser, smarter and more polite. I anticipate big things in Gallagher's future—as long as he doesn't try to tell Battalino how to run an investigation. Or get smart with him.

It had taken ten minutes for a Connecticut state trooper wearing a big Smokey the Bear hat to respond to my 911 call. I'd led him to Bruce's body in the guest cottage. As soon as he laid eyes on Bruce he called for help, which came in the form of Battalino and Gallagher from the Major Crime Squad Western District and a crew of crime scene technicians in blue-and-white cube vans. Also a death investigator from the state medical examiner's office. The crime scene investigators were still at the house on Candlewood Lake photographing and measuring the shoeprints and tire tracks in the snow. Bruce's body was being transported to the medical examiner's office in Farmington for an autopsy. The Weiners had been contacted at their home in Willoughby with the awful news. They'd have to drive to

Farmington in the morning to officially identify the body. The
mere thought of which filled me with grief. I felt complicit in
Bruce's death. I felt like shit. But I had to set my feelings aside
as I sat there with Battalino and Gallagher. Focus on concrete
physical evidence such as the killer's tire tracks. The ones that
I'd been trying to tell them led north out of the Warfield driveway.

Which was when Battalino decided to set me straight: "I
talk and you listen, got it? I'm not interested in your cute little
theories. And I expect you to shut up unless I ask you a direct
question, got it?" He gulped down some coffee, glowering at
me. "Let's talk about who hired you to find the victim."

"Was that a direct question?" I asked Gallagher.

Gallagher nodded, stone-faced.

"We were retained by the New York City law firm of Bates,
Winslow and Seymour. Peter Seymour was the partner who
contacted us."

"This was when?"

"Yesterday. He told us that Bruce Weiner had recently inherited a significant amount of money from one of their clients.
I don't know how much money. Or the client's identity. We
weren't made privy to the details."

"You do a lot of work for this law firm?"

"It was the first time they'd ever hired us. Seymour told us
they'd been trying to contact the victim for several days at his
school, Canterbury College in upper Manhattan. It was their
impression that he'd left campus. They hired us to find him."

"Why you?"

"That's what I do. Find young people."

Battalino smirked. "Whatever you say, tough guy. Talk us through it."

"Through what, Lieutenant?"

"Your activities in pursuit of the deceased, leading up to tonight."

"Okay, sure." I took a sip of my coffee, folding my hands before me on the table. "For starters, I spoke to Mr. and Mrs. Weiner last night at their house in Willoughby. They seemed to know nothing about any inheritance. Acted quite puzzled, actually. Plus they were under the impression that Bruce *was* on campus. Mr. Weiner phoned Bruce's roommate, Chris Warfield, while I was there and Chris assured him that Bruce was studying at the library."

"Uh-huh. And was he?"

"No. When I spoke to Chris in person about it today I was able to ascertain that Bruce was staying at the Warfield family home on Candlewood Lake."

"How were you able to 'ascertain' that?"

"By gaining his confidence."

"So that's something you're good at—gaining people's confidence?"

"I've had some success, yes."

"Then how come you're not gaining *my* confidence?"

I didn't respond. It didn't qualify as a direct question. Just sour gas. I wondered if Battalino had a wife. I wondered if she made him undress in the dark.

Now it was Gallagher's turn: "Any idea why the victim went to Candlewood Lake, Ben?"

"To cram for the Gauntlet. It's a week of midterm exams they have at Canterbury."

"He was alone up here?"

"As far as I know."

"Did he have any personal problems? Was he into drugs?"

"Not that I'm aware of."

"So why did the roommate lie to the victim's parents about his whereabouts?"

"I assume because Bruce asked him to."

Gallagher thought this over. "Candlewood's a mighty lonely spot this time of year. Maybe he had a nice, warm girl with him for company."

I let that go right on by. Offered not one word about Bruce's sexual orientation. And for damned sure nothing about his romantic relationship with Charles Willingham. If the finest college basketball player in America was going to get dragged into this it wasn't going to be by me. *Volunteer nothing.* That's another thing my dad taught me. Especially if you don't know what in the hell you're in the middle of. And I really, really didn't know what in the hell I was in the middle of. "My job was to locate Bruce Weiner," I said. "His body was still warm when I found him. I called my employer with the bad news. Then I called you."

"He died about a half hour before you phoned it in," Gallagher acknowledged. "The death investigator has confirmed as much. And the tire tracks and shoeprints do indicate that someone besides you has been at the scene since last night's snowfall. Any idea who that individual might be?"

"None."

"Is it your belief that what happened to the victim was not the result of a random break-in?"

"I seriously doubt it was a random break-in. But don't ask me what it was because I seriously don't know."

Battalino glared at me across the table. "I don't like it."

"I don't either, Lieutenant."

"You're not hearing me. What I don't like is the load of shit you're shoveling at us. There's something more going on here. What aren't you telling us?"

"Lieutenant, I'm being as helpful as I can. Believe me, when you speak to Peter Seymour you'll find him considerably less cooperative."

"Well, yeah, he's a high-priced New York City lawyer." Evidently, Battalino considered them to be even more of a petty annoyance than New York City private investigators. On a par with, say, the heartbreak of psoriasis. "How much did Seymour tell you when he hired you?"

"As little as possible. He refused to name his client. And he covered his tracks by paying us through a holding company."

Battalino stuck his lower lip out at me. "Where are you going with that? Is he going to deny he hired you?"

"I'm guessing he tells you he's never even heard of us."

"And now the kid who *you* say he sent you to look for is dead. Plus the kid's laptop and cell phone are gone. That just about makes you the putz of the century, am I right?"

"You could not be more wrong," a woman stated from the doorway behind me. It was Mom, who stood there looking like a million bucks, in her long sable coat. "Peter Seymour can try to play it that way. But it won't wash."

"Is that so?" Battalino eyeballed her up and down freely. "And you are? . . ."

"Abigail Golden of Golden Legal Services. I'm this gentleman's employer."

"You two are related?"

"It's a family business. My late husband, Meyer Golden, founded it."

Battalino raised his dense growth of monobrow, impressed. "*Briefcase Bob* Meyer Golden?" To me he said, "You're Meyer Golden's kid?"

"I am."

Mom strode briskly across the interview room and grabbed my duffel coat, motioning for me to stand up. "Lieutenant, we happen to enjoy excellent relations with the NYPD. If you have any doubts regarding the veracity or professionalism of my investigator then I urge you to place a personal call to Police Commissioner Dante Feldman. His direct extension number is—"

"That won't be necessary, ma'am," Battalino assured her, all four paws up in the air now. He wanted his furry belly rubbed. Like he had a prayer.

"And Peter Seymour *will* acknowledge that he retained our services," she added. "It so happens that I tape recorded our meeting. I'll be happy to make the tape available to you should it become necessary, although I doubt it will. We're all on the same side. We all want Bruce Weiner's killer brought to justice."

"That we do, ma'am," Battalino acknowledged.

"You weren't planning to detain my investigator overnight, were you?"

"No, ma'am, we were just about—"

"Do you have all of the information you need for the time being?"

"Yes, I believe that we're—"

"In that case we'll say good night now. It's late and we have a long drive home. Come on, Benji, let's blow this pop stand."

And with that we were out of there.

Like I said, Mom knows how to handle men.

THE TEMPERATURE HAD FALLEN into the teens there in the hills of Litchfield. An arctic wind was howling.

"How did you get out here?" I asked her, shivering as we started across the parking lot toward the Brougham.

"Wally rented me that green Toyota over there." Wally managed the garage where we kept the Caddy. He did a profitable side business renting out gently used cars. "I asked him if anybody's been hanging around our car lately. He said an exterminator was putting down rat poison a couple of days ago. Told Wally the building hired him. I've got Doug the techie coming in first thing tomorrow morning to sweep our office and apartments for bugs. Rita's installing new firewalls in case they've hacked into our computers—which we have to assume they have. And I got us some prepaid cell phones." She dug into her purse and handed me one. "Lose yours."

I tossed my phone in a nearby trash can. It touched bottom with a loud clank. In Connecticut they actually empty their public trash cans from time to time. Imagine that.

"Now tell me what you *didn't* tell those stateys," Mom commanded me.

"Like what?"

"Like who would want to kill that kid."

"My money's on the Canterbury board of trustees. I'm guessing the college's finances are even worse than they've owned up to. They desperately need to ride Charles Willingham all of the way to the Final Four and they can't have a gay sex scandal messing things up. Word must have leaked out somehow about Charles and Bruce. Seymour was approached by someone on the board to take care of it, quietly and discreetly. He hired us to find Bruce. And the Leetes people have been shadowing us every step of the way."

"It explains a lot," Mom conceded, hands burrowed in her coat pockets. "Except for why Seymour walked in our door peddling that inheritance yarn."

"A cover story. He made it up."

"That's not how men like Peter Seymour operate. They shade the truth. They blur it, bend it, stand it on its ear. But they don't introduce anything that constitutes an outright lie."

"So do you think this *is* about an inheritance?"

"Maybe so. Maybe Seymour's client wanted Bruce found and eliminated because he, or she, stood to gain from it."

"If that's the case then we'll have one hell of a time getting to the truth. In fact," I added glumly, "I doubt we'll ever know for sure what just happened."

"You sound down, Bunny. Are you okay?"

"I'm not even close to okay."

"I'm not either. That bastard made fools out of us. But we'll get even with him. Nobody scams the Goldens and gets away with it." She dug her keys out of her purse and unlocked the Toyota. "You lead the way home. I'll follow you."

"Whatever you say, boss."

"And *don't* call me boss."

I got onto Interstate 84 and steered us back through the darkness toward the city, with the heater cranked up high and Mom glued onto my tail. She is one of the world's worst tailgaters. Stayed no more than six feet off of my rear bumper the entire way home. I listened to WINS news radio as I drove. They had nothing on the shooting death at Candlewood Lake of Canterbury College senior Bruce Weiner. They did report that Coach John Seckla's Canterbury Athenians had edged out the Syracuse Orangemen 76-75 at a sold-out Madison Square Garden on a buzzer beater by Charles "In Charge" Willingham, who finished the game with 44 points, eight assists, six rebounds and four steals.

The traffic began to pick up as we drew closer to the city. The city is always awake. Cars and trucks are out on the roads no matter the hour—which was just past 3:00 A.M. when we pulled into Wally's twenty-four-hour garage. I removed my Chief's Special from the glove compartment, pocketed it and walked Mom home in brooding silence.

A cluster of cabs was double-parked outside of Scotty's allnight diner. Through the wraparound corner window I could see the cabbies hunched wearily over their coffee. Hector, Scotty's night man, was manning the big coffee urns. Most of the booths by the window were empty. But seated at one of them, gazing mournfully out at the street, was someone I recognized.

And when that someone caught sight of me she came running out the door of the diner and threw herself into my arms, sobbing. "I've been waiting *hours* for you, Benji. I was afraid you were *never* coming home."

"Sara, what are you doing here? How did you even . . . Mom, this is Sara Weiner."

"I'm very sorry about your brother, dear," Mom said gently.

"Thank you, Mrs. Golden," she snuffled. "I-I sneaked out of the house and Trevor gave me a ride to the Willoughby train station. I caught the midnight Metro-North to Grand Central and took a cab here. I just *had* to get away, you know? I can catch the five a.m. train back."

"Not a chance. I'm driving you home."

"Whatever. First we have to talk, Benji."

"I really meant to call you, Sara, but I was stuck with the state police until just now. I'm so sorry about what happened."

"Don't be. It wasn't your fault."

"Yes, it was. I should never have gotten you involved."

"No, *listen* to me, will you? If anyone's to blame it's *me*."

"Why you?"

"Because I wasn't totally straight with you, okay? That's why I'm here. I-I have to come clean about something right away or I'm going to flip out."

"Let's go back inside Scotty's," Mom suggested. "Normally, I'd invite you up to our office, dear, but I'm afraid our walls may have ears."

I took Sara by the arm and steered her back through the door into Scotty's. She was wearing a red ski parka and blue jeans. Her big brown eyes were swollen from crying. Mom escorted her to the farthest booth. I fetched us mugs of coffee from Hector and joined them there.

Sara dumped one, two, three spoonfuls of sugar in her mug. Took a nervous swallow, then ran a hand through her beautiful mane of honey-colored hair. "I have some money of my own. I want to hire you guys."

"Hire us to do what?" I asked.

"Find out who killed Brucie."

"The police will do that."

"No, they won't. They have no idea what's going on."

"And you do?"

She hesitated, her plump lower lip fastened between her teeth. "Remember that weird woman I told you came up to Brucie at the mall over Christmas?"

"I remember."

"I think they were . . . connected."

"As in romantically involved?" Mom asked.

Sara stared at her. "You do know my brother was gay, right?"

"I know that he was in a relationship with Charles Willingham," Mom responded. "That doesn't mean he hadn't been in relationships with women, too. But let's set that aside. What exactly do you mean by 'connected?' "

"I mean . . ." Sara took a deep breath. "Maybe she was related to him somehow—unlike me. We weren't really brother and sister, okay? My parents adopted Brucie when he was a baby. They told me they'd been trying to start a family for years, and couldn't, so they adopted Brucie. And then, like out of nowhere, my mom got pregnant with me. I hear that happens a lot. But I'm never, ever supposed to mention that he was adopted. My folks are super private about it. That's why I didn't tell you, Benji. From the time I was a teeny-tiny girl they always said, 'It's strictly a family matter. No one else's business.'"

"Which is perfectly understandable," Mom said.

Me, I was thinking about that inheritance story Peter Seymour had walked in our door with. How he'd explicitly told me not to reveal his law firm's name to Bruce's parents. How Laurie Weiner had reacted when I had. "Sara, this woman who came up to Bruce at the mall—how old was she?"

"I told you last night. Thirty, maybe thirty-five."

"Old enough to be his birth mother?"

Her eyes widened in surprise. "I thought she could be his older sister or something. His *mother?* I don't see how, unless she had him when she was, like, twelve. Why, are you thinking that's who she was?"

"I'm not thinking anything yet. Was there a physical resemblance?"

Sara thought this over, her small, soft hands wrapped around her coffee mug. "Real hard to say. She was such a total mess. Like she'd been sleeping out on the street for weeks. I do know Brucie wasn't happy to see her." She lowered her gaze, swallowing. "And there's more. I told you I couldn't hear what they were talking about. But I could. Only, it didn't make any sense. What they were saying."

I leaned over the table toward her. "Which was? . . ."

"Brucie said, 'I'm not one of you.' And she said, 'Yes, you are. You're a kid you always will be.' And he said, 'No, I'm not. I'm *not* a kid.'"

I could hear Mom draw in her breath. My own pulse was already off to the races. My mouth felt dry.

Sara gazed at us imploringly. "That doesn't make any sense, does it?"

I looked at Mom. Mom was looking at me. Because it did make sense. All of it. Mr. Classy Guy showing up in our crummy little office. The nice, fat missing-person case he'd slipped us by way of the Aurora Group. The mystery client whose name he dared not speak. The professional grade skullbuggery that had turned me into a high-priced bird dog and left Bruce Weiner dead. All of it made perfect sense—provided you stuck a second letter *d* on the word *kid* and capitalized the letter *K*. Sara may not have grasped what it meant but we sure did: Bruce Weiner may have been born a Kidd. One of *the* Kidds. Which meant that maybe, just maybe, there was a whole lot more at stake here than a distinguished small college and its shining sports hero. Maybe, just maybe, there was an entirely different reason why someone had wanted Bruce dead. Make that somewhere around three billion reasons—depending upon the ups and downs of the stock market. It meant that maybe, just maybe, we were talking about the upcoming race to decide who was going to be the next governor of the sovereign state of New York.

Or maybe, just maybe, it meant nothing at all. That would be up to me to find out. No maybe about it.

CHAPTER FOUR

I KNOW ALL ABOUT THE LEGEND of Black Jack Kidd. I grew up hearing it. Every kid in New York grows up hearing it. Black Jack Kidd was the flesh and blood embodiment of the impossible dream that was, is and always will be the engine that powers New York City.

He was born, fittingly enough, on the Fourth of July, 1902, in Rockaway Beach, Queens, which in those days was a seaside resort popular with New York City's Irish immigrants. His father, Paddy, ran a saloon there and was also a boxing promoter, loan shark and business partner of Mayor Van Wyck's bombastic police chief, William "Big Bill" Devery. According to popular legend, which in my experience is as good, if not better, than the truth, Big Bill presided over the single most corrupt police department in the history of New York City. And if you know anything about the history of New York City that's saying something. One of Paddy Kidd's joint ventures with Devery was buying up Baltimore's professional baseball team, moving it to New York City, renaming it the Highlanders and selling it for three hundred thousand dollars in 1915 to a consortium headed by beer brewer Jake Ruppert. The team was renamed the New York Yankees.

Young Jack left school at age fourteen to work in Manhattan as a bellhop at the Plaza Hotel, which at the dawn of the Jazz Age was becoming *the* hot spot for the city's wealthy young smart set. The Plaza's high society clientele found handsome young Jack to be bright, eager and—thanks to his father's contacts—very useful. If you wanted to place a bet on a horse or a boxing match, Jack was your man. If you wanted a clean, attractive girl sent to your room for an hour, or a night, Jack was your man. And, with the advent of prohibition in 1920, if you wanted a bottle of bonded whiskey, Jack was most definitely your man. Quickly, he became the go-to guy for booze among the flapper set. Which, if you're keeping score at home, made him a thriving bookmaker, pimp and bootlegger by the time he was eighteen years old.

Black Jack was no ordinary bootlegger. The man was a true visionary. He tapped into his father's powerful political and criminal connections and set up the fabulously lucrative operation off the Long Island coast that came to be known as Rum Row. It was Black Jack's fleet of fishing boats that met up three miles out to sea with William "The Real" McCoy, the fabled rumrunner who was bringing up boatloads of the stuff from the Bahamas. Until, that is, the US Coast Guard broke up their whole operation in 1923.

Undaunted, Black Jack put his money and well-connected friends to good use by becoming a Wall Street stock trader. And a mighty shady one at that. The man was a gleefully unscrupulous engineer of elaborate price fixing and insider trading schemes. There was no scoundrel more skilled at artificially puffing up a stock price, making a killing and then bailing on it before it fell back down to earth. Most of the trading laws that were put into place after the crash of '29 were put there because of Black Jack Kidd and his merry band of cohorts. Many of those cohorts lost their shirts in the crash. Not Black Jack. He sold out early and moved his money into real estate, eventually buying up large chunks of midtown Manhattan for pennies on the dollar from cash-strapped Wall Street titans.

By 1932 he was considered one of the five wealthiest men in New York City. He was a mere thirty years old and a true American success story. He wooed and wed the sensitive, lovely young Clarissa Lodge, a genuine blue-blooded Fifth Avenue aristocrat. They had one child, Tommy, a boy of fabulous wealth and privilege who went on to attend Harvard, where he was a classmate and friend of Bobby Kennedy.

Tommy Kidd devoted his entire adult life to atoning for the crimes and sins of his father, who died of a heart attack in 1950 while in the act of shtupping his mistress, Mabel Gray, age sixteen. Tommy's life was an exemplary one of public service and philanthropy. He was an advisor to President John F. Kennedy. A diplomat, an ambassador. Also a good son to his mother, an emotionally fragile woman given to bouts of what was known in those days as "nervousness." Clarissa Lodge Kidd died of an apparent accidental overdose of sleeping pills in 1964. Soon after that, Tommy, age thirty-seven, married a strong, sensible Bostonian named Eleanor Saltonstall, one of *the* Saltonstalls, and began to give away many of Black Jack's ill-gotten millions to New York City's major hospitals, libraries, and museums. He didn't part with any of the vast chunks of New York City real estate that his father had left him. The man was generous. He wasn't dumb.

Tommy and Eleanor had two children, which brings us up to the now generation. Robert, who is known to every reader of the New York tabloids as Bobby the K, just turned forty. His sister Kathleen is six years younger than he. Dubbed the "Quiet Kidd," Kathleen hasn't sought the Big Apple limelight. She attended school in Europe and has lived most of her adult life in Paris. She returned home to New York last year to be a comfort to her elderly mother, who has been a widow since Tommy's death in 1994. Kathleen has never married, is discreet about her romantic involvements and avoids high-profile causes. She draws almost no attention from the media.

Her brother Bobby, Harvard class of '93, sucks up enough of that for both of them. A flamboyant extrovert and world-class playboy, Bobby the K earned his PhD in sex, drugs and rock 'n' roll. And he inherited Black Jack's swashbuckling entrepreneurial gifts to go along with Tommy's vast fortune and social connections. Bobby the K was still in his early twenties when he started bankrolling a succession of downtown dance clubs, art galleries and restaurants. All of them chic, hot and hugely successful. Soon he was managing and producing rock bands, performance artists and comedy troupes. All of them—again—chic, hot and hugely successful. Next Bobby the K launched the Gotham Bus Company, a production and distribution hub for music, films, theater and television programming. Everything the Gotham Bus Company touched made money. He started buying up newspapers and magazines, too. By the time he was thirty, Bobby the K had transformed himself from a billionaire brat into a rapacious, unabashedly liberal media baron whose only rival on the New York scene was the rapacious, unabashedly conservative Rupert Murdoch. Bobby the K wasn't a man burdened by a lack of self-esteem. He was incredibly sure of himself and he took whatever he wanted, same as Black Jack had. Handsome like his grandfather, too, with twinkling blue eyes and a boyish mop of hair that had turned gray while he was still in college.

Given the man's constant need for attention, it was inevitable that he'd end up in politics. Which explained his choice of a wife. As a twentysomething man about downtown, he'd been linked with succulent supermodels, glam actresses, singers, tennis stars—you name her, he'd done her. Everyone in the tabloid press assumed he'd eventually marry a superbabe. But in 2002 he opted for brains and married Meg Grayson, a Yale Law School graduate and daughter of the late US Senator Andrew Grayson of New York, not to mention the niece of New York's former governor Kenneth Grayson. The Graysons have been one of the most powerful families in Democratic politics for generations. And the two families were already related by marriage—Kenneth Grayson was married to a cousin of Bobby the K's mother, Eleanor. Bobby and Meg had known each other since they were children. She was an accomplished downhill skier, horsewoman and skeet shooter. Not to mention a shrewd, sharp-elbowed campaign strategist. There'd been talk of Meg running for the US Congress, but she preferred to operate behind the scenes.

Which made them the ideal team. Bobby was the charmer

who drew people into his orbit. Meg was the fiercely driven hard-ass who kept everyone in line. First, they started a family. A boy and a girl. And then, with great stealth and precision, they started recrafting Bobby the K's flamboyant image. He divested himself of the Gotham Bus Company, selling it off for God knows how many billions. And then Meg joined him on his celebrated "listening tour" of New York State, where he logged face time with mayors, police chiefs and union leaders in decidedly unchic places like Buffalo and Syracuse. Bobby the K won over these longtime Grayson family loyalists one by one. The same traits that had made him a wildly successful entrepreneur translated easily to the political arena. He was a charismatic public speaker. He had top writers on his payroll. And he had a simple message: "Voters are tired of do-nothing politicians. I'm Mr. Do Something."

Also Mr. Can't Miss. He had Meg by his side. Her family's political machine in his back pocket. Media contacts and savvy of his own. A campaign war chest no one else could match. The man was a shoo-in to win the Democratic Party's primary for governor of New York. And a lock to win it all in November. At the still-young age of forty, Bobby Kidd was going to be the next governor of the state of New York. There was no stopping him.

Unless, that is, something or someone popped up out of nowhere to trip him up.

A UNIFORMED CAMPUS COP stood guard at the players' entrance to the historic Stuyvesant Field House. To get past him I had to flash my laminated Canterbury College student photo ID and my press credentials from the *Daily Athenian,* the on-line student newspaper. Both cards were courtesy of Rita. When the campus cop grudgingly let me in, I found myself in a subterranean maze of dank, dimly lit concrete corridors. The historic Field House had been built just after World War I and probably would have been condemned decades ago if some genius hadn't slapped the word "historic" on it. The bare light-bulbs flickered and sizzled. The exposed overhead pipes leaked. There were puddles everywhere. I saw one, two, three rats as I splish-splashed my way past the home and visitor locker rooms, which gave off the familiar scent of mildew, soggy gym towels and soiled jock straps. As I neared the entrance to the arena I could hear husky yells and the thudding of footsteps on hard-wood flooring.

Out on the court, the Athenians were running full court drills and their young head coach, John Seckla, was giving them a real earful. There was no way to tell from his tone or manner that his players had actually beaten mighty Syracuse last night. Another security guard intercepted me as I made my way down to the court. Again, I flashed my campus credentials. Again, I was allowed to pass. I slid into a seat a few rows behind the bench.

"Billy, get *on* him, will you?" Coach Seckla hollered at the pimply scrub who was trying to keep up with the Charles Will-ingham in the open court. "Honest to God, son, my *mother* can defend tighter than that! *Move* those feet!"

Mostly, my eyes were glued on Charles and the fluid, seem-ingly effortless way he flowed up and down the court, weaving his way through defenders, changing speeds, stopping, starting, pivoting. Charles was never off balance. Never out of position. Never out of breath. He was a faster, stronger animal than the others. But it wasn't just his physical superiority that set him apart. It was his court awareness. He had a precise idea of where he was going and why he was going there. The others were just running up and down the floor.

When the shoot-around was over, Coach Seckla blew his whistle and gathered his players around him at midcourt. He spoke to them quietly for a moment. When he was done, each player piled an outstretched hand atop another's and—as one—they hollered "*Team!*" Then they broke practice and made their way slowly back toward the locker room. Over by the bench, a team manager tossed Charles a towel. Charles paused there to wipe his sweat-drenched face as the others filed out.

I made my move, feeling like a tiny little boy the nearer I got to him. He towered over me by a foot. "I'm sorry for your loss, Charles."

He frowned at me. "What loss? We beat them by one point."

"I'm not talking about the game. I'm talking about Bruce. I'm the person who found him last night."

Charles's eyes widened. He glanced over his shoulder, then turned back to me, swallowing. "This isn't a good time, man."

Coach Seckla noticed me there with his star player and started toward us. "Everything okay, Charles?"

"I'm with the *Daily Athenian*, Coach," I said, holding up my press ID.

"Sure, that's fine, son. Just haven't seen you before, that's all. What happened to Neal?"

"He's still around. I don't usually write about sports. My thing is the theater."

The coach stared at me blankly. "Theater?"

I waved an arm at the empty seats around us. "It's all theater, don't you think?"

"Son, are you high on something?"

"No, sir."

"And you cleared this interview with Bucky?"

"Yeah, he did, Coach," Charles spoke up. "It was Bucky who set it up."

Coach Seckla shrugged. "Don't keep him long, son. He needs to hit the shower." Then he headed off the court with the others, leaving the two of us alone by the team bench.

"Who's Bucky?" I asked.

"Our sports information director," Charles replied. "And just exactly who are you?"

"My name's Benji Golden. I'm a private investigator."

"No way."

"Way."

Charles took a seat at courtside, stretching his long legs out before him. He exuded the physical vitality of a world-class athlete from every pore. Also an athlete's tremendous physical calm. But while his body was at rest, his mind wasn't. His large, liquid brown eyes watched me warily as he sat there, hands resting on his knees. They were enormous hands. He had the longest fingers I'd ever seen.

"I'm surprised you made it to practice today," I said.

"Don't have any choice. I'm expected to be here. I can't just not show up because a buddy of mine got capped."

"No, I guess not. Except Bruce wasn't just a buddy, was he?"

Charles stared at me long and hard. "What's that supposed to mean?"

"Look, I know the real story, okay? Sara told me."

Charles ran a hand over his hair, which he wore high and tight to his skull. "Why would she go and do that?"

"Because she was worried about him. He could get really depressed sometimes. She wanted me to make sure he was okay."

"So you were working for his family?"

"Not exactly. It's a bit more complicated than that."

He peered at me, his gaze softening. "How did he look when you found him?"

"Very peaceful. He didn't suffer."

"Sara texted me right after the police called her family. I was up all night surfing every news site I could find. The news reports were real sketchy—just a couple of sentences about a botched home invasion. Sounded like it was a couple of meth heads maybe. You don't think about something like that happening in a million-dollar lakefront home in Connecticut. What did the fool bastards get out of it anyway—a lousy TV set?"

"It was only one bastard. And he was no fool."

Charles Willingham's face tightened. "What are you trying to tell me?"

"That it was no home invasion, botched or otherwise. Bruce was murdered by a professional hit man."

"That's bull. Who would want Bruce dead?"

"I was hoping you might have some idea."

"Why me?" he demanded. "Do you think *I* had something to do with it?"

"Not directly, no. But the two of you *were* involved."

He ducked his head, sighing hugely. "Bruce was the only slice of normal I had. He kept me together. I don't know how I'm going to get through this."

"His parents will be sitting shiva today. Are you planning to go?"

"I can't, man. I-I just can't." He swiped at his face with the towel again. "What is it that you want?"

"I'm trying to figure out what happened." I told him how Bates, Winslow and Seymour had hired us to find Bruce. How I'd managed to locate him but had unwittingly led his killer right to him. Doug, our techie, had swept the office earlier that morning. Found the place crawling with bugs. Our office phones were being tapped, too.

"So you're telling me," Charles said slowly, "that a slick attorney scammed you into finding Bruce in order to have him killed."

"Exactly. It was a professional job all of the way."

"But who on earth would want to do that to Bruce?"

"You tell me, Charles."

"Tell you what, man? How would I know anything? I'm a ball player."

"You're a *gay* ball player. Who knew about you and Bruce?"

"Nobody. My mom. Bruce's roommate, Chris, and Sara. That's it. As far as my teammates and Coach Seckla are concerned, Bruce and I were friends who shot hoops together. No

one ever suspected that anything more was going on. Why
would they? I've hung with a lot of girls since I've been here.
Even had a steady thing going last year with a Nigerian girl.
Her dad's in the oil business. Terrific girl. Smart, beautiful. But
there was no spark, know what I mean?"

"I know."

"For me, there was never anyone special. Not until I met
Bruce. And what we had going on . . ." He cleared his throat
uncomfortably. "That was something neither of us had ever
done before."

"And what about the NBA?"

He stared at me. "What about it?"

"You're going to be worth hundreds of millions when draft
day arrives. I know there are NCAA rules governing who you
can and can't talk to before you turn pro. I also know those
rules are made to be broken. I need to know the real deal. Do
you have a handshake agreement with a management agency or
sneaker company or anyone else who might believe they have a
financial stake in your future?"

"Absolutely not," Charles insisted vehemently. "I've stayed
clear of those people. Coach Seckla has been real good about
keeping them away from me. He's an honorable guy. There's
no one, I swear." He gazed out at the court for a moment. "Besides, I'm not even sure I'm going to play pro ball."

"You mean you may not?"

"Just because you can do something reasonably well doesn't
mean that you want to devote your life to it. That was the
truly whack thing about Bruce and me. He loved the game
of basketball much more than I ever have. Every facet of it—

practice, the weight room, being on the bus with the guys. Me, I'd just as soon start law school in the fall. I want to help other people."

"And you don't think you are?"

"By playing ball? This is strictly theater, like you said."

"Charles, did you know that the Weiners weren't Bruce's birth parents? That they adopted him when he was a baby?"

He raised his chin at me. "Sure, I knew. And it was no big deal. Or at least it wasn't until his birth mother suddenly decided she wanted back into his life. She provoked contact, as we say out on the court. Approached him right here on campus."

"When was this?"

"The day after we played St. John's. That was a week before Thanksgiving."

Which translated to several weeks before Sara said that a woman had accosted Bruce at a mall in Willoughby. "And how did Bruce feel about it?"

"He was freaked out. This total stranger coming up to him out of nowhere, wanting to start up a relationship. He wanted no part of it. Or her."

"He'd never expressed any interest in meeting his birth mother?"

"Never. The Weiners were his parents, period. Don't ask me how this woman found him because I don't know."

"Did you meet her?"

"No, I didn't. I can't tell you much else about her—except that she really got under his skin. After that he started obsessing about his adoption. Asking his parents about the details. The name of the adoption agency, that kind of thing."

"Were the Weiners forthcoming?"

"Anything but. They wouldn't talk about it at all. When he asked to see his original birth certificate they gave him the run-around about that, too."

"When you say 'original' you mean? . . ."

"The Weiners had to apply for US citizenship for Bruce after they adopted him."

"So he was born overseas?"

"Apparently. Bruce never found out where. Or got a look at his birth certificate. They have it hidden away somewhere and wouldn't show it to him. He had no idea why. It really bothered him. It was . . . a sore subject. Whatever that lady told Bruce was eating at him. He went up to Candlewood Lake because he needed some time alone to figure things out. But h-he . . ." Charles broke off, his face etched with misery. "I would have been there for him, you know? Whenever I was down, he was right there to pick me up. We would have handled it. Together, we could handle anything."

"Charles, do you have someone who you can be with?"

"My mom," he replied, his eyes puddling with tears.

I opened my daypack and showed him the two New York State driver's license photos that Rita had pulled from the DMV's database. "Have you ever seen either of these women on campus?"

He studied the photos carefully before he said, "No, I don't believe I have. Although this one here looks vaguely familiar. I may have seen her picture in the newspaper. Is that possible?"

"Yes, it's possible. And what about this other one?"

"I don't recognize her at all." He narrowed his gaze at me. "Who are these women?"

"That, my friend, is a very good question."

"I'm SORRY FOR YOUR LOSS," I said when Paul Weiner opened his front door.

The street outside of the house was lined with parked cars. I'd had to park ten houses down Powder Horn Hill Road.

Paul stared at me, bewildered and blown away. He looked like a man who'd just gotten poleaxed with a two-by-four. "What . . . are *you* doing here?"

Sara rushed toward the door and said, "Daddy, I invited him, okay?" Then took me by the hand and tugged me inside.

Sara had her hair pulled back with a clasp. She was wearing a white silk blouse and a short, rather tight black skirt with low heels. Her smooth white legs were bare. Her eyes were puffy. She'd been up late last night, I happened to know. It was nearly four A.M. by the time I delivered her home from Scotty's diner. She dozed for the last hour of the drive, her down jacket thrown over her like a blanket. I had to wake her up when I pulled up outside of the house. Before she got out she kissed me on the cheek, her breath warm on my neck, and said, "G'night, Benji. Thanks for being such a sweetie."

I thought about her breath on my neck the whole way back to the city.

There was a box of yarmulkes by the door in the entry hall. I put one on and followed her toward the cavernous showroom of a living room. It was full of mourners that day. Full of a heavy, quiet sadness. At least three dozen people were sitting shiva for Bruce. Most of them were older people. Relatives and family friends, I imagined. Bruce's mother, Laurie, sat crying on the sofa. Two women were trying to comfort her. When Laurie caught sight of me in the doorway, holding Sara's hand, she glared at me and murmured something to the women next to her. They glared at me, too.

A group of big, husky young guys were seated in there. I figured them for Bruce's high school basketball teammates. His Canterbury roommate, Chris Warfield, was there, too, yarmulke perched high atop his mop of curly blond hair. When Chris spotted me he came right over to give me a sympathetic hug. He was still under the impression that I was Bruce's cousin—a deception that made me feel slightly soiled under the circumstances.

"Real sorry about what happened, bro," he said softly.

"Me, too. It was real nice of you to come, Chris."

"Hey, least I could do for my roomie."

"Chris, will you please excuse us for a sec?" asked Sara. "Benji and I have to talk."

She led me toward the kitchen, which smelled of fresh-brewed coffee and marble cake. A half-dozen women were bustling away in there. Working the phone. Slicing the cake. Getting plates, cups and silverware ready.

"Your mother needs you to unload the dishwasher," one of them barked at Sara.

"In a minute, Aunt Stella," she responded, leading me out the door that was next to the pantry.

It was a bit chilly out in the attached garage, but not too bad.

The garage door was down. Two cars were parked inside—a Lexus SUV and a BMW convertible. One wall of the garage was lined with steel industrial shelving. Sara reached around behind a carton on the top shelf and came away with a small package wrapped in tissue paper. I thought it might be her dope stash but it wasn't. That was on a different shelf, tucked inside of a Twinings Tea tin. She removed a joint from it and returned the tin to its hiding place. Then she started toward a cast-iron spiral staircase that led to an enclosed loft space over the garage.

That was when the kitchen door opened and out came Laurie, who wore a black dress that was so shapeless she looked like a stick figure inside of it. Her shoulders were hunched, her complexion grayish. "What's going on out here?" she demanded.

"*Nothing*," Sara shot back defensively. "We're *talking*."

"About what? What is this person even doing here?"

"I invited him."

"How dare you? And how dare you sit shiva for your brother without wearing any stockings?"

"What the fuck difference does *that* make?"

"Don't you talk to me like!—"

"I'm very sorry for your loss, Mrs. Weiner," I interjected.

"Young man, I want you to leave my house right this second. You came here the other night with some cockamamie story about some cockamamie inheritance and now my son is dead."

"You've had contact with Bates, Winslow and Seymour before, haven't you?" I suggested.

Laurie lowered her eyes. "Why, no. Whatever do you mean?"

"Mom, he knows all about Bruce being adopted."

"How would he know that?"

"Because I told him," Sara answered.

Laurie took two steps toward her and slapped her hard across the face. It made a loud smack. "Young man, I want you to leave."

"I want him to stay!" Sara cried out, a red splotch forming on her cheek.

"I do not have time for this right now. I have a house full of people. But we *will* talk about this later," Laurie vowed, shaking her finger at Sara. Then she stormed back inside the house, slamming the door.

"I hate you!" Sara hollered after her.

"Maybe she's right. I'd better take off."

"No, please don't, Benji." Sara held her hand out to me. "Come upstairs with me, okay?"

There was a ton of clutter up in the room over the garage. Assorted half-finished craft projects that seemed to involve seashells, dried flowers, pebbles, bits of colored glass and a variety of X-ACTO knives, clamps and glues. I had no idea what any of them were supposed to be. I've never understood the concept of crafts. There was a desk in there. A daybed. One window that faced the street. Another that looked out over the Weiners' backyard, which appeared to be at least two acres of snow-covered lawn and iron-gray bare trees.

I sat down on the daybed. Sara flicked on an electric space heater, then found a book of matches on the desk and lit the joint, toking on it deeply as she stood there. "This is supposed to be my mom's studio. She has this lame idea that she's artistic. Trevor and I come up here to bone if she's home, which she almost never is because she's out boning her boyfriend. Get this, he's—"

"The principal of her school, I know."

She gazed at me curiously. "How did you find that out?"

"Part of the job."

"God, Benji, my life is *so* messed up right now that I-I . . ." She let out a sob and threw herself into my arms.

I sat there with her, hugging her protectively. I was starting to feel responsible for Sara Weiner. Bruce was gone. She needed someone. That someone was me.

"Sorry, I didn't mean to blubber all over you," she sniffled. "That just keeps happening."

"Let it happen. It's healthy."

She took a deep breath and let it out, composing herself. Then moved over to the desk chair and sat, crossing her bare legs.

I perched on the edge of the daybed, trying not to stare at her smooth white thighs. I reminded myself that she was seventeen, grief-stricken and vulnerable. I reminded myself that I was not the sort of horny, low-class boor who would ever take advantage of such a girl in her parents' garage while they were inside sitting shiva for her dead brother. That wasn't me. Nope, not me.

Sara relit the joint, toking on it. "Want some, Benji?"

I shook my head.

Now she held that small, tissue-wrapped package out to me. "I made this for you," she said shyly.

I unwrapped it. Inside, I found a hand-woven purple-and-pink striped bracelet.

"It's a friendship bracelet," she explained, coloring slightly. "And see? It has a silver bunny-rabbit clasp. That's because your mom calls you Bunny. I-I only make them for special people. I've never made one for Trevor, okay? Here, give me your wrist. . . ." She put the woven bracelet around my right wrist, fastening it in place with the clasp. "Now, remember, you can't *ever* take it off. Not until it breaks on its own. Otherwise something heinous will happen to you. Promise?"

"I promise," I said, admiring it there on my wrist.

"You think it's totally girlie-girl and stupid, don't you?"

"Sara, I think it's the nicest present anyone's ever given me."

"Now you're just making fun of me."

"I'm not, I swear."

Her big brown eyes searched mine. "Really?"

"Really. I feel honored."

She smiled, showing me those dimples of hers. "Cool."

"So, listen, I sat down with Charles this morning."

Her face fell. "How is he?"

"A wreck. He's going to stay with his mother for a few days."

"That must be nice," Sara said, fingering her splotchy cheek. "Being able to share his grief with his mother, I mean. Mine's the total bitch from hell. God, it's just so awful here. My mom and dad hate each other. And they don't even know I'm alive, I swear. Can I go back to New York with you, Benji? I really need someplace sane to crash for a few days."

"Your place is here, Sara. Your parents need you, whether it seems that way or not. Besides, you have school, don't you?"

"I guess," she acknowledged grudgingly. "They gave me today off. I don't want to go back tomorrow. Everyone's going to be totally weird about Bruce and everything. Staring at me like I'm some freak."

"You have your friends. You have Trevor. It'll be okay."

"No, it won't, Benji," she said quietly. "It won't ever be okay."

I studied Sara carefully, not liking what I was hearing one bit. Because I'd heard it before. She was another runaway in the making. I wondered if she'd show up at my door some night very soon, even though I'd told her not to come. I wondered what I'd do if she did. "Charles told me that Bruce had been trying to find out the details of his adoption. Your parents wouldn't talk about it."

Sara nodded. "They never talk about it. Ever. You'd swear the stork just left him on their doorstep."

"Have you ever seen any of his birth records or adoption papers? Anything like that?"

"Nothing, Benji."

"Do they keep a safety deposit box at a local bank out here?"

"I really wouldn't know."

"That woman who you told us approached Bruce at the mall . . ."

"What about her?"

"She'd already approached him at Canterbury a week before Thanksgiving. Charles didn't see it happen, but I showed him a couple of photographs anyway. I was hoping maybe he saw one of the women around campus."

"And did he?"

"I'm afraid not."

"Did you bring them with you?" she asked anxiously. "Can I see them?"

I had the DMV photos tucked in my coat pocket. I held them out to her.

Sara peered at them—and immediately tapped one of the photos with her finger. "That's her, Benji. She's the one."

"Are you positive?"

"Totally. She's the woman who I saw at the mall. She looked messier in person, but it was her." Sara lifted her gaze at me. "Is she Bruce's real mother?"

"I don't know."

"Well, what's her name? Who is she?"

"A great big pile of trouble."

"SARA IDENTIFIED HER," I informed Mom over my disposable cell phone as I drove away from the Weiner house. "The woman who accosted Bruce at the mall was none other than Bobby the K's sister—Kathleen Kidd."

I could hear Mom draw in her breath. "She's positive it was Kathleen?"

"I showed her two pictures. One was of Bobby's wife, Meg Grayson Kidd, who Charles Willingham thought he recognized from the newspaper. The other was of Kathleen. Sara went right for her. No hesitation. I'll pay a call on Kathleen as soon as I get back to the city. I have to talk to her. According to her driver's license she lives at 131 Riverside Drive. That's the Dorchester on the corner of West 85th, isn't it?"

"Yes, it is."

"If she won't see me I'll stake out the building. She has to come out sometime. She'll talk to me."

"She won't be doing any talking, Bunny," Mom informed me. "She took a dive off of her sixteenth-floor balcony two hours ago. Kathleen Kidd is dead. It's all over the Internet.

According to a family spokesman she had a long history of emotional problems, which explains why she avoided the lime-light all of these years. The Kidd family's been shielding her. Hell, hiding her."

I didn't hear that last part real well. There was too much whirring going on inside of my head.

"Bunny, are you still there or did that cheap phone just crap out?"

"I'm still here," I said quietly. "Mom, what in the hell have we gotten ourselves into?"

"I don't know."

"I don't either. But I'm going to find out. And when I do . . ."

"Yes, Bunny?"

"Somebody's going to be really sorry."

"YO, HOW ARE YOU, LITTLE BUD?"

"I've been better, Legs."

"Your message said you have something for me about our jumper."

"That I do."

"Then I guess you'd better lay it on me."

"I guess I'd better."

Detective Lieutenant Larry Diamond and I were hunched over cups of coffee at a Greek coffee shop on Broadway and West 89th Street, not far from where Kathleen Kidd had gone splat all over the sidewalk. It was 4:30 in the afternoon and the place was packed with grumpy, half-deaf old timers who were partaking of that day's Early Bird Special—one-half of a roasted chicken, vegetable, potato, soup and complimentary

glass of red or white wine. It was a bit like meeting up at a senior center.

My dad had been Larry Diamond's rabbi back when Legs
joined the force out of Brooklyn College, where he'd graduated
with a degree in English literature. My dad changed his diapers
and whispered in the right ears when Legs wanted to make detective. He saw a rising star in Legs Diamond. Someone who
was super intense, super smart and wasn't afraid to ruffle feath-
ers. Someone who cared. Legs is six years older than I am and
is like a big brother to me. A big brother who happens to be a
homicide detective working out of the two-four, which encom-
passes the neighborhood where Kathleen lived. Since she was a
Kidd I figured that meant Legs's boss would assign his best
man to the case. Legs Diamond is the two-four's best man.

He sipped his coffee, waiting me out. Our young waitress
passed by and topped off his cup for him, undressing him with
her eyes. Legs is the kind of guy who women stare at that way.
He has a lot of wavy black hair, soulful dark eyes and a goatee.
He wore an aged leather trench coat over a black turtleneck
sweater, blue jeans and motorcycle boots. To be honest, he's kind
of my idol in the looks department. The only thing I don't envy
about him is his wary restlessness. The man never relaxes. Ever.
He also has some nagging name-recognition issues, as in he really, really doesn't like to be called Larry.

"They're calling Kathleen's death a suicide," I said over the
din of fifty or more old people slurping their soup. "Is there any
chance it wasn't?"

He sat there, one knee jiggling. "Meaning you think somebody pushed her?"

"I'm just asking. It never hurts to ask."

"Actually, that's not true. It can hurt a lot." Legs ran a hand through his hair, thinking it over. "I examined her body and it plays suicide all of the way. No fresh bruising. No scratch marks. Her fingernails were clean. . . ."

"How about her apartment?"

"She was an artist of some kind. Had abstract paintings taped all over the walls. And her living room's strewn with tubes of paint, brushes, canvases. The place is a real pigsty. Dirty clothes and dishes everywhere. But there was no sign of a break-in or a struggle. No furniture overturned. No scuff marks on the tile flooring out on the balcony." His eyes searched mine. "We're family. I'll recheck everything from top to bottom if you give me a good reason why. But so far I'm not seeing one." He pulled a notepad from his coat pocket, flipping it open. "Her doorman told us she had no visitors in the time frame leading up to her death. He also said the lady was a recluse. Seldom went out. Had everything delivered. Her psychiatrist, a Dr. Joseph Schwartz, told us we'd likely find a combination of antidepression medications in her system. The medicine chest in her bathroom is full of them. She practically has a pharmacy in there. Wasn't supposed to drink alcohol on top of what she was taking but we found a half-empty bottle of Bordeaux and one glass on the coffee table in her living room. Also several empties in the trash in the kitchen. We've got her mixing booze with powerful meds and no sign of a break-in or a struggle. What does that tell you?"

"That whoever pushed her off of her balcony was someone who she knew—or felt she had no reason to be afraid of."

Legs looked at me doubtfully. "It could be just exactly what it looks like."

"Trust me, it's not. Did anyone sign in downstairs shortly before her death? Someone who came to, say, visit another tenant or repair somebody's cable TV?"

"Absolutely. It's a huge building. A hundred and sixty-one tenants. We have a list of everyone who signed in with the doorman in the two hours leading up to her death. And we've got a man checking them out, one by one, just to determine if they saw or heard anything."

"Can I see the list?"

"I don't have it on me, but I can get it for you."

"Was anything missing from her apartment?"

"You mean like jewelry?"

"I mean like a laptop computer."

Legs stared at me. "Now that you mention it, I didn't notice a laptop."

"How about her cell phone?"

"I don't know. They're still cataloguing everything." He reached for his own cell. "I'll check."

I sipped my coffee while he did, serenaded by the cheery sound of soup spoons bouncing off of artificial teeth.

"No cell phone," Legs reported after he rang off. "Not in her purse. Not anywhere." He peered at me suspiciously now. "Where are you going with this? Because to me it plays suicide all of the way."

"Of course it does. That's what they want you to think."

"Okay, who is *they*?"

"Will there be an autopsy?"

"Has to be. It's an unnatural death."

"Will the autopsy results be made public?"

"She was a Kidd. We're talking about the wealthiest, most politically connected family in the city."

"Does that mean no?"

"It means," Legs replied, "that the family lawyer has already done some heavy leaning on Commissioner Feldman. Her autopsy results are to be kept sealed. First thing I was told when I was handed the case."

"That's because the Kidds know what it'll show."

"Which is? . . ."

"That Kathleen had a baby at a certain point in her life."

"*What* point in her life?"

"I'd say right around when she was thirteen years old. This Kidd family lawyer who leaned on Feldman—was his name by any chance Peter Seymour?"

"How did you know that?"

"Because he's the classy cocksucker who set me up."

Legs Diamond took a slow sip of his coffee before he turned his penetrating gaze on me and said, "Start talking, little bud."

I started talking. I told him everything I could, which is to say everything short of the name Charles Willingham and why Bruce Weiner had been staying in a borrowed guest cottage on Candlewood Lake. There was no need for Legs to know that. But I told him the rest. How Mr. Classy Guy had shown up at our office two days ago offering us big bucks to find the elusive Bruce. How I'd found him at the Warfield place on Candlewood Lake with three nine-mil slugs in him and his laptop and cell phone gone. How I'd learned from his sister, Sara, that Bruce had been adopted. And that Bruce had been approached on campus before Thanksgiving by a woman claiming to be his birth mother. Sara had seen a woman in her thirties approach Bruce at a mall in Willoughby over Christmas. And had heard the woman say, "You're a kid and you always will be." Kid as in Kidd. She'd identified the woman from her DMV photo as Kathleen Kidd.

"My car was bugged," I informed him. "A three-watt UHF transmitter and a GPS tracker. Our office and our phones were bugged. The whole thing smells of the Leetes Group. We know that they're involved—Seymour had them prepare the file he gave us on the Weiners. He used me to find Bruce so that Bruce could be taken out. And now Kathleen is dead, too. There's no way her death is a random, coincidental suicide. It's all part of a calculated plan to keep some awful secret from coming out."

Legs let all of this soak in, his head nodding. "Yo, I see where you're coming from. It plays. But it's pure speculation. If I take it to my captain I'll get nowhere. Not without hard evidence. And I'll for damned sure get nowhere with Jake Leetes. He's as tough and nasty as they come." He paused, mulling it over. "Who's handling the Weiner shooting out in Connecticut?"

"Some total prick on the major crime squad in Litchfield."

"He's not a Battalino, is he?"

"Yeah, how'd you know that?"

"Because half of the guys who have juice out there are Battalinos. They're one big happy family. Which one is it—Rico, Tommy, Richie? . . ."

"Marco. Since when are you such an expert on the Connecticut State Police?"

"I've been seeing a woman named Claudia who's a homicide investigator on major crimes out there. Met her on a case a few weeks back."

"Hey, that's great, Legs."

"Well, it is and it isn't," grumbled Legs, whose relationship train always seemed to come grinding to a halt at dysfunction junction. "She lives three hours away. The best we can manage is weekends, except we're both workaholics so who has a weekend? Mostly, we just sext back and forth twenty times a day— which gets old in a hurry, believe me."

"Oh, I do."

He shot me a look. "You mocking me?"

"Never."

"Good, because I can still pound the snot out of you."

"What you two need is a week in the Bahamas together. Why don't you both put in for vacation time and book a trip?"

"I have a better idea. Why don't you and me get back to what we were talking about, okay, Dr. Phil?"

"Whatever you say."

He tugged at his goatee thoughtfully. "If he's a Battalino then he's probably not overly blessed in the smarts department."

"You can just go ahead and dispense with the word 'probably.'"

"But he'll be turfy. It's *his* case and he won't want any hotshot from New York City within ten miles of it. *Maybe* I could sell him that our two cases connect up. But first I'd have to sell my own captain. And I'm going to need more before I can do that."

"You have two dead bodies. Kathleen Kidd's is in the custody of the Manhattan medical examiner. Bruce Weiner's is at the State of Connecticut's lab in Farmington. Can't you just take a DNA sample from each of them to verify that she was his birth mother?"

"Yes but no."

"What does that mean?"

"It means I'd have to fill out a requisition. That means it has to be part of an official investigation. And there *is* no investigation into Kathleen Kidd's death. If I mess around in this it could cost me my shield. By the way, did I remember to thank you large for dumping it in my lap?"

"I wouldn't think of dumping it anywhere else. Can you do it or not?"

"Only if it's off the books," he replied, puffing out his cheeks. "It'll have to come in through the back door on tiptoes. I'll talk to my girl Claudia. See if she knows someone in Farmington who'll do her a solid. And there *might* be someone in our ME's office who'll help me out. But I'll still need a whole lot more to get my captain on board."

"Like what?"

"Like a paper trail. Bruce Weiner's birth certificate, the adoption records. All of that ought to be recorded somewhere. Trouble is, if you're right about any of this . . ."

"Oh, I'm right."

"Then as soon as I start nosing around a really loud alarm bell will go off and the Kidd family will shut me right down." He stared down into his coffee cup. "This sister of Bruce's . . ."

"Sara? What about her?"

"If they've got her on tape talking to you then her life may be in danger."

"Legs, if anything happens to that girl I'll never forgive myself."

"Same goes for her parents," he added. "They're the ones who legally adopted Bruce. They know a lot. Too much, maybe. Where is it that they live?"

I gave him their address in Willoughby.

"I'm going to ask the Willoughby PD to keep an eye on that house."

"Does this mean you believe me?"

"It means I'd rather be safe than sorry. Who was Bruce tight with?"

"His roommate, Chris Warfield."

"Okay, I can reach out to the campus police. Anyone else?"

"No one else," I stated firmly.

He looked me in the eye and said, "Yeah, there is."

"Legs, there's no one else."

"Yeah, there is."

"Why do you keep saying that?"

"Because you suck as a liar."

"Really? I always thought I was pretty good."

"Maybe with other people. Me, I can see right through you. Who else was Bruce tight with? And don't you dare hold out on me."

"Charles Willingham," I said, swallowing. "*The* Charles Willingham. The two of them were extremely close, okay?"

He stared at me. "When you say 'extremely close' are you saying? . . ."

"I'm saying it."

"Okay, that particular nugget we keep to ourselves."

"Thank you."

"But I'm for sure putting a man on him. Any idea where he?—"

"He's staying with his mom, Velma, for a few days. She lives in the Martin Luther King projects. And Charles confides in her."

"Anybody else?"

"That's everybody."

Legs shook his head at me. "Not so, doofus. There's *you*."

"They could have taken me out last night at Candlewood Lake. If they wanted me dead I'd be dead."

"Don't be too sure. That was last night. Today's a whole new scenario. Kathleen's dead. And now you've reached out to me. That might change everything as far as they're concerned. Are you packing?"

I patted the pocket of my duffel coat, nodding. "But Mom never carries a weapon. Neither does Rita."

"I'll ask somebody to keep an eye on them off the clock. For Meyer Golden's widow I bet I can scrounge up more than three-dozen volunteers. Your father was beloved. I was proud to know him."

"So was I."

"I've been granted some brief, respectful face time with Kathleen's mother, Eleanor, tomorrow morning. It falls under the category of routine follow-up. I'm guessing that Bobby the K and Meg will be there. Also this attorney of theirs, Peter Seymour."

"Wait until you get a load of his shoes."

"His what?"

"You were saying? . . ."

"Maybe I'll find out something about Kathleen that'll shed a light on what's going on here. But I'll have to tread super careful or Seymour will show me the door."

"That you can count on. Any chance I can tag along?"

"In what capacity?"

"I'm working for the Weiner family."

"You are?"

"Well, no. Although Sara did try to hire us last night."

"Did I remember to thank you for dumping this in my lap?"

"I believe you did."

Legs Diamond drained the last of his coffee, looking down into his empty cup. "Let's say, just for the sake of argument, that Kathleen Kidd *did* have a baby way back when she was thirteen. Let's say she *was* Bruce Weiner's birth mother. Why suddenly take them out now, after all of these years?"

"Her brother does intend to be our next governor."

"Yo, I totally get that. And I get that the tabloids would go hog wild if this ever came out. But so what? The Kidds have been tabloid fodder for as long as there have been tabloids. What's there to be *so* afraid of? Seriously, who cares if his emotionally unstable sister got herself knocked up twenty years ago?"

I drank the last of my own coffee. "Good question, Legs. I don't have an answer. But *somebody* cares."

SHE LIVED IN A FOUR-STORY brownstone on West 12 between Fifth and Sixth, which happens to be a really nice Greenwich

Village block of really nice brownstones. Hers was especially nice. It had tall windows with window boxes. A polished hardwood front door with gleaming brass work. I tried the door but it was locked. There was no walk-in vestibule with the usual row of mailboxes and apartment buzzers. There was only the hardwood door and one buzzer. I pushed it and waited there on the front steps. But I wasn't buzzed in. That's because it wasn't a buzzer. It was a doorbell.

When she opened the door I was pleased to discover that Sonya Posner was the exact same height as me in her bare feet. Mind you, I was wearing my thick-soled hiking boots. But it was nice to know that I could go nose-to-nose with her. It made it that much easier to get lost in those utterly mesmerizing pale green eyes of hers. As I stood there, gazing into them, my heart went pitter-patter all over again.

"I was *so* glad you called, cookie."

"Really? I was afraid it was kind of short notice."

"Are you kidding me? I was sitting here by the phone, praying it would ring and it would be you inviting me out to dinner tonight. I'm the one who came by your office, cupcakes in hand, remember? Come on in. It's *freezing* out here."

I followed Sonya into the entry hall, careful not to tromp on her slender bare feet. Her toenails were painted lime green. She was wearing a pair of tight jeans and a burgundy silk blouse with nothing, but nothing, underneath it. I heard music playing somewhere inside—the cast album of *Gypsy*.

"Your mom told me you're huge into Ethel Merman," Sonya explained. "So I downloaded a bunch of her Broadway shows from iTunes. Seriously, are you *sure* you're not gay?"

"Positive."

"I'm so glad." To show me just how glad Sonya gave me a friendly, full-body hug—then drew back from me, arching one eyebrow. "Is that a gun in your pocket or are you just happy to see me?"

"Actually, it's a gun in my pocket."

"Shut up! Let me see!"

I pulled it from the pocket of my duffel coat and showed it to her.

She gaped at it. "What do you call that thing?"

"It's a Chief's Special."

"Is it loaded?"

"Yes, it is." I returned it to my coat pocket.

"Forgive me for asking, Benji, but why are you carrying that?"

"There's been a bit of trouble with a case I'm working on." I took off my coat and hung it from the peg rack in the entry hall. "I'd rather not go into it if you don't mind."

"I don't mind. Are you kidding me? You're gorgeous, dangerous *and* mysterious. Men don't come any hotter. And I just love what you're wearing."

I was wearing a navy blue turtleneck sweater and jeans— sort of like I'd seen Legs Diamond wearing. Okay, exactly like I'd seen Legs Diamond wearing. He's my fashion icon. Some guys have James Dean. I have Legs.

Sonya led me into the living room and dining area. The building had been gutted and renovated not long ago. It was airy, clean and modern. There was recessed lighting. Polished parquet flooring. New wiring and plumbing, no doubt. Hell, I bet it even had an energy-efficient furnace that didn't seize up three times a week. The sleek, Danish-y looking sofa and armchairs were upholstered in white leather. The dining table was an oval-shaped glass thingy surrounded by a set of eight Eames molded plywood chairs.

"Nice place," I observed, noticing the carpeted stairs that led upstairs and down.

"You want the full basement-to-garret tour?"

"You rent the whole building?"

Sonya colored slightly. "Actually, I own it."

"You *own* it?" I tried to sound calm. Really, I did. But a renovated townhouse on a prime West Village block was worth many millions.

"My father bought it for me as a present when I graduated from Wesleyan."

"Nice present. I don't mean to sound crass, Sonya, but are you rich?"

"Why, is that a problem?"

"No, not at all. I'm extremely open-minded. I just always figured your Uncle Al was—"

"A cheapie? A chiseler? A small-timer of a bookie who never has more than two nickels to scrape together? He totally is. But my father is Generation Next. He graduated from Harvard Business School and is in charge of operations for one of the gigantic Indian casinos in Uncasville, Connecticut. When I told him I wanted to teach school in the city he said okay, but he didn't want me living in some rundown dump with clanky pipes. Know what I mean?"

"Only too well. And I would."

"You would what, cookie?"

"Like the full tour."

"Well, right now you're looking at the living room and dining room, obviously," she said, leading me toward the glass dining table.

"Sonya, is that cupboard in the wall over there what I think it is?"

She smiled at me. "Why, what do you think it is?"

"A dumbwaiter."

"Don't you just love it? It still works, too. I insisted we keep it when they renovated the place. I've always had a thing for dumbwaiters. Come on, I'll show you the kitchen. But we'll have to take the stairs. The dumbwaiter won't hold both of us. Your mom is a real doll, by the way," she chattered, her hips wiggling enticingly in those tight jeans as she led me downstairs. "And is she ever built. No wonder you're still unattached. There isn't a girl on the planet who can measure up."

Sonya's huge restaurant kitchen seemed to be constructed entirely out of stainless steel. Her six-burner Viking stove had an island unto itself. The dumbwaiter had a wall to itself. A breakfast table was situated before a set of French doors that led out to her floodlit patio and garden.

"Are you okay with Chianti Classico?" she asked, reaching for the open bottle that was breathing on the granite counter.

"More than okay."

She poured two glasses and handed me one, her gaze grabbing hold of mine and not letting go. "I don't mean to pry but I'd like to know a little more about what you do for a living. Your mom was really, really vague. 'We help lawyers,' was all I could get out of her. And now I find out you carry a loaded gun. Benji, you're not some kind of baby-faced thug, are you?"

"No, nothing like that. I'm a private investigator."

"Get out! You're a private eye? How on earth did you? . . ."

"It's the family business. My dad started the agency after he retired from the force. I worked for him as an operative while I was in school. Now I do it full time."

"A real-life private eye. Benji, that is *so* exciting. Do you spy on cheating husbands?"

"Sometimes I even spy on cheating wives."

"Can I come with you some time on a stakeout?"

I took a sip of my wine. "Why would you want to do that?"

"I teach kindergarten. I'm with five-year-olds all day. You have no idea how little excitement I have in my life. Don't get me wrong. I love the little brats. But sometimes I feel like life is passing me by. I'm going to be twenty-eight in September. And the only guys I ever seem to meet are assholes and putzes." She tilted her head at me curiously. "You must meet gorgeous women constantly in your line of work."

"Not that many."

"And you really don't have anybody special in your life?"

"I really don't, Sonya."

"So who gave you that bunny bracelet?"

I glanced down at Sara's bracelet on my wrist. "A very mixed-up seventeen-year-old girl who needs a friend."

Sonya topped off our glasses. "Are you ready for the rest of the tour?"

"I'm ready. This is really good wine, by the way."

"You like it? Daddy's wholesaler sends it to me by the case."

The entire third floor of Sonya's brownstone was a plush master bedroom suite. She had a king-sized bed and a queen-sized dressing room with a walk-in closet paneled in cedar. Her bathroom had a Jacuzzi. On the top floor she had a guest bedroom and an office.

"Sonya, this place is amazing. I can't believe you have it all to yourself."

"Well, I'm hoping to share it with someone someday," she confessed, leading me back downstairs to the living room. She sat on the sofa with her legs curled beneath her. I sat down next to her. "And not just *any* someone, Benji. The right someone. I want a husband. I want kids. I want a great big smoochy dog. I want the whole *megillah*." She sipped her wine, eyeing me somewhat guardedly now over the rim of her glass. "I'm telling you this because I don't want you to get the wrong idea about me. I don't jump into bed with some guy who I've just met. I like to take things slow."

"Good."

She blinked at me in surprise. "Good?"

"Absolutely. I wouldn't want to get involved with someone who doesn't think that sex between two people is something really, really special."

"Okay, I cannot believe you just said that."

"Why, Sonya?"

"Because I've never heard those words come out of the mouth of any living creature who has a penis. You *do* have a? . . ."

"Yep. Fully equipped here."

She took another sip of her wine, looking at me shyly. "I shouldn't admit this, because it's totally uncool, but I got a funny feeling when I met you in the basement of B'Nai Jacob this morning."

"Funny ha-ha or funny weird?"

"Funny as in you're someone who is going to become important to me."

"I know."

"You do?"

"Absolutely, Sonya. I felt the same exact way about you. Instantly. And now *I'm* the one who has to confess something."

"You *don't* have a penis?"

"No, no, I do. Trust me." I took a deep breath and let it out slowly. "Nothing like this has ever happened to me before."

"That's so sweet, cookie. Really?"

"Really."

"I'll let you in on a little secret. It's never happened to me either."

We clinked glasses on that, gazing into each other's eyes.

I cleared my throat. "Are you a *hungry* old-fashioned girl?"

"Starved."

"Good. Where would you like to eat?"

"I thought we could eat here. I love to cook. I was thinking linguine with white clam sauce. Are you okay with garlic?"

"I love garlic. You want to eat now or after?"

"After what, Benji?"

"After I tear that blouse off of you."

She looked at me through her eyelashes. "Just the blouse?"

"It's a start."

"My, my. What happened to going slow?"

"Trust me, Sonya, I am going slow. I didn't jump you when

I walked through your front door. Or when we were down in the kitchen. Or up in your bedroom. I've been really, really patient—considering that all I've wanted to do since I met you this morning is strip you naked and ravage you from head to toe."

Sonya shook her head at me in disbelief. "Does your mother know you talk like this?"

"Who do you think taught me how to talk like this?"

She didn't say anything to that. Just drank down the last of her wine and set her empty glass on the coffee table. Her hand trembled slightly, I noticed. And a vein was throbbing in her forehead. She sat back on the sofa and ran her hands through her shiny black hair, staring at me with an extremely dark, serious look on her lovely face.

"I apologize if I shocked you," I said. "But when I see what I want I don't know how to hold back. Plus I am *so* tired of being alone. I've never been so tired of anything in my whole life. But I really did mean what I said before. If you want to take it slow we'll take it slow. It's just that, well, in our case I don't see the point, do you?"

In response, Sonya Posner unbuttoned her blouse and tossed it aside. Those stupendous girls of her were now staring me right in the face. "No, I don't, Benji," she said in a husky voice. "I don't see any point at all."

IT WAS 3:30 IN THE MORNING by the time I limped out of there—hobbled, bruised and covered with a million little bite marks and scratches. I would have been perfectly willing to spend what little was left of the night right there in Sonya's bed, but Sonya thought I ought to go home. She was thinking of my mom.

"Abby will be wondering where you are," she pointed out as we snuggled there together under the covers.

"No, she won't. I guarantee you she's fast asleep."

"I guarantee you she's not. The poor woman's wide-awake at this very minute. And scared to death that something has happened to you."

"Sonya, my mom doesn't keep tabs on me."

"Of course she does."

"What makes you say that?"

"Because I'm a woman and *I* would, every minute of every day. I don't want her hating me, Benji. Besides, I have school in the morning and if you stay over I won't get any sleep. I'll just try to start something with you again."

"Good luck with that. We've already broken my single-night record." Eclipsed it, in fact. Think Bob Beamon's long jump at the 1968 Olympic Games in Mexico City. "But maybe you're right. About my mom, I mean."

"Of course I'm right."

So I got dressed and she led me downstairs in her robe, kissing me lightly on the mouth after I put on my coat.

"Cookie, is this the start of something or am I crazy?"

"You're not crazy, Sonya. I'll call you."

"You'd better."

A light, chilly rain was falling as I made my way down West 12th Street toward Sixth Avenue. I had the street to myself at that hour, and I was feeling pretty damned good about one Benji Golden. Never before in my life had I experienced such a night of wild humpage. We did a grand total of five different things that I'd never done before. And we did them exceedingly well. I had the insatiable, freakishly limber Sonya's word for that. A beast, she'd called me. *Me.*

I was feeling so good that I decided to treat myself to a cab when I got to Sixth. I deserved it. Besides, there was no telling how long I'd have to wait for an uptown train at that hour of the night.

I was nearly at the corner of Sixth when the first shot rang out. It hit a trash can about three feet away from me—and sent me diving headfirst down the basement steps of the nearest brownstone as two more shots *chunked* into the side of the building. I've seen people make that headfirst dive all of the time in the movies. Those people are stuntmen. I'm not a stuntman. I whacked my kneecap on the edge of a step and came down so hard on my left shoulder that my hand went numb instantly.

I pulled my weapon and poked my head up to the sidewalk, eyes scanning the street, ears straining. I saw no one. But I did hear footsteps retreating into the night. Someone was running away.

Then all was silent.

I crouched there, gasping for breath, my mind racing. The shooter must have been waiting for me outside of Sonya's place, meaning he'd tailed me there from West 103rd Street earlier in the evening—even though I'd been on high alert for a tail. Or I thought I'd been. Yet I hadn't made him. Not then. And for damned sure not now. He was a pro, no question. So much of a pro that I knew this much: If he'd wanted me dead I'd be dead.

This had been a warning. Something told me I wouldn't be warned again.

Next time he'd shoot to kill.

CHAPTER FIVE

"WELL, YOU WERE RIGHT."

"Right about what?"

"Someone took a shot at me last night on West 12th. Three shots, actually."

Legs Diamond's eyes widened at me in the weak winter sunlight. We were rocketing down Broadway in his battered unmarked sedan, his hands gripping the wheel tightly as he bounced us in and out of every pothole. And I do mean bounced. The sedan's suspension? Shot. Alignment? Shot. Shock absorbers? Don't think so. "Did any of them come close to you?" he demanded.

"Not really." Although my right knee still throbbed from that headfirst dive I'd taken.

The morning tabloids lay on the seat between us. Both the *Daily News* and the *Post* had gone with giant banner headlines about Kathleen Kidd's suicide leap. It was big news, no question. Although their news accounts offered little in the way of details beyond a quote from an unnamed family spokesman, presumably Peter Seymour, who allowed that Kathleen was "a

troubled soul who had been rather depressed in recent weeks."
The family was grieving. They wished to have their privacy at
this time. Not a whole lot else, except for the standard boiler-
plate sidebars on the history of the fabled Kidd family—with
the emphasis tilting toward Kathleen's much higher profile
brother, Bobby the K, and his wife Meg.

I'd already scoured the stories on the web over my morning
coffee and fried egg sandwich from Scotty's while Lovely Rita
kept shooting suspicious looks across her desk at my red-
rimmed eyes. I could have sworn she knew that I'd just had the
shtupping of my life. But how was that even possible? I hadn't
said a word. It had been past four A.M. by the time I got home.
A Chevy Tahoe was parked outside of our building. Two of my
dad's old running buddies, Sam Glickstein and Bobby O'Brien,
were seated in the front seat keeping an eye on the place. They
were still sitting there when Legs picked me up at nine o'clock
sharp. Retirees, both of them. Happy to do Meyer Golden's
widow a favor. Besides, they had nowhere else to be.

"Did you phone it in?" Legs demanded as we spelunked our
way in and out of a crater-sized pothole at West 86th.

"Didn't see any need to." I reached into my coat pocket and
removed the Ziploc sandwich bag with the slug inside. "I dug
this out of the wall of the building with my pocket knife. It's a
nine-mil."

"Yeah, I can see that," he growled, snatching the bag from
me.

"Bruce Weiner was shot with a nine-mil."

"You're not peddling a same gun, same shooter scenario, are
you?"

"Why, what's wrong with it?"

"Any pro who works for the Leetes Group is careful, that's what."

"Maybe he's figuring he doesn't have to be careful."

"Why the hell not?"

"Because he knows no one's going to connect a shooting in Northwest Connecticut with a shooting in Greenwich Village. And even if they do they'll never follow up on it."

"Because? . . ."

"They'll be told not to."

"Okay, now you're just starting to piss me off."

"The hell I am. You're loving this. We're working our first big case together. You feel like a proud uncle. Admit it."

Legs didn't admit it. What he said was, "I won't feel real proud if you get yourself killed. You should have called me."

"It was late."

"You should have called me," he said again. "I've got no police report of a shooting on West 12th. No chain of evidence. This damned slug could have come from anywhere. Plus you probably got your greasy prints all over it."

"I had gloves on. And I left the other two slugs there. This one passed through a full trash barrel before it hit the wall. I figured it would be the least mangled, not that it matters."

"Why doesn't it matter?"

"Something tells me we're not going to crack this case with traditional ballistics evidence."

"Who's this *we*, white man?"

"These are powerful people, Legs. They've gone to a lot of trouble to silence Bruce and Kathleen. And they'll go to even more trouble to shut down any official investigation into their deaths." I held on for dear life as he made a hard left on two wheels at West 81st Street. "We'll have to resort to other methods."

"You may be right about that," he admitted, peering at me curiously. "Your voice sounds deeper today. Did you get laid last night?"

"There is that possibility."

"You got a girl on West 12th?"

"I got a girl on West 12th."

"Good for you, little bud."

We started our way across Central Park on the 79th Street Transverse. Some traces of slush were still clinging to the bare frozen ground there.

"I reached out to your boy Marco Battalino in Litchfield," Legs reported.

"And? . . ."

"And he pretty much confirmed what you told me—he's a complete douche. But Claudia schooled me on how to play it. I convinced him that not only is he in total charge, but that the high and mighty NYPD desperately needs his expert help. Worked like a charm. He gave up all sorts of details on the Candlewood Lake crime scene."

"Like what?"

"Like the shoe prints they found in the snow. They had Bruce's—he was a huge guy who had on a pair of size-fourteen Nikes. They had your size-nine Rockports. You know, you have awfully big feet for such a little guy."

"Trust me, I've got size where it counts."

"Are you always this unbearable after you get laid? Wait, what am I saying? You never get laid. Who is this girl?"

"A kindergarten teacher-slash-sex maniac. I met her at shul."

"Of course you did."

"They found a third set of shoe prints, am I right?"

He nodded. "Presumably the shooter's. He wore a pair of size-eight Vibram soles that are typical of a hiking boot."

"So he's not a big guy."

"It isn't an exact science. He could be a six-footer who happens to have smallish feet. Although he doesn't weigh a whole lot. Based on the depth of his shoe impression in the snow, Marco's techies estimate he goes about a buck-fifty."

I mulled this over, my mind straying to someone on the smallish side who knew that Bruce was staying at Candlewood Lake—Chris Warfield. But why on earth would Bruce's roommate, the son of a Park Avenue pediatric neurosurgeon, want him dead? And what possible connection could Chris have had with Kathleen Kidd? Besides, Chris was a college student, not a Leetes Group pro. Chris hadn't bugged our car and our office. Chris hadn't taken three shots at me last night on West 12th Street. That made no sense it, did it? "How about the shooter's tire prints?" I asked Legs Diamond.

"The techies identified them as a well-worn set of Goodyear Eagle RS-A four-season radials. That particular tire was factory spec on the 2009 Jeep Grand Cherokee. Wheel base measurements happen to be a dead-nuts match for a Grand Cherokee. I told your boy Marco I'd be happy to check the tollbooth cams for any and all Grand Cherokees that entered the city late that evening."

"That was smart of you."

"Yo, I'm a smart guy. Trouble is, so's our shooter. He probably ditched the Grand Cherokee out there somewhere and returned to the city—*if* he returned to the city—in a different ride. Or maybe he checked into a motel out there and came back the next morning. Marco liked the motel angle. He's got his people checking the area to see if anyone registered that night who happened to own a Grand Cherokee. That reminds me . . ." Legs dug into the pocket of his aged leather trench coat and yanked out a folded computer printout. "That's everyone who signed in with the doorman of Kathleen Kidd's building in the two hours prior to her death."

"Thanks." I slid it into the chest pocket of my sincere Harris Tweed jacket to peruse later. If I tried to read it while he was veering in and out of the transverse traffic I would lose my fried egg sandwich. "What about Bruce's DNA?"

"Done deal. Marco gave me his word that he'll share if I'll share. He's fast tracking it through their forensics lab in Meriden."

"And how about Kathleen's?"

He puffed out his cheeks. "I got us what we need but it's going to cost me."

"How so?"

"On a certain fixed date in a few weeks I have to put on a tuxedo and escort a certain assistant medical examiner named Tat—that's short for Tatiana—to her sister's wedding."

"She has a crush on you?"

"She's a nice young lady of the Ukrainian persuasion who's somewhat plain of face and has a job that most men find horrifying."

"And she has a crush on you."

"Maybe a tiny one," he allowed.

"So you're playing her."

"*She's* playing *me*. I have to go a freakin' Brighton Beach wedding. It'll take my liver a week to detox from all of the vodka." He glanced over at me. "You were right. Kathleen did give birth to a child. Tat found vaginal scarring. She took a blood sample for me. As soon as your boy Marco coughs up Bruce's DNA we'll know if we have a match. She also ran Kathleen's blood for alcohol and drugs."

"And? . . ."

"The drugs in her system match the prescription bottles we found in her medicine chest. Kathleen was taking a combination of lithium and Seroquel XR. That's strong shit. There were no red flags in terms of how much she had in her system. But her blood alcohol level was .16—twice the legal limit to drive in the state of New York. The lady was hammered when she went off of that balcony. I spoke to her psychiatrist, Dr. Schwartz, again. He harrumphed at me about doctor-patient confidentiality but he did allow as how Kathleen suffered from 'black moods.' He wouldn't rule out suicide." Legs' face tightened. "Except Tat found something on Kathleen's body that doesn't fit with the suicide scenario."

"What was it?"

"Fresh bruises around her upper arms that are consistent with finger indentations."

"Wait, I thought you told me there were no—"

"I didn't see them when I examined her on the sidewalk. She was wearing a long-sleeved sweater, okay? That's why the

ME's office does a more thorough examination. They find things we don't."

"So someone squeezed her by the arms?"

"Someone squeezed her by the arms."

"Can they can get fingerprints off of her sweater?"

"There was no trace evidence. He was probably wearing gloves."

"Big hands?"

"Not particularly."

"Which is consistent with the shoe prints they found at Candlewood Lake."

"So you're assuming it's the same guy."

"You're not?"

"If the Leetes Group is behind this we could be talking about a whole crew."

"Does this give you enough to open a homicide investigation into her death?"

"Officially? No. Officially, none of this is making it into Kathleen's autopsy report. Tat told me her office has been ordered to fast-track it and *not* get bogged down in details. The Kidds want it to go down as a suicide. So it's a suicide."

"Do you have any contacts inside of the Leetes Group?"

"You'll never get a peep out of Jake Leetes or anyone who works for him. He pays them to keep their mouths shut."

"Does he pay them to carry out contract hits?"

"The Leetes Group is a licensed, law-abiding detective agency. I've heard of unfortunate things happening to certain undesirables who were harassing, bilking or otherwise pissing off certain well-heeled clients. I've also heard that Jake keeps ex-Special

Forces guys on the payroll. But that's strictly chatter. And if you're thinking what I think you're thinking forget it. I can't compel the Leetes Group to cooperate. I'd need a court order and I'll never get one because—wait for it—I have no actual evidence to take to the DA, remember?"

We came bursting out of Central Park at Fifth Avenue, where Legs made a sharp right and joined the taxis and limos that were inching their way down toward Midtown. As we drew closer to East 69th the traffic came to a total standstill. Wasn't hard to see why. I could make out the bulge of TV news vans that were double-parked there from two blocks away. We ditched the car in a no-parking zone and hoofed it the rest of the way.

A raucous mob of reporters, TV cameramen and paparazzi was crowded outside of the elegant, prewar doorman building overlooking Central Park where Eleanor Saltonstall Kidd, Kathleen's elderly billionaire mother, maintained her New York City residence. I think the old lady had something like eight or ten other residences scattered around the world. I also think she owned the entire building, which occupied a half block of precious Fifth Avenue frontage and seventeen stories of air space. The media people were standing out there in the bitter cold hoping for some kind of a statement from her. Or, better yet, from Kathleen's high-profile brother. All they were getting was a pair of pink-faced cops in uniform and a harried young Kidd campaign aide who seemed to be losing her mind.

"If you people would *please* show the family just a little respect," she was pleading, which had to be the funniest line I'd heard all year.

Legs flashed his shield at the building's white-gloved doorman. We were admitted to the lobby. There were fresh flowers
in a vase at the reception desk, where another uniformed doorman was waiting for us. This one wasn't wearing white gloves
but his hands looked real clean. He called Mrs. Kidd's apartment on the house phone. Spoke softly into it, then listened a
moment before he hung up.

"Mrs. Kidd will see you," he said, motioning us to one of the
three elevators.

We got in the elevator, which was a whole lot nicer than the
one we have in our building. In fact, it was the nicest elevator
I've ever been in. It had walnut paneling, thick pile carpeting
and gleaming brass work. If there'd been a bath I'd have moved
right in and called it home. There was no need for us to push a
button for the floor we wanted. There were no buttons to push.
They were on a console at the front desk, to insure that visitors
were delivered to their intended floor and nowhere else.

When the elevator door opened we discovered that we'd been
delivered directly into the marble entry hall of Mrs. Kidd's
palatial digs, which seemed to occupy the top two floors of the
entire goddamned building. There was a grand curving staircase up to the second floor. A bronze fountain burbled away
right there before us in the entry hall. And way, way up over
our heads there was a crystal chandelier that looked as if it
could light up the new Yankee Stadium.

I stood there with my mouth open. I'd known that such
apartments existed, same as I knew that rock stars have a great
deal of casual sex and cotton candy isn't made out of cotton. But
I'd never been inside such a place. It was like walking into the

main entrance of the Metropolitan Museum of Art. This was life on a whole different scale.

But the lawyer was still the same. My old nonfriend Mr. Classy Guy stood there under the chandelier waiting to greet us. Or I should say glower at us. Peter Seymour wore a custom-tailored navy blue suit today, a crisp white shirt, muted maroon tie and those same spotless mink-lined shoes. Unless he owned more than one pair and rotated them.

"Don't forget to check out his shoes," I murmured at Legs.

"Check out his what?"

"Good morning, gentlemen," Seymour said, as he looked Legs Diamond up and down with starchy disdain. The aged leather trench coat. Rumpled sweater and jeans, goatee. Clearly, he'd been expecting a proper suit from One Police Plaza. Someone more presentable, who smelled of polite deference and Aqua Velva. "I'm Peter Seymour, Mrs. Kidd's legal counsel," he stated in his burgundy baritone. "Detective Lieutenant Diamond, is it not?"

Legs nodded. "That's me."

"Shall I call you Larry?"

"Only if you want me to call you an ambulance."

Seymour's eyes widened slightly. "As you wish. Mrs. Kidd is prepared to make herself available to an appropriate individual from the NYPD for a brief few minutes. Frankly, I advised her against having this conversation. She overruled me. She said that the police have a job to do and it has always been the policy of the Kidd family to cooperate whenever, however possible." He swiveled his patrician blade of nose in my direction. "However, she is *not* expecting young Mr. Ben Golden here."

"I asked Ben to accompany me," Legs said.

"In what capacity?" Seymour demanded to know. "While it's true that he was recently retained by Bates, Winslow and Seymour, that particular matter has no bearing whatsoever on this tragic event. Furthermore, he is no longer in our employ."

"I'm working for someone else now," I informed him.

"And who might that be?"

I smiled at him. "Sorry, that's confidential."

"This is totally inappropriate. Ben, I insist that you take that elevator back downstairs right this minute."

"Not going to happen, Counselor," Legs told him. "Ben's with me."

"Mr. Seymour, why didn't you want me to mention your firm's name to Paul and Laurie Weiner?"

"I have no comment to make on that. It was . . . most unfortunate what happened to the young man."

"All sorts of unfortunate things seem to be happening lately. Why do you suppose that is?"

"I can see where you're going with this, Ben," he said with a shake of his sleek head. "And I have a word of advice for you: Don't. There's no connection whatsoever between Bruce Weiner's murder and Kathleen Kidd's suicide."

"Yeah, there is," Legs pointed out. "There's *you.*"

"I'm a senior partner of an immense law firm. We have many, many partners and literally hundreds of clients."

"One of whom was looking for Bruce Weiner. How come?"

"I have nothing to say on that matter, Lieutenant."

"Okay, then who bugged our car and our office?" I pressed him. "Who tailed me to Candlewood Lake?"

"I have no direct, personal knowledge of any such behavior."

Legs tugged at his goatee thoughtfully. "That sure sounded like plausible deniability to me. Did that sound like plausible deniability to you?"

I nodded. "Kind of did."

"Lieutenant, you have been invited into Mrs. Kidd's home as a courtesy." There was more than a trace of irritation in Seymour's voice now. "I am not going to stand here and be given the third degree by you. You will cease this line of inquiry immediately."

Legs stepped in closer to him. A lot closer. "Let's get something straight, Counselor," he growled, poking Seymour in the chest with his index finger. People like Mr. Classy Guy really don't like to be poked in the chest. "I don't work for you. I run an investigation how I choose to run it. And if you don't like it you can take it up with my superiors."

"Oh, I will." Seymour whipped out his cell phone, fuming. "I'm calling Commissioner Feldman right now. I will have you thrown off of this case before your feet hit the street."

"You will do nothing of the sort, Peter," boomed Eleanor Saltonstall Kidd as she came striding toward us. The reigning doyenne of Fifth Avenue society was a tall, regal, silver-haired woman in her eighties who positively filled the vast marble entry hall with her aura of money and power. There was no question that she was someone of great privilege who was accustomed to having things done her way. None. She was dressed plainly in a matching sweater and skirt of dark green cashmere and a pair of sturdy cordovan oxfords. No jewelry. Just a wristwatch that I swore looked like it was a Timex. "It was my intention to extend every courtesy to the NYPD," she said. "Not to issue threats."

"Mrs. Kidd, I owe you an apology," Seymour said hurriedly. "I thought that Commissioner Feldman and I had an understanding. However, he's chosen to send us a slovenly, ill-mannered young lieutenant who has brought along a private investigator with no connection whatsoever to this or any other—"

"Oh, will you *please* shut your mouth, Peter?"

Peter Seymour shut his mouth. I sure wish I had it on film. It would have been fun to replay it over and over again.

"The commissioner has 'chosen' to send us none other than the highly decorated Detective Lieutenant Larry Diamond." Mrs. Kidd studied Legs, looking him up and down as if he were an exotic breed of mastiff at the Westminster Kennel Club Dog Show. "His grooming may not be what we're accustomed to, but I am assured that he's the sharpest detective in all of Manhattan—which is to say all of New York City. I was expecting him. I was *not* expecting anyone else, but if Lieutenant Diamond has asked this young man to accompany him then I'm certain he has his reasons. And we shall respect those reasons." She extended her hand to him. "I'm Eleanor Kidd, Lieutenant. Kindly excuse my attorney's bellicosity. He gets paid a great deal of money to behave that way. Although, frankly, I doubt he behaves any differently when his meter's not running. And your young companion is? . . ."

"Ben Golden of Golden Legal Services, Mrs. Kidd," Legs told her. "Ben tracks missing young people. And if his name sounds familiar that's because his father was Meyer Golden."

The old lady raised her eyebrows. "*The* Meyer Golden? I'm honored to meet you, Ben."

"I'm sorry it's under such sad circumstances, ma'am."

She sighed heavily. "Kathleen was a troubled soul. I hope that she's found some small measure of peace now. Please join us in the library, will you? I'll ring for tea."

The library was no more than three times the size of my entire apartment and was lined from floor to twenty-foot ceiling with bookcases filled with leather-bound books. There were rolling library ladders on rails so you could reach the books on the top shelves if you ever needed to. And there was another chandelier in there, too. I guess you can never have too many. Two deep leather sofas and a matching pair of leather club chairs were set before the fire that was roaring in the fireplace. A life-sized oil portrait of the late, great Black Jack Kidd himself was hanging over the mantel, where an antique clock was tick-tocking away. It was five minutes slow, according to my dad's Omega. Four tall windows looked out over Central Park. From where I stood, I could see the skating rink, the Sheep Meadow and the rowboat lake. Hell, I could see all the way across the park to the apartment towers on Central Park West, the Hudson River, New Jersey and, way off in the distance, the Grand Tetons. Okay, I lied. But trust me, the view was so amazing that it was hard to pull my eyes from it.

When I finally did, I managed to focus on the two people who stood there, shoulder to shoulder, looking extremely ill at ease. Their faces were plenty familiar to me. They were *the* hottest New York power couple of the moment.

Our would-be next governor wasn't nearly as tall as I'd

expected he'd be from his photos. I doubt whether Bobby the K topped off at more than five-feet-eight. But he gave the impression of size because he was built thick through the chest and shoulders. Plus he had a really huge head. Seriously, the man had the most humongous melon I'd ever seen. His thick shock of hair was pure silver just like his mother's, which was unusual for a man who'd barely turned forty. His features, in contrast, were strikingly youthful. He had round apple cheeks and bright robin's egg-blue eyes. In photographs, those blue eyes usually gleamed with boyish enthusiasm. Not today. He wore a dark gray suit, white shirt and dark blue tie. His feet in their polished black loafers were no bigger than mine, I noticed. They might even have been smaller.

"Pleased to meet you," he said somberly. The hand that shook mine was small, too, and on the soft side. "Sorry you fellows had to come to us."

"We're essentially trapped here because of the media horde," Meg explained. "They follow us everywhere we go. Comes with the territory. Most unfortunate."

Meg Grayson Kidd had a thrusting chin and didn't move her lips when she talked. That particular affectation used to be called Locust Valley Lockjaw. I don't know if it still is. It's some sort of a WASP boarding school thingy. She was the same height as her husband in her low-heeled pumps. And wore a nicely tailored pair of gabardine slacks over what was clearly a size double-wide butt—which, again, you wouldn't know from the photos. Those strictly zoomed in on her sharp edges—the high forehead, the sculpted cheekbones and that trademark Grayson chin. Meg wore her light brown hair cropped short.

No makeup. Just a touch of lipstick. She wasn't an unattractive woman, but she wasn't pretty either. Mannish, I guess you'd call her. There was absolutely nothing girlie-girl about her. Her gaze was extremely direct. The lady didn't so much as blink. If a housefly was dozing on a lampshade fifteen feet away, I swear she knew it was there. Her grip, when she shook my hand, was way firmer than her husband's. The many magazine profiles I'd read about Meg always emphasized how outdoorsy she was—especially her passionate love for skeet shooting. Her being a gun owner and proud member of the National Rifle Association played well with conservative upstate voters.

I sat down on one of the sofas next to Legs. Mrs. Kidd sat on the sofa across the coffee table from us, with Peter Seymour by her side. Bobby the K and Meg took the club chairs. A maid in an honest-to-god uniform brought in our tea on an honest-to-god teacart. The matching five-piece tea service looked to be genuine silver and quite old. She set a cup and saucer before each of us and poured the tea, then rustled out, closing the door softly behind her.

Mrs. Kidd said, "Please be aware, Lieutenant, that while I am willing to cooperate with the NYPD, I will only discuss Kathleen with you on this one occasion. I will be as candid and brutally honest with you as I can be, even though I find the prospect tremendously painful. Nothing that I say to you this morning is for public attribution. I do not wish to see one word of it in any newspaper or television news report. If I do, I will know the source and I will have your badge." She turned her regal head in my direction, her blue eyes glinting at me. "And you will lose your license to operate in the state of New York. Furthermore,

I want both of you to give me your word, as gentlemen, that what we say here in this room will remain confidential."

"You have it," Legs said.

"Absolutely," I assured her.

The old lady took a sip of her tea. It looked like a stage sip to me. I don't think she actually swallowed anything. She was just collecting herself. "Kathleen was a sunny and outgoing child," she began. "Smart as a whip and a gifted artist. She drew instinctively and beautifully. She was also a lovely child with long, flowing blond hair. She had many, many friends. Everyone adored her. 'Our little gift,' we called her. Tommy and I had tried to have another child after Bobby and we'd all but given up when I discovered I was pregnant with Kathleen. Tommy was nearly fifty by the time she was born. She was six full years younger than Bobby. There was such an age gap between them that they barely grew up in the same house together. He was already off to boarding school by the time she was nine." Mrs. Kidd fell silent for a moment. The fire crackled. The mantel clock tick-tocked. She took a deep breath and continued. "As Kathleen underwent puberty her personality began to change for the worse. By the age of twelve she became wildly moody. She'd be listless and withdrawn for days at a time, then burst forth into sudden excitement or shockingly violent anger. She'd shriek obscenities at us, throw things, break things. Naturally, we were quite alarmed. It was all of a pattern that Tommy had experienced before. His poor mother, Clarissa, was emotionally fragile in much the same way."

"She died from an accidental overdose of sleeping pills back in the sixties, didn't she?" Legs put in.

"It was no accident, Lieutenant. It was a suicide. And whatever genetic demon it was that plagued Clarissa got passed on to poor Kathleen, I'm afraid. She was no longer happy at the private school she'd been attending here in the city. She was disruptive in class. Got into fights with the girls who'd been her nearest and dearest friends. Not just arguments. Kathleen actually bloodied several prized Park Avenue noses. One day, in a fit of rage, she punched her fist through a classroom window and severed a vein in her wrist. They had to rush her to the hospital. After that episode, her pediatrician sent her to Dr. Marvin Levin, the top child psychoanalyst in the city."

"Is he still practicing?" Legs asked.

Mrs. Kidd narrowed her gaze at him ever so slightly. "Why, no. He passed away at least ten years ago. Dr. Levin was extremely reluctant to stigmatize Kathleen with any sort of a label. He told us that children who are experiencing the hormonal changes of puberty often exhibit extreme personality changes. Even the most extreme behavior may simply be a phase that the child will outgrow in a year. Kathleen was a bright and accomplished girl, after all. She had no neurological disorders of any kind. He suggested that we place her in the Barrow School up in Millbrook. Barrow was, or I should say is, a private residential middle school for troubled young teenagers such as Kathleen. The classes are small. They offer daily counseling and group therapy sessions. And they keep the children extremely busy. The school was once the country estate of a railroad baron. There are two hundred acres of grounds. Chickens and goats to mind. A vegetable garden to tend. Dr. Levin told us many of Barrow's students were able to return to traditional

schools after a relatively short stay." Mrs. Kidd gazed into the
fire for a moment, her jaw tensing. "I remember the day we sat
Kathleen down in this very room and talked to her about going
there. She was in one of her morose moods. Didn't care whether
she went there or not. Didn't care about a blessed thing. So off she
went."

"And when was this?" Legs asked.

"It was in . . . 1989," Mrs. Kidd replied. "We visited her regularly, of course. That first semester Tommy and I must have
gone up there practically every weekend. We'd have a picnic
together if the weather permitted. She *seemed* happy there.
Didn't you think so, Bobby?"

"Yes, I did, Mother," Bobby the K confirmed, as Meg
watched him attentively. "I didn't see Kathleen real often in
those days. I was away at Choate. But I distinctly remember the
weekend when I went up there with you. Kathleen seemed real
upbeat. She had that light back in her eyes again."

"Dr. Levin was cautiously optimistic," Mrs. Kidd recalled.
"He felt that she was making excellent progress. Tommy and I
were thrilled, of course. We wanted nothing more than for
Kathleen to be our—our little girl again. . . ." She broke off,
struggling to retain her composure. "But the Barrow people let
us down. They didn't supervise the children properly."

"It was outright negligence," Peter Seymour spoke up. "I still
say you should have let me file a civil suit against those people."

"That was *not* an option," Mrs. Kidd said with a shake of her
head. "We didn't wish to call attention to the matter—even
though we were utterly furious. I had never seen Tommy so
angry in my entire life."

"Mrs. Kidd, exactly what happened to Kathleen up there?" I asked.

She sat there in stony silence for a moment before she cleared her throat and said, "One of the boys . . . he got Kathleen pregnant. An older boy. He was fifteen years old. Kathleen was barely thirteen."

"He raped her?" Legs asked.

"According to the laws of this state he did," Seymour huffed. "She was nowhere near the age of consent, as you know perfectly well."

"Exactly what happened was never clear to us, Lieutenant," Mrs. Kidd said quietly. "Kathleen never told the school administrators the same story twice. Neither did the boy. We do know that they somehow managed to find a time and place to be sexually active. We were also told that the boy's older brother attended college nearby at SUNY New Paltz and kept him supplied with marijuana and cocaine. Quite a few of the Barrow kids had drug problems. That's why they were there in the first place. Not Kathleen. The administrators were certain she was never involved in *that* sort of behavior."

"I can't imagine those people were in a position to be certain of anything," Meg said.

"Kathleen did *not* use illegal drugs," Mrs. Kidd said to her pointedly.

Meg's eyes widened. "No, of course not, Eleanor."

"What was this boy's name?" Legs asked.

Peter Seymour sat there with his thin lips pursed before he gave Mrs. Kidd a slight shake of the head.

"I see no reason to drag the young man and his family into

this conversation, Lieutenant," she responded. "The incident at Barrow occurred more than twenty years ago. And it has no bearing on what happened yesterday. Is that understood?"

Legs nodded politely but didn't back off. "So Kathleen got pregnant when she was thirteen. You proceeded how?"

The old lady glowered at him across the coffee table. She'd indicated that she wished to move on. She took another stage sip of her tea before she said, "Tommy was a devout Catholic who did not regard terminating her pregnancy as an option. I'm Episcopalian, but I don't happen to believe in abortion either. We pulled Kathleen out of Barrow—for good, needless to say—and arranged for her to have the baby at a private location that was safe from prying eyes. Peter found a good family to take the baby. It was a boy. I don't know the name of the family that adopted him. I never wanted to know."

"And exactly where was this private location?" Legs asked.

"Why on earth does that matter?" Mrs. Kidd demanded.

"Just answer the question, please."

She heaved a royal sigh. "Kathleen had the baby at our winter home in the Caribbean. It's a restored sugar plantation on the island of Nevis. We've had it for many, many years. I typically spend the month of February there. In fact, I'm intending to go down next week after h-her funeral. Kathleen stayed there for the final trimester of her pregnancy. I was with her, naturally. She gave birth toward the end of January."

"Of 1990?"

"That's correct. She was so young that our family physician flew down with his nurse to be there with her for the last few weeks. And he made certain that our home was as well equipped as any hospital—just in case there were any complications."

"And were there any?"

"No, there were not. He took every precaution."

"And his name is? . . ."

"John Sykes. John was a fine fellow. Passed away, let's see, nine years ago." That made two doctors who were dead so far. "He always wanted to open a free clinic down there. We made it financially possible for him to do so. I miss John. Don't care for this current fellow at all. He treats me like a dotty old featherhead. Which I assure you I am not, Lieutenant."

"I believe you, ma'am. So Kathleen's child was born in Nevis?"

"Not officially," Peter Seymour answered. "It was a home delivery. The birth was never recorded there. Dr. Sykes and the nurse brought the baby to New York when it was medically safe to do so and proceeded with the adoption."

"Sorry, I don't understand," I said. "Was the baby a citizen of the US or of Nevis?"

Seymour stared at me from behind his rimless spectacles. "He was born overseas to an American mother but there was no recorded birth certificate. Got it?"

"Not really, but I'm not super bright."

"Kathleen remained behind with me in Nevis for a few more weeks," Mrs. Kidd continued.

"How did she feel about the baby being taken from her?" Legs asked.

"She wept for days," Mrs. Kidd recalled sadly. "And remained deeply, deeply depressed. We sent her abroad to a school in Geneva that was noted for its work with emotionally challenged young people. They placed her on an assortment of prescription medications, which she continued to take for the remainder of her life. Kathleen was . . . incapable of experiencing the emotion of joy, Lieutenant. This made her extremely angry. Her art was the only thing that gave her some solace. She moved to Paris after she got out of school so as to pursue it further. She had a generous income from her trust fund and was able to live quite comfortably. Paris remained her home for a number of years."

"Was there a man in her life?"

"When she was nineteen she got married to some awful hunk of eurotrash," the old lady sniffed. "He was strictly after her money. Tommy paid him to go away and he went away. It lasted less than a month." She gazed out the tall windows at her panoramic view of Central Park. "Last year she decided to give up Paris and buy the apartment on Riverside Drive. She didn't tell us why she came home. Kathleen never explained herself. She simply did what she did."

"Did you see a lot of her after she came back?"

"I tried to. I haven't many friends left. They're either dead or they've moved to Florida, which is as good as being dead in my opinion. I'm always looking for someone to go with me to the ballet or the opera. I asked her to join me dozens of times, but she always declined—*if* she bothered to return my phone call. I'm well aware that the media thinks Kathleen moved back to New York so as to be with me in my declining years. But the truth is, she wanted nothing to do with me."

"Or me," Bobby spoke up. "I called her a million times. So

did Meg. But all Kathleen ever wanted to do was stay in her apartment and paint."

Legs said, "Her doorman told us she seldom went out and almost never had visitors. When was the last time you folks saw her?"

"It w-was Christmas . . ." Mrs. Kidd replied, choking back a sob. "She . . . showed up here an hour late looking like something the cat dragged in. Unkempt and filthy. She had nothing to say to us. Just got roaring drunk on eggnog and left without so much as opening her presents. I-I still have them."

"She was seeing a psychiatrist named Joseph Schwartz. Are you familiar with him?"

"I've never heard of him." Mrs. Kidd glanced at Bobby. "Have you?"

Bobby shook his head. "She didn't get his name from me. She never asked me for anything, Lieutenant. Never wanted anything. We weren't close," he said regretfully. "Hardly spent any time together when we were kids—except for when we summered on Nantucket. Even then I hardly ever saw her. I was too busy having fun with my friends. And then she was off in France for most of her adult life, like mother just said. I wish I'd made more time for her after she moved back to town. I should have but . . ." He lowered his bright blue eyes, swallowing. "I've just been so busy with my campaign."

"Don't blame yourself for what she did," Meg said to him sternly. "It's not your fault."

"I should have tried harder," he insisted. "If I had maybe she wouldn't have felt so desperate and alone."

Legs said, "Mrs. Kidd, are you aware that Kathleen had been

reaching out to a Canterbury College student named Bruce Weiner? She confronted him publicly on two occasions that we know of in the past three months. Apparently, she was under the impression that he was her birth son."

The old lady shook her head. "Why, no. I've never heard the name Bruce Weiner before in my life."

Legs stared across the coffee table at her. "So you're not aware that this same Bruce Weiner was shot to death the night before last at a vacation home on Candlewood Lake?"

Mrs. Kidd's eyes widened a bit but she had nothing to say.

Peter Seymour had nothing to say either. He wasn't going anywhere near it. Just sat there like a six-hundred-dollar-an-hour mute. Bobby the K was likewise mute. The library fell into guarded silence.

Until Meg said, "Lieutenant, are you attempting to link his death with Kathleen's?"

"It does raise questions, don't you think?"

"I honestly have no idea *what* to think," Meg answered brusquely.

Mrs. Kidd cleared her throat. "All I know is that Kathleen gave birth to a baby boy when she was terribly young and vulnerable. She never saw that baby boy again. The experience was traumatic for her. Her whole life was filled with trauma. She was a tortured soul. We could never make her happy. We let her down. Everyone let her down. And now . . ." She halted, her eyes brimming with tears. "And now my beautiful little girl is *gone*," she sobbed.

Bobby rushed to the old lady's side to console her.

Seymour said, "This interview is over, Lieutenant Diamond."

Legs nodded grimly. "Thank you for your time, Mrs. Kidd. I'm sorry for your loss."

She didn't hear him. Just sat there and cried.

Meg shook my hand again, although this time her gaze was chillier. She'd sized us up and decided we represented a potential threat to her.

"I'll show you guys out," offered Bobby, wiping his own eyes.

Meg stayed there in the library with Mrs. Kidd. So did Peter Seymour, who was avoiding us so we wouldn't pepper him with more questions.

Bobby led us across the marble entry hall toward the elevator. Again, I was struck by how much shorter he was than I'd thought. "I want to thank you guys for your courtesy. You both seem real decent. Watch your backs, okay?"

Legs said, "Meaning? . . ."

"You're dealing with a situation here that's gotten out of control."

Legs's dark eyes narrowed. "You think your sister's suicide might have been something other than a suicide?"

Bobby pushed the button for the elevator. "I'm with my wife on this one. I honestly don't know what to think."

"You must have an inkling," I said. "What's really going on here?"

"I wish I knew," he sighed. "But if I were you guys I'd steer clear of it. If you don't, you're liable to get pulled in so deep you'll never get out."

"Is that some kind of a threat?"

Bobby showed me his best campaign smile. Well, almost his

best. His eyes weren't totally into it. "Just the opposite, Ben. I'm trying to look out for you. Understand?"

"Not really, but I'm not super bright."

The elevator arrived. We got in and started back down to the lobby.

"That rich old lady just chumped us," Legs grumbled at me. "All she gave up were cherry-picked morsels. And she was spinning them all of the way."

"Damned good acting job," I said admiringly. "I guess she's had plenty of practice over the years. More than Bobby. What was *that* just about?"

"Dude's scared shitless."

"Of what?"

"His political future, what else?"

"Legs, why were Bruce and Kathleen murdered?"

"Because they knew too much."

"About what?"

"That's what we have to find out." He glanced at his watch. "Millbrook's a two-hour drive, tops. I'm going to drop that nine-mil slug of yours off at the lab and then take a quick run up to the Barrow School. Maybe somebody still works there who was around back in eighty-nine and remembers the real deal. I'm guessing the Kidds paid everybody off—but a pissed-off janitor might have slipped through the cracks." He glanced over at me. "Any idea what you're going to do?"

"Actually, I have a very good idea."

THE WINDSOR HOTEL ON LEXINGTON caters mostly to out-of-town business travelers who want a midtown location, a bed and not much else. It's not a tourist hotel. And for sure not a luxury hotel. The lobby's barely a lobby at all. There's no fancy seating area with plump armchairs. No piano bar. No coffee shop or gift shop. Just a front desk, a bell captain's station and a whole bunch of busy people bustling in and out. One of those busy people was a tall guy with receding black hair who stood just inside of the front door, glaring impatiently out at the street. He appeared to be waiting for somebody who was late. He was pretty good at it, too, but I made him anyway. My dad taught me well.

No one answered when I knocked on the door to room 613. I stood there in the hall and listened to the moaning and groaning that was going on inside. I knocked again, harder this time.

"Who is it?" a man's voice finally demanded.

"Room service."

"I didn't order anything."

"Compliments of the concierge, sir."

He undid the chain and dead bolt and opened the door. Paul Weiner was naked except for the towel he'd wrapped around his plump middle. His face was flushed. His thinning hair was mussed. He blinked out at me in horror. "What are *you* doing here?"

"I was hoping to talk to you."

"B-But how did you find me?" he sputtered.

"This is how I make my living, remember?" I replied. There was no need for him to know that when I'd called his house, Sara told me he'd come into the city to catch up on work. Or that when I'd called his office, they told me he was home in Willoughby due to a death in the family. Or that I knew he was a dues-paying member of the Gladiator Club. Or that I'd

shmeared the bell captain fifty bucks and slipped past the plain-
clothesman who was staked out downstairs. There was no need
for Bruce's father to know any of that. "May I come in?"

He hesitated, swallowing uncomfortably.

"We can have this conversation right out here in the hallway
if you want."

He let me in. It was a tiny room, barely big enough for a
double bed, dresser and TV. There was a bath. There was a
closet. He padded over to the bed and sat on the edge of it,
shifting uneasily in his towel.

The Asian girl who was naked in the bed didn't do a thing.
She didn't even bother to pull the sheet over her bare breasts.
Didn't care if I looked at them or not. Just lay there calm as can
be, her gaze more than a bit unfocussed. My guess? She popped
something heavy duty to get herself through the unpleasant-
ness of her work day. Unless, that is, a nooner with a pudgy,
balding forty-eight-year-old toe sucker was her idea of a good
time. She wore a lot of makeup but it didn't hide the sprinkling
of pimples on her forehead. Or the fact that she appeared to be
about fifteen years old.

Paul Weiner cleared his throat. "Would you mind excusing
us for a moment?" he asked her, gesturing to the bathroom.

She shrugged her narrow shoulders and got up out of the
bed, making no effort whatsoever to cover herself. She was so
thin I could see her ribs, front and back. Her breasts were a
child's breasts. Clearly, this was a kid with serious troubles. But
right now they weren't my troubles. She went into the bathroom and closed the door softly behind her.

"She's eighteen," Paul pointed out defensively.

"If you say so. That would make her just about Sara's age, wouldn't it?"

He heaved a pained sigh, his soft white shoulders slumping. "Look, I had to get out of the house, okay? Away from Laurie. Away from our friends and relatives and th-that creep who keeps calling from the funeral home. You have *no* idea how much he's charging me to bury Bruce. I don't even know how I'm going to pay for it. I'm *drowning* in debt."

And yet he'd come up with fifteen hundred dollars to spend on an Asian cupcake for the afternoon. Priorities. Sound financial planning is all about priorities.

"You don't have to explain yourself to me," I said sympathetically. "You've suffered a real blow. You're just trying to cope. I understand that."

I heard the toilet flush. Then the shower came on.

"She's really a very sweet girl," he said helplessly. "Laurie . . . hired you to follow me, is that it?"

"I haven't been in contact with Laurie at all. And she doesn't have to know about this. You have my word. Assuming, that is, I get something in return."

Paul pondered this slowly. "Sure, I understand. Just give me two minutes to throw my clothes on and I'm gone. She's very capable and she'll do *anything*. Her name is—"

"I don't want to know her name. And you don't understand."

He frowned at me. "What is it you want, Ben?"

"The truth about Bruce's adoption. I want to know the details of how it went down."

"Why do you care about that?"

"Because he's dead, that's why. Someone hired me to find

him. That someone was Peter Seymour, who specifically told me not to mention the law firm of Bates, Winslow and Seymour to you. Tell me why and I'll leave you and your little girlfriend in peace."

"There's really not much to tell," he said. "Bruce's adoption was a-a private arrangement. We didn't go through an agency."

"You bought yourself a baby, is that what you're saying?"

"Other way around. We didn't buy Bruce. We were paid to take him."

"Paid how much?"

"Fifty thousand dollars."

"For what?"

"Our silence."

"And who paid you?"

"Bates, Winslow and Seymour. Or the Aurora Group, to be more precise. Some shell company of theirs."

"You're a smart guy, Mr. Weiner. Didn't this arrangement seem a bit strange to you?"

"Of course it did. But I didn't care. *We* didn't care. Laurie and I had been trying to have a baby for years. You have no idea how worthless she felt. Her friends, her cousins, they were *all* having babies. We were desperate. The adoption agency that our rabbi recommended had stuck us on a waiting list that was backed up for years. And the other adoption agencies scared us. You could end up with some kid who has brain damage or God knows what. Sure, it was a bit unusual. But Peter Seymour wasn't exactly a scuzzball. He was a partner in a white-shoe law firm."

"How did you hook up with him?"

"Through a client of mine named Frankie Donahue. I used to handle Frankie's investment portfolio."

"You don't anymore?"

"No, he passed away three, four years ago."

I sighed inwardly. *Everyone* was dead.

"Frankie was an old-school New York City permit expeditor. One of those fellows who you hire if you're trying to get a construction permit or liquor license or what have you. He knew who to pay off and how much it'd cost. Took a healthy percentage for himself, of course, but he worked like a dog and had put away close to a half-mil by the time he came to me. We were reviewing his investments over lunch one afternoon when I happened to mention our situation. Frankie said he might be able to help us out. That every once in a while he'd hear about an honest, reliable party that was on the lookout for an honest, reliable couple—no questions asked. He said it might not be right away but if he heard of anything he'd let me know."

"And I'm guessing he did."

Paul nodded. "About six months later. It was a bright blue Sunday morning in May. I remember the exact date—May the fifth, 1990. He called me at home and told us to meet him in one hour at an address on East 39th Street. We still lived in our apartment on York Avenue in those days. Laurie was more than a little skeptical. Hell, so was I. But we jumped in a cab and went to the address he'd given me. It was a brownstone apartment. Frankie was waiting there for us. And so was Peter Seymour, acting like he was real hot stuff."

"Yeah, he still does that."

"Also a doctor and nurse."

"Do you remember their names?"

"We weren't introduced. The doctor was in his fifties maybe. The nurse was younger, no more than thirty. They were both very tan, I remember. Not many New Yorkers are tan in early May. The baby was in a crib in the back bedroom. It was a new-born boy. Two weeks old, tops. He seemed healthy and well cared for."

"What were you told about the circumstances of his birth?"

"Absolutely nothing."

"Did the baby have a birth certificate?"

"He did. It said that he'd been born in Nevis on January the twenty-fourth. Which obviously was not the case. Like I said, he was two weeks old—not three-and-a-half months. Laurie had been around a million newborns and was quite positive. But that's what his birth certificate said, and the arrangement we'd agreed to was strictly no questions asked. So when we ap-plied for Bruce's US citizenship we entered his date of birth as January the twenty-fourth."

I mulled this over, my wheels turning. It jibed with what El-eanor Saltonstall Kidd had told Legs and me—that Kathleen gave birth in Nevis at the end of January. The old lady had been good and specific about that. How come? Why the discrepancy about the baby's age? And why had Seymour insisted that no birth certificate had been filed? "Was the mother's name listed on this Nevis birth certificate?"

"Yes and no," Paul replied. "She was listed as Jane Jones. The baby was simply listed as Male Jones."

"I understand that Bruce was anxious to get a look at his birth certificate."

"It was something he'd gotten curious about," Paul acknowledged. "But one of the terms of our adoption agreement was that we stash it in our safety deposit box and never, ever let him see it."

"Any idea why?"

"Well, sure. Nevis is a tiny island. If he found out that he'd been born there, chances were good he'd be able to track down the identity of his birth mother."

"Were you and Laurie told anything about her identity?"

"Not a thing. We were not allowed to ask about her. Or to contact Peter Seymour about anything. Ever. That's what the fifty thousand was for. That and 'transitional expenses.' Setting up a nursery in our apartment and so forth."

"But you must have come up with a theory about who she was."

"Of course we did. That's human nature. We figured she was a single young woman who came from a wealthy family. A family that didn't want to go through official adoption channels because they wanted her pregnancy kept quiet. It *was* kept quiet. And we never heard the name Peter Seymour again—until you showed up the other night. Frankly, we were both quite shaken."

"Mr. Weiner, why would Peter Seymour want to hire me twenty-one years later to locate Bruce?"

"Honestly? I don't know."

"Does the name Kathleen Kidd mean anything to you?"

"She committed suicide yesterday. I saw it on the news. What of it?"

"Have you ever had any personal contact with her?"

"No, the Kidds are way out of my league. My clientele is

strictly middle-class." He ducked his head, plump hands folded in his lap. "Bruce was our boy, okay? We raised him since he was a baby. We have good memories, Ben. And we want to hold on to those memories."

"What are you trying to tell me?"

"If you find out something, I want you to keep it to yourself. Please don't upset my wife. She's not a strong person."

The Asian girl in the bathroom turned off the shower. Then she opened the bathroom door. She was still naked, but now she was wet and naked. She raised one bare foot onto the edge of the tub and slowly, carefully began to wipe each one of her toes dry with a towel, gazing over her shoulder at Paul through her false eyelashes. He stared at her, transfixed. I had to give her credit. For a stoned-out teenager she was a total pro.

But I did not like being a witness to this little seduction ritual of theirs. "I'll be going now," I announced.

He looked up at me guiltily. "You won't tell my wife about this?"

"Your secret is safe with me."

I couldn't get out of that hotel room fast enough.

"I DON'T *BELIEVE* THIS!"

"Why, Sonya? I told you I'd call." I was talking to her on my cell as I strode from the Windsor to the subway station. I needed to talk to her. Needed to forget about Paul Weiner and that girl up in 613.

"I know you did, but guys never actually follow through. It's just an empty, meaningless promise they make as they go fleeing out the door into the night, never to be heard from again."

"I'm not like that, Sonya."

"You're so sweet. And you're *just* what I needed today."

"Why, what happened?"

"Oh, it's totally stupid. You don't want to hear about it."

"Believe me, I do."

"There's a little stomach bug going around my school."

"And you picked it up?"

"No, little Shoko Birnbaum did. And she threw up all over my brand-new white cashmere sweater. I was just putting it in the sink to soak."

"So does that mean you're not wearing a top right now?"

She let out a gasp. "Are you trying to start something on the phone?"

"What if I am?"

"I knew it. You're a naughty boy. Guess what, Benji? I like naughty boys."

"Good. When can I see you again?"

"Cookie, you are *so* not doing this right. You're supposed to keep me wondering and worrying and sobbing. Men always play hard to get."

"I don't know how to play. I just know that I want see you again."

"Wow, I must be dreaming. . . ."

"You're not dreaming, Sonya."

"How about dinner tomorrow? But we'll have to make it an early night because I can't handle a roomful of five-year-olds on two hours of sleep. Plus I could barely sit down this morning. My friend Tovah asked me if I'd been hit by a bus."

"Dinner tomorrow sounds perfect. But I'm in the middle of a

crazy case right now and not totally in control of my schedule. So if I have to cancel please don't take it the wrong way, okay?"

"Sure thing. Oh, hey, Benji? You were right."

"About? . . ."

"I'm not wearing a top. Just this flimsy little silk camisole that you can see right through. And I'm washing my sweater in *freezing* cold water. . . ."

"I'm hanging up now," I growled, pocketing my phone hurriedly.

I have a ton of male pride. I didn't want her to hear me whimper.

A SHINY BLACK CADILLAC LIMO was parked out front. A uniformed chauffeur sat behind the wheel reading the *Daily News*. When I made it upstairs to our office, I discovered we had company.

Bobby the K was seated on the sofa in Mom's office. Gus was curled up in his lap, purring away shamelessly.

"Ah, here's Ben now," Mom exclaimed with a dazzling smile. "I believe you already know Mr. Kidd, don't you?"

"Why, yes." I sat in one of the chairs that faced her desk. "Good to see you again, sir."

"And you, Ben," he said quietly, his bright blue eyes fastened on Mom's worn Afghan rug. "I hope you folks don't mind me just showing up this way."

"Not at all," Mom assured him.

"Of course not." Lovely Rita came sashaying in with a container of coffee from Scotty's. "Here you are, Mr. Kidd. Black, two sugars."

"Thank you. Sorry to put you to so much trouble, Rita."

"It was no trouble at all." Rita set it down on the end table next to him, beaming with girlish delight that the great man had remembered her name. Or I should say swooning. I half expected her to plant a kiss on his huge melon of a head. To my surprise I felt a pang of resentment. No, jealousy. It was definitely jealousy.

He sipped his coffee, gazing across the desk at Mom. "Forgive me for staring, Mrs. Golden, but I keep thinking that we know each other from a long time ago."

"Happens all of the time." She and Rita exchanged a knowing look. "My maiden name is Kaminsky if that's any help."

"Did you used to teach?"

Mom let out a bubbly laugh. "Well, I certainly schooled a lot of people."

"I'm really good with faces and I'm *positive* I know yours. I came in contact with a lot of rock groups when I was first starting out. Did you used to perform with a grunge band?"

"I used to perform," Mom allowed. "But not in any grunge band."

"You had a solo act?"

"I did. If it will help jog your memory my professional name was Abraxas."

"Abraxas . . ." Suddenly, it hit him. "My God, you gave me a lap dance once."

Mom arched an eyebrow at him. "Are you sure it wasn't more like twenty lap dances?"

Bobby colored slightly. "So you remember me."

"Of course I remember you, Mr. Kidd. You offered me a

thousand dollars to go for a ride around the block with you in your limo."

"And you turned me down cold. I could look but I couldn't touch. You were very . . . professional."

"I still am," Mom assured him. "Rita danced, too, you know."

He eyeballed Rita up and down. "I don't remember you. And God knows I would. You went by? . . ."

"Natural Born," she replied primly.

"Which meant? . . ."

"Let's not go there, Mr. Kidd."

"You're right," he said with a quick nod. "It was a long time ago. I haven't been in one of those clubs in a million years."

"We all move on," Mom commented sagely.

Rita excused herself and went back out to her desk, closing Mom's door.

Mom folded her hands before her on the desk. "How may we help you today, Mr. Kidd?"

He sat there stroking Gus for a moment before he turned to me and said, "By answering a direct question. Was my sister pushed off of her terrace?"

"Why? Do you have some reason to believe that she was?"

"I don't know, Ben. I wish I did."

"That's what you said this morning when you gave Lieutenant Diamond and me that vague, cryptic warning about watching our backs. You must have *something* more to tell us or you wouldn't be here. By the way, does anyone in your family know that you are?"

"No one knows I'm here."

"Then let's get to it, okay? We're busy people, Mr. Kidd. Our time is valuable."

Mom gaped at me in astonishment. She isn't used to being around me when I've just gotten laid.

"Ben, I honestly . . . I don't know what the devil is going on," Bobby began, choosing his words carefully. "What I do know is that my mother didn't exactly give you an accurate picture of why Katherine was sent away to the Barrow School. In fact, that story she fed you was a fairy tale."

"Why would she do that?"

"Because she can't deal with the reality of what actually happened. It makes her too uncomfortable. My mother . . . needs her illusions. She's lost without them. That's why I didn't speak up this morning. Can you understand?"

"Sure I can," I said. "What's the real story?"

Bobby's eyes returned to the carpet. "Kathleen wasn't sent away to the Barrow School by Dr. Levin because she was becoming disruptive in class. She was sent there because she was abusing drugs and alcohol *and* sleeping with any and every boy who'd have her." He paused to take a sip of his coffee. "I didn't know a thing about it until I came home from Cambridge for Thanksgiving. I couldn't believe what I was seeing—high school boys coming in and out of her bedroom all day long while our mother was off playing bridge. Kathleen would take on three, four, five of them in a single afternoon. They were practically lined up out in the hallway. I-I was shocked. Especially because she'd been such a nice, sweet girl when I went away to school at the end of the summer."

"Why don't you tell us more about that summer, Mr. Kidd," Mom suggested.

"Happy to," Bobby said obligingly. "We spent it on Nantucket. Kathleen loved it there. She loved the water. And I have very happy memories of that summer. The Graysons had a place right up the beach from ours and that was the summer when I fell in love with Meg. She was sixteen. I was eighteen. We swam together every day. Sailed together, played tennis. She always had to beat me at everything. She was *so* competitive," he remembered fondly. "So was her dad, Senator Grayson. He and my old man, the Ambassador, used to play high-stakes cribbage on our veranda every afternoon. They'd drink gin and tonics and curse up a storm. No one plays cribbage anymore. Have you noticed that?" On our silence he added, "When I left for Cambridge just before Labor Day, Kathleen was a healthy, blossoming twelve-year-old girl. She was well behaved, studious, *normal*. Somehow, in a few short months, she'd gotten totally out of control."

"Did you try talking to her?" Mom asked him.

"You bet I did. She laughed at me. Hell, she even accused me of hassling her because *I* secretly wanted her, too. And couldn't have her. It was just plain sick, the stuff that came out of Kathleen's mouth. She was *twisted* inside. She was angry and mean. That's why they sent her away to Barrow. But it hurts my mother too much to talk about it."

"What happened when Kathleen got to Barrow?" I asked.

"Nothing changed. She was in constant trouble. And not because of any mythical bad boy whose big brother at New Paltz was supplying him with dope. It was Kathleen who was getting drugs sent to her—from her doper friends in the city. And she was screwing every boy in the school. The sad reality is, my parents had no way of knowing who the father of her baby was. It could have been anyone. It wasn't the school's fault. The authorities at Barrow did everything humanly possible, short of insisting that my folks lock her away in an institution. And my parents felt no animosity toward them. Hell, my father gave the Barrow School two million bucks after Kathleen left, for a new performing arts building. Would he have done that if he'd thought they were responsible for what happened to her?"

"I wouldn't think so," Mom murmured.

"The story that your mother told us about taking Kathleen down to Nevis to have her baby—was that fiction, too?"

"No, that part was true. Dr. Sykes and his nurse did fly down and Kathleen did give birth there, like Mother said."

"In January of 1990?"

"That's what I was told." He frowned at me. "Why, do you have reason to believe otherwise?"

"Nope. Just wondered."

"After that, Kathleen was sent away to Geneva, like my mother said. But when it came to men, Kathleen was a trouble magnet her whole life. That eurotrash bum who married her for her money—he wasn't the only one who used her. A lot of men did. One of them took filthy photos of her having sex with two of his closest friends and threatened to sell them to the British tabloids if my father didn't pay up. Which my father did. Another one stole her credit cards and cleaned out her bank accounts. On and on it went. My father always had to ride to the rescue. About five years ago, she started seeing a new therapist in Paris, who finally seemed to get somewhere with her. Or maybe it was just the new generation of meds she was on. But she seemed to be doing better. Started to paint again. Stayed out of trouble."

"You know this how?" I asked him.

He blinked at me. "Excuse me?"

"Did you visit her over there?"

"No," he answered shortly. "We weren't close, as I told you this morning."

"So how do you know this? Through your mother?"

Bobby let out a humorless laugh. "Hardly. Kathleen and my mother could barely stand to be in the same room together. We got periodic updates about her from Peter Seymour. Peter's the one who she stayed in touch with. She had to. He held the purse strings."

"So he's maintained a relationship with Kathleen over the years?"

Bobby's face tightened. "Of a sort."

"What sort?"

"Where are you going with this, Ben?"

"Just trying to figure things out."

"You won't. Not where Kathleen's concerned. She was impossible to figure out. When she decided to move back to New York we were . . . encouraged, I guess. But, as my mother said, Kathleen kept to herself. She wasn't comfortable around other people. Not even us. Especially us."

"What do you know about Bruce Weiner?"

"Not a thing. I'd never heard of him until you guys mentioned him this morning. I gather, from what you were saying, that Kathleen had become obsessed with trying to establish a relationship with him."

"Do you have any idea how she was able to locate him?"

"No idea whatsoever."

"Who was privy to the identity of the couple that adopted her baby?"

"Besides Peter Seymour, you mean? No one."

"Your mother didn't know?"

"My mother didn't want to know. No one in the family did. I sure didn't. Nor did Meg," he added hesitantly. "Or at least I don't think she did."

"Okay, I'm a bit confused now," I confessed. "Is there a reason why your wife might have known who Bruce was?"

Bobby cleared his throat. "Well, yeah. She's a Grayson."

"Which means? . . ."

"Look, can we talk real world here?"

"By all means," Mom said to him encouragingly.

"Meg's running my campaign and she is strictly old school. A Grayson, through and through. Don't get me wrong—she's loving and kind and a wonderful mother. But she's also one of the most ruthless people I've ever met, with the possible exception of her dear, departed father, the Senator. The Graysons take no prisoners. And that name still carries a lot of clout with certain people around this state. Like union bosses who know how to get out the vote and will bust heads if they have to. Meg has devoted herself—body, mind and soul—to making sure that I'm sworn in as New York's next governor. For all I know, having some goon fling Kathleen off of that balcony could simply fall under the category of 'preventive damage control.'"

I looked at him in disbelief. "Are you suggesting that Meg may be involved in your sister's death?"

"I'm saying I don't know. I'm saying that when it comes to politics *nothing* is off limits as far as she's concerned."

I looked at him some more. "Why are you telling us this?"

"Because I want to know who killed my sister."

"So you *don't* think she committed suicide."

He puffed out his cheeks before he said, "No, I don't."

"Real world, Mr. Kidd," Mom said. "What's going on here?"

"I wish I knew, Mrs. Golden. I really do." He glanced at his watch, then nudged Gus out of his lap and stood up. "I have to be going. They'll wonder where I am. I hope this was helpful." And with that, Bobby the K grabbed his topcoat and hustled on out of there.

"There he goes, ladies and gentlemen," I said quietly. "Our next governor."

Mom shook her head at me. "How weird was that?"

"Plenty weird. He called his mother a liar, his sister a slut *and* he cozied right up to accusing his wife of murder."

"I wonder if we should believe what he said."

"You didn't?"

"He *seemed* credible. And genuinely upset. But I just don't know." She said it again. "How weird was that?"

The two of us were sitting there mulling over just how weird when Rita let out a cry of shock from her computer.

Someone had just fired shots at Charles Willingham outside of the Stuyvesant Field House on the campus of Canterbury College. Charles was no longer in charge. He was dead.

CHAPTER SIX

HE'D BEEN SHOOTING HOOPS AT THE FIELD HOUSE with Coach Seckla, according to the latest news accounts I could find on my computer. Apparently, Charles wanted to get in some extra practice despite the mandatory three-day study break he'd been given for the Gauntlet. He was leaving the Field House when he and Sergeant Fred Ayeroff, a twelve-year veteran of the NYPD, were both shot dead by an unknown assailant. Ayeroff was one of the two officers assigned by Legs Diamond to watch over Charles. Coach Seckla, who had departed the Field House moments earlier to fetch his car, was unharmed.

The shooting death of Charles Willingham set off an instant torrent of grief—on the Canterbury campus, in the projects where'd grown up, across all of New York City. Hell, across the whole damned country. He was a huge star. A role model. A hero. I happen to know he was also a nice guy. A makeshift shrine was already being erected outside of those tall, wrought-iron campus gates. People by the hundreds were leaving flowers, candles and cards. The same thing was happening outside of the front door to his mother's apartment building.

As I sat there at my desk, blown away, I got two phone calls. The first was from Sara Weiner, who sounded even worse than I felt.

"Benji, why did they have kill *Charles?* Why is this happening?"

"I don't know, Sara. But I promise you we'll find out. Are you okay?"

"No, I'm *not* okay. Some man is parked outside of our house."

"He's with the Willoughby police. Just making sure no one tries to mess with you."

"Well, then why doesn't he start with my parents? Because they are *totally* messing with me. My mom was out boning her boyfriend all afternoon. She just came staggering in smelling of wine. I can hear her in her bathroom throwing up. And my dad went—"

"To the office, I know. You already—"

"How can he *work* at a time like this? I mean, doesn't he have *any* feelings? I'm freaking out here, Benji. I really, really don't know how I-I'm . . ." She broke off, snuffling into the phone. "I told Trevor."

"Told Trevor what?"

"That I made you the bracelet."

I glanced down at the purple and pink woven bracelet on my wrist. It still seemed foreign there. "Was that wise?"

"I don't know, but I needed to be truthful. It's how I am. He was actually jealous, which is just so childish and s-so *Trevor.* But he's not here for me right now. No one is—except for you. You're here, right?"

"Always. You can count on me, Sara," I promised, thinking

that what Sara Weiner really needed right now was a professional grief counselor. Not to mention a mother who wasn't self-medicating between the sheets all afternoon and a father who hadn't run off to the city to bang a teenaged hooker. It wasn't fair. Sara was a victim of this hot mess same as her brother had been—except she was still around to feel the pain.

"Benji, will you come to Bruce's funeral tomorrow?"

"I'll sure try."

"Don't say you'll try. Say you'll be there. I *need* you there. I'll totally lose it if you're not holding my hand."

"Sara, I'll be there."

"Thank you, Benji. Can I ride back to the city with you after the funeral and spend the night?"

I sighed inwardly. "We'll talk about you and me tomorrow, okay?"

"That sounds like no."

"Sara? . . ."

"Yes, Benji?"

"I really like my bracelet."

"You'd better," she said.

I hung up the phone. Rita was staring across her desk at me, and my new bracelet, with keen-eyed disapproval.

"Okay, what is it?"

"That little girl's madly in love with you."

"She just needs someone to hold onto right now."

"*And* she's madly in love with you. Tell me, does she know about you and the ferret?"

"Would you be referring to Sonya?"

"If Sara Weiner finds out that you're sleeping with the

ferret she'll be crushed. You can't toy with a girl's feelings this way. "

"That's not what I'm doing. I'm trying to be a friend to her."

"Trust me, friendship isn't what she's after. She wants to jump you, same as the ferret did. You're quite jumpworthy in your own adorably helpless way. Just don't make a mess of things, okay?"

"Does that mean you think I am?"

"It means I think you're a grown man and therefore you haven't got the slightest idea what you're doing."

"Not to worry, Rita. I've got everything under control."

"Sure, you do, little lamb."

Now I got my second phone call—this one from Legs Diamond.

"It's getting tense out on the front lines," he informed me in a taut, edgy voice. "We just had a mini-riot outside of Velma Willingham's building in the King projects. Fifteen, twenty bangers started throwing rocks and bottles at our men. Back-up had to be called in. The situation was contained, but the whole department's on high alert now."

"Are you working his shooting?"

"I just left the crime scene. And we have *two* victims, don't forget."

"I haven't. Did you know Fred Ayeroff well?"

"Yeah, I knew him well. Listen, I'm ten blocks uptown from your place. Grab your coat and head downstairs. I'm picking you up."

"Where are we going?"

"We'll talk about that when I see you. Yo, little dude?"

"Yeah, Legs?"

"Tell your mom you may be home late."

When I stuck my head in her doorway, Mom was sitting at her desk gazing out the window at Broadway, lost in thought. I wondered what she was thinking about. Maybe she was missing my dad. Maybe she was wishing he was around to take care of this shitstorm instead of me. I didn't blame her. I wished he was still around, too. I tapped on the door and told her Legs was coming by for me.

She heaved a sigh and said, "Take care of yourself, Bunny. And don't forget your gun."

"I won't, Mom."

I put my duffel coat on over my Harris Tweed sports jacket, feeling the snug weight of my Chief's Special in my right-hand coat pocket. I told Rita I'd see her in the morning. She didn't say anything in response. Seemed to be lost in thought, too. Missing Clarence, I imagined. It was that kind of a day.

By the time I made it downstairs Legs was pulling up out front. I got in and off we zoomed down Broadway, Legs with his foot to the floor, me holding on for dear life. He was incredibly wired. His left knee was jiggling. His head was bobbing. It was a wonder he could keep the car on the road.

"Where are we going?" I asked him.

"Command performance," he said tightly. "We are into some uber-bad shit now."

"Tell me what the press doesn't have, will you?"

"No prob, although it wasn't easy getting anything out of Coach Seckla. The man's a total wreck. Charles was like a son to him. He called the coach at home in Riverdale from his mom's place right around noon. The coach said he sounded real down."

"Did Charles tell him why?"

"Yes and no. He told him a close friend had just been murdered. That he was having a hard time dealing. And he was going to go nuts if he didn't get in the gym. Coach Seckla drove straight to the King projects and picked him up. Fred Ayeroff and his partner, Mark Olman, were there keeping an eye on Velma's building. They tailed Coach Seckla and Charles to the Field House. Ayeroff went inside with them."

"How did Ayeroff explain his presence to the coach?"

"Charles took care of it. He told Coach Seckla that it had to do with the shooting of his friend. A precautionary measure. Coach Seckla was fine with it. He was accustomed to having extra security for Charles. Crowds of people wanted a piece of him wherever the team went. They shot hoops together for a couple hours. Coach told me they didn't talk a lot. Charles didn't want to talk. Just shoot. Ayeroff sat and watched them the whole time."

"And where was Olman?"

"Parked outside in their ride, maybe fifty feet from the door."

"Did he see anyone?"

"Not a soul. He told me the grounds outside of the Field House were deserted."

"What about the security guard who's on duty outside the door?"

"He's only there when the team is using the Field House. The place was locked up tight. Coach Seckla used his key to get in. When Charles was ready to leave, the coach went on ahead to get his car while Charles stopped off in the locker room to take a leak. Ayeroff stayed with Charles. When they exited the Field House they were both sprayed with a TEC-9. Real gang-banger special. Charles died instantly. Ayeroff died in Olman's arms before the ambulance got there."

"Was he able to tell Olman anything?"

Legs shook his head.

"What about the shooter?"

"Got away."

"How's it possible that Olman didn't see him?"

"The door's surrounded by a bunch of big old London plane trees. Plus it's nearly dark there by four o'clock on a winter afternoon. He was hiding in the shadows somewhere. Shots were fired from no more than ten feet away, according to our techies."

"How about Coach Seckla? Did he see anyone?"

Legs shook his head again.

"Did the shooter take anything?"

"I put that question to Coach Seckla. He was so shook it took him a while to notice that Charles's backpack was gone. I asked him what Charles kept in it."

"Let me guess—his laptop."

"Swish," he confirmed as we hit Columbus Circle and bar-reled on down toward the theater district. "His cell phone's gone, too."

I sat there mulling it over. "Are you thinking the shooter tailed them to the Field House?"

"No, he was already set up there. He had his getaway pre-planned. Must have had a tap on Charles's phone. We are dealing with a stone-cold pro here. The mayor's *furious*. Wants to make a bow tie out of somebody's balls." Legs glanced over at me. "Olman did see a dark green vehicle go streaking down the block a few seconds after the shots were fired. It was a Jeep Grand Cherokee."

"Oh, yeah? Did he get a license number?"

"Too far away. But I'm doubling down on the number of eyeballs that we've got scanning the tollbooth videos from the night Bruce was shot. We'll catalogue every dark green Grand Cherokee that entered the city after ten p.m. And question every owner. But, real, this is a large metropolis. Your boy Marco Battalino still has people canvassing the motels near Candlewood Lake. They haven't turned up anything yet."

"You said we're dealing with a stone-cold pro here."

"Most definitely."

"You're assuming it's one guy?"

"It's one guy. He's precise and he's surgical. Bruce's death looked like a home invasion. Kathleen's like a suicide. And now Charles looks like he was taken down by a gangbanger. Trust me, this is an intelligent, highly skilled lone operator."

"Are your cop instincts telling you this?"

"Well, yeah," he said, steering us through the traffic of Times Square. "Plus I know something you don't. The rifling pattern on the nine-mil slug you dug out of that building on West 12th matched the slugs the Connecticut State Police pulled out of Bruce's body. Came from a Glock 17, they think. Same gun, same shooter."

"If he's so smart why did he use the same gun?"

"Because he's taunting me, that's why. And the arrogant son of a bitch is really starting to piss me off."

"Legs, you still haven't said where we're going."

"Little Italy."

"What for?"

He didn't tell me. Just drove.

"Did you find out anything at the Barrow School?"

"Never made it up there. You?"

I told him about our little visit from Bobby the K. What he'd told us about Kathleen's wicked, wicked ways. And how the circumstances surrounding her pregnancy weren't exactly how the old lady had portrayed them.

Legs listened without comment until I got to the part where Bobby had hinted that the Grayson political machine might be behind the deaths of Bruce and Kathleen. "Wait, he told you that his dead sister was a teen skank *and* he threw his own wife under the bus?"

"Pretty much."

"Whoa, he's some cutie."

"And he's going to be our next governor. Makes you proud to be an American, doesn't it?"

By now we'd hurtled our way downtown past Herald Square and the Flatiron Building. When we reached the Village, Legs Diamond worked his way east on Houston Street, then hung a right on Mott and took that down to Little Italy. He parked in front of a corner grocery on Mott and Grand. We got out and he led me inside of the little grocery store and straight on through to the back room, where a steep stairway took us down to the basement storeroom. There was a long, dimly lit concrete corridor down there that led, seemingly, to the basements of every store and restaurant on the block. We walked all of the way to the end of this subterranean corridor, where it made a sharp right and continued on. I heard car traffic over my head now. I'm fairly certain we were crossing under Mulberry Street. Then we made another right turn and connected up with another corridor that led us past more basement storerooms and narrow staircases.

"These passageways are left over from Prohibition," Legs explained over his shoulder as he strode along, his motorcycle boots thunking on the concrete floor. "There's a whole network of them in lower Manhattan. There's even one that used to go from the basement of City Hall right to the speakeasy across the street. No lie."

We had arrived at the basement of a restaurant. Legs led us upstairs past the bustling, fragrant kitchen—where absolutely no one looked us in the eye—and straight on up to a private second-floor dining room. I could hear the voices and laughter of the people in the restaurant below us. I don't know what restaurant it was. Or even what street we were on. The wooden shutters over the windows were closed.

A table in the private dining room was set for five. Three men were already seated there. Our host rose to greet us.

"Thanks for coming," said New York City Police Commissioner Dante Feldman. "Sorry for the cloak and dagger shit but I didn't want anyone to know we were getting together. Take off your coats and join us."

We took off our coats and joined them. I was well aware of

who the other two men were. Peter Seymour I knew person-
ally. The other man was someone who was always on television
making damned sure everyone knew who he was—Jake Leetes,
the one-time NYPD chief of detectives who was the founder and
president of the Leetes Group.

"Good to see you again, Ben," said Commissioner Feldman,
who delivered a real nice eulogy at my dad's funeral. "How's
that beautiful mother of yours?"

"She's fine, sir. Thank you for asking."

Dante Feldman was famously demanding and volatile. They
called him the Human Hemorrhoid around One Police Plaza,
although never to his face. It was a hawk-like face. He had a
prominent beak of a nose. A carefully combed snowy white
pompadour. Thin, pale lips and the hooded, penetrating glare
of a man who had spent decades in interrogation rooms breaking every tough customer who came along. He was in his late
fifties, tall, taut and a real sharp dresser. His navy blue suit was
an Armani. And the pale blue shirt he wore had French cuffs
with gold cufflinks. He was constantly shooting his cuffs and
smoothing his pompadour. It was a thing that he did. Don't
know if he was aware of it or not.

Jake Leetes got up from his chair and shook my hand. "I
knew your old man real well, Ben."

Leetes was, in his own way, as intimidating a figure as Feldman. He was a simmering bunched fist of a man with a shaved
head, bulging eyes and thick, liver-colored lips. A man who
gave you the feeling that he could barely contain his inner rage.
Leetes was no more than five-foot-nine but he had to weigh at
least 220 and it was all muscle. He wore an English tweed suit

with a suede vest, knit tie and tattersall shirt. He was aiming to look classy and gentlemanly the way Peter Seymour did. To me, he looked like a well-tailored bulldog.

Mr. Classy Guy didn't say a word to me or to Legs as we joined them at the table. Just sat there sipping his mineral water and measuring the mood in the room—which was highly charged. Commissioner Feldman and Jake Leetes had come up together on the force and were two sides of the same coin. Both were ruthless, fiercely ambitious empire builders. Both had succeeded beyond their wildest schoolboy dreams. But Feldman had done it within the system while Leetes had created a system—and rules—of his own. Which meant there was a deeply felt enmity between them, a shared contempt for the other's chosen life path. It was so apparent that it hung there in the air along with the scent of sautéed garlic from the kitchen downstairs.

Our food had already been ordered for us. A waiter brought up the first course, which was bean and pasta soup drizzled with olive oil. There was a basket of crusty bread on the table. Also two bottles of Chianti Classico. Leetes was having wine. Commissioner Feldman was sticking to mineral water same as Seymour was. Mr. Classy Guy wasn't eating. Apparently, he had other plans for dinner. I didn't. Neither did Legs. We both dove in as soon as our soup was set before us. I poured myself some wine. Legs drank water.

"This is a bad day for the City of New York," said Feldman, pausing to taste his soup. "I've got a special young man, a transcendent hero to the black community, dead in a hail of gunfire along with a fallen hero of our own. I've got the mayor screaming at me. I've got the media screaming at me. What I haven't got is time for polite small talk. I'm on the air with Rachel Maddow in . . ." He shot his cuff, glancing at his watch. "Less than seventy-five minutes. And I've got three other on-air appearances to make before this night's over. Kids from Charles Willingham's neighborhood are throwing rocks and bottles at our men in uniform. The usual activists are already mouthing off. I've got to convince the black community that we're doing everything we possibly can to bring his killer to justice." He dipped a chunk of bread in his soup and shoved it into his mouth. "I brought you all here so we could talk frankly and openly about just exactly what the fuck is going on. It's dicks on the table time, understood?"

Leetes and Seymour listened to him in steadfast silence, their gazes revealing nothing.

Legs and I worked on our soup. It was good soup. As we were finishing it, two waiters brought up our main course and side dishes on family style platters. There was a platter of veal piccata, another of roasted potatoes with peppers, another of spinach sautéed in olive oil and garlic. The waiters removed our soup bowls, topped off our water and wine glasses and then left us, closing the door discreetly behind them.

Commissioner Feldman helped himself to mammoth portions of everything and passed the platters around. As we were serving ourselves he turned his hooded gaze on Legs and said, "Lieutenant, what do *you* think is going on?"

Legs took a sip of water. "Bottom line? Someone's systematically eliminating every single person who might know about Bruce Weiner's connection to Kathleen Kidd, his birth mother."

"*Alleged* birth mother," Peter Seymour interjected right away. "What you're stating is not an established fact."

"We're dealing with a consummate pro here," Legs continued, ignoring him. "He stays one step ahead of us and makes sure he removes all traces of e-mail and cell phone contact between the parties. He took Bruce Weiner's laptop and cell. Also Kathleen Kidd's. And now Charles Willingham's."

Feldman mulled this over before he said, "Keep talking."

"We're concerned about the safety of the Weiner family. The Willoughby PD has their house under surveillance, and we're keeping a body on any family member who goes out. Also on Bruce's roommate, Chris Warfield."

Jake Leetes shook his gleaming bald head. "Hold on a sec, Donnie. I'm missing something here."

Feldman stared across the table at him. "And that is? . . ."

"I don't see any connection between Charles Willingham and Kathleen Kidd," he said.

Which I took to be Leetes jerking our collective chains. He knew every single dirty detail of what we knew—and a whole lot more. The Leetes Group was up to its eyeballs in this. By playing dumb he was simply trying to get Feldman to show him his hand.

Feldman glowered at him, no doubt thinking the exact same thing. Leetes glowered right back. What I was witnessing was a battle of wills between two extremely formidable men. Leetes was winning round one by refusing to concede a thing.

Feldman cut into his veal, chewing on it savagely. "What I'm about to say must never leave this room. It's my understanding that Charles Willingham was secretly involved in a romantic

relationship with Bruce Weiner. And that what happened outside of Stuyvesant Field House this afternoon wasn't a gang-
related shooting or a mugging gone bad. It was really about
the circumstances surrounding Bruce Weiner's adoption. Am I
correct so far, Lieutenant?"

"Yes, sir," Legs said.

"Unless," Peter Seymour countered, "it was really about
eliminating anyone who knew that Charles Willingham was a
homosexual."

Feldman swiveled his pompadour in Seymour's direction.
"*Including* Willingham himself? Are you shitting me?"

"Not at all. I'm offering you a perfectly viable alternative
scenario," Seymour answered in his rich baritone.

"What you're doing," Feldman shot back, "is trying to tell us
that none of this shit has a thing to do with Kathleen Kidd. That
you, the Kidd family counsel, hired Golden Legal Services to
find Bruce Weiner on a totally unrelated matter. And that it's
just one big, fat coincidence that *all* of these folks are getting
murdered one right after another."

"I'm merely stating that I don't think we're in possession of
enough of the facts yet to say for certain what is clear."

Feldman gaped at him in mocking disbelief. "Is that so? Because I think it's plenty fucking clear—unless you purposely
fog up the lens. What do *you* think, Jake?"

Leetes took a slow sip of his wine and swallowed it, shoving
his thick, moist lower lip in and out. "Let me just say this, Donnie, because I think it needs saying: If I discover that anyone in
my organization is involved in the shooting death of a New
York City police officer, I will come forward with the facts in a

heartbeat. I am talking full disclosure. You have my word on that."

"I appreciate that, Jake." Commissioner Feldman waited for Leetes to say something more. Like something useful.

Except Leetes had nothing more to say. He just went back to shoveling veal and potatoes into his mouth. He chewed with his mouth open and made a weird little *num-num-num* humming noise while he ate which was kind of endearingly cute— except not.

Feldman promptly lost it. "*That's* the sack of shit you're going to hand me?" he screamed at him. "You're going to look me right in the eye, eat my food and hand me *that?*"

"The food's good here." Leetes calmly took another sip of his wine. "Where the hell are we, anyway?"

"Listen to what I'm telling you, Jake!" Feldman roared, stabbing the table with his index finger. "If you're involved in this I *will* find out and I *will* put you out of business!"

Leetes grew a bit chestier now, his eyes narrowing. "Don't make empty threats in front of other people. You sound like a blustering fool. I run a legitimate operation. I don't have hired killers on my payroll."

"But you know how to hire them."

He let out a laugh. "Who doesn't? So what?"

"And what about *you,* Counselor?" Feldman's face was growing redder by the second. They didn't call him the Human Hemorrhoid for nothing. "Have *you* got anything more to say?"

"The Kidd family is going through an extremely difficult time," Seymour answered. "Beyond that, I can say very little.

With all due respect, Commissioner, we're straying into the realm of attorney-client privilege."

"Fuck your respect!" Feldman hollered at him. "And fuck your attorney-client privilege! I've got people dropping like flies. I need answers!"

Seymour's mouth tightened. "You say you need answers. And you have the resources of the largest police department in the United States at your disposal. If that's the case, then why are we sitting here with an ill-mannered rock and roller and his little sidekick, Mister Bunny Bracelet?"

"I'm not supposed to take it off," I offered as explanation. "If I do something heinous will happen to me."

Seymour stared at me coldly. "I cannot believe we're having this conversation."

"You're the one who brought it up. You're also the one who got me into this mess in the first place."

"A mistake I shall be regretting for the rest of my life."

"You mean because I found Bruce? Did you think I wouldn't? Did you hire me to fail?"

Seymour refused to dignify my questions with a response.

"Lieutenant Diamond happens to be my best man," Feldman told him brusquely. "There's no one else who I'd rather have on this case. And Ben's here because you put him here, like he said. If there's a weak link at this table, Counselor, it's you. All I've gotten out of you so far is silky-smooth bullshit. Will you at least acknowledge that Kathleen Kidd was Bruce Weiner's birth mother? Can we get that one simple fact straight?"

Seymour moistened his lips with the tip of his pale pink

tongue before he said, "Yes, she was. Should there be a DNA test, it will confirm that fact."

"Who was the father?" Legs wanted to know.

Seymour blinked at him from behind his rimless spectacles. "We already discussed that this morning. It was a troubled teenaged boy at the Barrow School."

"And where is he now?" Legs pressed him.

"It's my understanding that he lives in Colorado. He has a wife and two children. He's leading a productive life. And he has had no contact whatsoever with the Kidd family."

Briefly, the private dining room fell silent—aside from the *num-num-num* sound Jake Leetes made while he chewed on his dinner.

Feldman shot his cuffs and smoothed his pompadour. "So Kathleen Kidd's baby was adopted by the Weiners, and twenty-one years later, here we are. Kathleen is dead, her son Bruce is dead and Bruce's lover, Charles Willingham, is dead—along with one of my men. Why now? Why do all of these people suddenly have to die?" He glanced at Legs. "Do you have anything more for me?"

Legs's gaze flickered. He did have something more, but was in no mood to volunteer it in front of Jake Leetes and Peter Seymour. "Nothing that I'm prepared to discuss at this time, Commissioner."

"Why not?"

"It's unconfirmed, sir. Nothing more than rumor."

Feldman swiveled his hawk's beak back toward Peter Seymour. "Why did you hire Ben to find Bruce Weiner? Who wanted him found?"

"A client," he answered. "I can't tell you anything more than that."

"Jake, did your people prepare the background file on the Weiners that he passed to Ben?"

"We did," Leetes allowed. "Pretty standard stuff."

"Why weren't you hired to find Bruce? Why was Golden Legal Services brought in?"

"Because," Seymour explained, "we had been told that Ben has a special gift for finding missing young people."

"Maybe the kid does," Feldman conceded. "But Jake's got hundreds of people on his payroll. Maybe even thousands. Is it thousands, Jake?"

"It's thousands," Leetes confirmed. "I've got offices in seventeen states now, Donnie. Still, if a client prefers to outsource a certain aspect of a job, that's his right."

"I'd like to know who bugged our office and our car," I said, staring across the table at Leetes.

He brushed me off like I was a piece of carpet lint. "Son, I'm not here to answer your questions."

"I'd like to know that, too," Legs said to him.

But Jake Leetes had no intention of answering him either.

Feldman glowered. "Jake, when your people were preparing the file on Bruce Weiner did they find out that he and Charles Willingham were romantically involved?"

Leetes furrowed his brow. "Honestly?"

"That would be nice."

"My people were aware that the two young men shot hoops together and went out for beers. But they were also aware that Charles had dated a number of attractive female students during his stay at Canterbury. I'm talking black, brown *and* white. The fact that he dated white girls wasn't common knowledge, and it's something you may want to look into. Certain types of people can get real upset about the interracial thing. My point is, there was no reason to suspect that Charles had anything out of the ordinary or weird going on in his personal life."

"Being gay isn't out of the ordinary or weird," I pointed out.

"You're absolutely right. I apologize for how that sounded."

"Who's behind these hits, Jake?" Feldman demanded. "Do you know?"

"There's a million freelancers out there," Leetes replied with a shrug.

"There aren't a million who are this good. And you didn't answer my question. Do you know?"

"I have no personal knowledge of who is responsible."

"Bullshit," Feldman snarled at him.

Which kind of threw a wrench into the whole frank, open talk thing. Not that there had been any frank, open talk. But at least we were speaking. Now we were just sitting there in smoldering silence.

Feldman heaved an exasperated sigh and tried again. "We believe that Katherine made her initial attempt to contact Bruce shortly before Thanksgiving. What we don't know is how she found out that Bruce was her biological son."

"She got the information from you, didn't she?" I said to Peter Seymour.

"She most certainly did not. That's an absurd notion. Why would you even think such a thing?"

"Because you and Kathleen were close. You're the one

person who she stayed in contact with when she was living abroad."

"How do you know that?" he demanded.

I smiled at him. "You know I can't divulge how I come by my information. It's confidential."

"Commissioner Feldman, I have somewhere else to be," Seymour said indignantly. "Unless you have something more to discuss, something concrete, I'm leaving right now."

"No, you're not," Feldman snapped. "Cool your jets, Counselor. We're still not talking about what we came here to talk about. I mean the eight-hundred-pound gorilla in the room. Why all of this shit is happening *now*. What it does or doesn't have to do with Bobby the K's gubernatorial bid. Only a total fucking moron would fail to wonder whether somebody's trying to derail his campaign. And no one at this table is a total fucking moron. We go back a lot of years, Jake, but if you don't step up and tell me what I need to know right now, I swear I will make it impossible for you to do business in the City of New York."

Leetes held up his hands in a gesture of surrender. "I'll help you if I can, Donnie. You know that. What do you need to know?"

"Whether the smart money is for Bobby or against him. You know who I mean. The big boys with the big, deep pockets. Are they trying to put Bobby in or keep him out. Which is it?"

Leetes and Seymour exchanged a guarded glance before Leetes said, "In. Definitely in. This isn't some kind of a power play. The big money's all lined up behind Bobby the K. He's a shoo-in."

"Then who's behind all of this?" Feldman pressed him. "Why is it happening?"

"Donnie, I wish I knew. But I don't."

The commissioner shot a cold, hard look at Legs Diamond. "In that case, Lieutenant, I have two words of advice for you— find out."

"WHERE ARE WE GOING NOW?"

"Ronkonkoma," Legs informed me quietly as he steered us across the Williamsburg Bridge to the Brooklyn-Queens Expressway. He'd been pensive ever since we'd retraced our footsteps from the private dining room to his car.

"On the island? What's out there?"

"It's not a what. It's a who. Her name's Judith Heintz." He glanced across the seat at me. "I didn't share everything just now with the commissioner. Didn't much care for the company he was keeping."

"Really? Because I thought Jake was adorable."

"I told you the nine-mil slug you dug out of that wall on West 12th matched the slugs that killed Bruce Weiner, remember?"

"Believe me, I haven't forgotten."

"Well, there's another body on that gun. An identical slug was pulled out of a lady named Martine Price in Jackson Heights, Queens, three weeks ago. She was killed in a home invasion."

We were crossing the Kosciuszko Bridge now. On the other side of it we picked up the Long Island Expressway, Legs maneuvering his battered sedan with high-speed ease through the sluggish evening traffic.

"Martine was fifty-two and unmarried. She lived alone in one half of a two-family house. Her kitchen door was jimmied. She was shot twice. Her jewelry box was emptied. Her silver was taken. They didn't get a whole lot. She didn't have a lot, although she did own the building. Len Wood, the detective who handled the case, told me he had zilch to work with. Nobody saw anything, nobody heard anything. No prints or trace evidence. Just the two slugs. Martine's tenants and neighbors all described her as a nice, quiet lady who kept to herself. She was a registered nurse employed by Sanctuary Health, a private home-care provider. Saw to the needs of housebound patients in Brooklyn and Queens. Elderly, mostly." His eyes flicked up at his rearview mirror once, twice, three times. "She went to work for Sanctuary four years ago. Wood spoke to her supervisor there to see if maybe one of her patients has a relative with a sheet—a grandson or nephew who she might have pissed off or whatever. But that angle didn't pan out. Everyone who came in contact with Martine loved her."

"Forgive me, but I still don't see what this has to do with—"

"Stay with me. The Sanctuary people kept Martine's job application in their files. Prior to working for Sanctuary she was an ICU nurse at Lenox Hill Hospital for twelve years."

"And? . . ."

"And prior to that she worked for a high-end Park Avenue doctor named John Sykes."

I felt my pulse quicken. "The Kidd family's private physician. He brought a nurse with him to Nevis. That must have been Martine. She was there when Bruce was born. She brought him back to New York with Dr. Sykes. And she took care of him in that apartment on East 39th Street until the adoption went through. We've got ourselves another victim, haven't we?"

"You got that right." Legs's eyes flicked at the rearview mirror again.

"Are we being tailed?"

"I thought so for a sec, but it's just a juiced-up Trans Am cowboy." He frowned at me. "*What* apartment on East 39th Street?"

"I got the real deal from Paul Weiner today. How they got the baby, all of it."

"How'd you manage that?"

"Crowbar. Walked in on him banging a teenaged hooker in the Windsor. Paul talked to me so I wouldn't spill the dirty details to his wife."

"Kid, does your mother know what you do for a living?"

"She not only knows, she writes my paycheck—when I get a paycheck."

"Weiner's protection detail in Willoughby told us that he caught a train into the city this morning. One of my men shadowed him from Grand Central straight to the Windsor. He told me Weiner was hiking the Appalachian Trail with a working girl. What he didn't tell me was that *you* went up to Weiner's room. How is it that he didn't make you?"

"No one ever makes me. I totally disappear in public—unlike your man. Tall with receding black hair, am I right?"

"Yeah, that's him," he said grudgingly. "So what did Weiner tell you?"

"That a client of his named Frankie Donahue arranged the adoption. Donahue was a permit expeditor."

"You say he 'was.' Does that mean? . . ."

"Yeah, he's dead. Everybody's dead."

Legs nodded. "Or getting dead. Keep talking."

"The Weiners hadn't been able to conceive. They were getting nowhere through the conventional adoption route and they were desperate. Paul mentioned it to Donahue one day. Donahue told him he might be able to help them out."

"Meaning that permits weren't the only thing this dude expedited."

"Hey, a fixer's a fixer. They got a call from him on a Sunday morning in May. May the fifth, to be exact. He sent them to an address on East 39th Street. Donahue was there to meet them along with Peter Seymour, who Paul said acted like a real dick."

"Hey, a dick's a dick," Legs said.

"A doctor and nurse were there, too. Both really tan. Paul said the doctor was in his fifties. That would be Sykes. And the nurse was maybe thirty—Martine Price. The baby boy was in a crib in one of the bedrooms. They were offered the boy *and* a check for fifty thou for 'transitional expenses,' courtesy of the Aurora Group, which is the same shell company that Seymour used to pay us. The doctor assured the Weiners that the baby was completely healthy and normal. Which Paul said he appeared to be—aside from one small discrepancy."

"What discrepancy?"

"According to the baby's Nevis birth certificate—and contrary to what Seymour told us there *was* a Nevis birth certificate—he'd been born to a Jane Jones on January 25, 1990. That jibes with what Mrs. Kidd said, right?"

Legs nodded. "Right. . . ."

"And it means the baby would have been three and a half months old when Paul and Laurie took possession of him on May the fifth."

"He wasn't?"

"Two weeks old is more like it. Paul said Laurie was positive of it. Bruce was born at the end of April, not January."

"Hmm, interesting. But where the hell does that take us?"

"That's what I'd like to know. The Weiners wondered about it, but they wanted a baby. And for fifty thou they didn't ask."

"No questions, no details. Sure, I get it. And Martine Price was killed because she knew some of those details. We had no idea she was out there but the people who are behind this sure did." He glanced over at me. "That's good work, little bud. Not too late for you to take the test, you know. You'd make a hell of a cop. Pay's steady. Health and pension benefits are off the chart. And you'd have me for a rabbi. How cool is that?"

"That was my dad's life. It's not for me. And I still don't get something. We're dealing with a total pro here. Yet he used the same gun three weeks ago in Queens, two nights ago at Candlewood Lake and again last night when he shot at me. What kind of a pro does that?"

"A pro," he growled, "who's been told he doesn't have to worry about my investigation."

"The commissioner didn't talk like a man who's looking to shut you down."

"The commissioner talked a lot. Who knows how much of it he meant. I don't. I just know that he needs somebody's head on a platter for the Charles Willingham shooting. And it's *not* going to be mine."

"There's something else I don't get. Why didn't he kill me last night? He could have taken me out. Same as he could have taken me out at Candlewood Lake. Why am I still mucking around in the middle of this? It doesn't make any sense."

"Not to worry, it will. Maybe not tonight. Maybe not tomorrow. But we'll get there."

"I sure wish I had my iPod on me right now."

"Why's that?"

"I'd really like to listen to some Ethel Merman. Ethel's a huge help to me when I'm searching for clarity."

"Okay, I take back what I just said. You wouldn't last one week at the academy."

"Legs, why are we driving to Ronkonkoma to see a woman named Judith Heintz?"

"She's Martine Price's sister. Told me she wouldn't mind talking about her. Sounded eager to, in fact."

"What's her story?"

"She works a cash register at Waldbaum's. Her husband, Steve, drives for UPS. Plain, honest, working folk. Two kids, ages thirteen and sixteen." He glanced over at me. "She's going to think you're my sergeant. No need to set her straight, okay?"

"Sure thing, Loo."

Ronkonkoma is a decaying middle-class bedroom community set dead center in the decaying heart of Long Island—which isn't to be confused with somewhere near the water that's nice like the Hamptons or the North Shore. The Heintz family lived in a drab little raised ranch on a street of drab little raised ranches. Come to think of it, I've never seen a raised ranch that wasn't drab. And I ought to know. I grew up in one. There wasn't

much snow cover on the ground out there. Just a light dusting
on the bare, brown lawns. The street was clear and dry. A Dodge
Ram pickup and a Toyota Camry were parked in the Heintz's
driveway.

Legs kept on going past their house, circled around the block
and came back. Making sure we hadn't brought a tail with us.
We hadn't.

Judith Heintz opened the front door before we rang the bell.
She must have been watching for us out the front window.
"Come in, come in, please," she urged us breathlessly. Her voice
was unexpectedly fluty for such a large, fleshy woman. I got the
impression that she'd recently lost a lot of weight. She still
moved like someone who was circus fat, tottering from side to
side as she led us into the entry hall. And the skin hung loose
from her jowls and neck like rubbery dewlaps. Her graying
hair was cut short. She wore loose fitting navy blue sweat pants
and a matching sweatshirt that had several moist-looking tissues stuffed into its wristbands.

The house was small and cluttered. A television blared from
the living room, where the ceiling seemed unusually low to me.
Maybe because there was so damned much homey, crafty shit
crammed in there. Framed macaroni art hanging from the walls,
macramé planters from the windows. Everywhere I looked I
saw samplers, quilts, coverlets, stuffed animals.

Judith's lanky, balding husband, Steve, was stretched out on
the sofa watching *WWE Raw*. He did acknowledge that Legs
and I were standing there in his home. Sort of nodded our way.
But he refused to take his eyes off of his steroid freak show.
Talking to the police again was strictly Judith's thing, not his.

She led us into the kitchen and the three of us sat around a dinette set. It was the land of knit cozies in there. The toaster had one. The coffee maker had one. The salt and pepper shakers. The paper napkin holder. You name it and it had its own cozy.

"I was pleased to hear from you, Lieutenant," Judith said as she settled into her chair. "I hope you fellows will forgive me in advance but I'm still in mourning for my Marty and I can't seem to talk about her without . . . I-I just keep on . . ." She broke off as her tears began to flow. "Poor Steve's had it up to here with me. But I just miss her so much. She was my big sister and I've never been without her. I feel s-so *lost*." She yanked one of those damp tissues from her sleeve and dabbed at her eyes. "Excuse me for asking, but what happened to Detective Wood?"

"We've taken over the case," Legs explained.

"And have you caught Marty's killer? Because you were a little vague on the phone. Gosh, please forgive my manners. Can I get you fellows some coffee or a soda?"

We both told her we were fine.

"What we have is a new angle," Legs informed her. "This may sound strange, but an entirely different motive for Martine's death has emerged in the past few hours. We no longer think it was a routine break-in."

She blinked at him in surprise. "You don't?"

"No, ma'am. The gun that her killer used was also used in the murder of a young man in Connecticut two nights ago. We believe the two deaths are connected. We believe your sister's death has something to do with an adoption that took place about twenty years ago, back when she was in the employ of a Dr. John Sykes."

Judith's face darkened. "Oh, *him* . . ."

Legs leaned across the table toward her. "You knew Dr. Sykes?"

"Only to spit at," she answered viciously. "I tried not to judge Marty and her beloved Dr. John, even though it was just so wrong. He was another woman's husband. A married man with three children. I told her he would never leave them for her. I told her and I told her. But Marty didn't care."

"She and Dr. Sykes were lovers?" I asked.

"Dr. John was the great love of her life, Sergeant. It was because of him that she never married and had babies of her own. Who knows if he felt that way about her. At first, I figured he was just, you know, using her for the sex. She was young and awful pretty. But it was no casual fling, I can tell you that much."

"They were together for a long time?"

She nodded. "Years and years. Their romance, if you want to call it that, started when they were in the Caribbean on an island called Nevis. I'd never heard of the place until she went down there. Dr. John had to take care of a rich patient there for several weeks. He asked Marty to join him. This was . . . must be twenty years ago, like you just said, Lieutenant. I still have the photos and letters she sent me. I was just looking through them the other day." She got up, tottered to the front hall and came back with a shoebox filled with snapshots and envelopes. She searched through the pictures and put one on the table for us to look at. "Here's my Marty. Wasn't she pretty?"

Martine Price was frolicking on a beach. She was big boned and on the horsy side. Not my idea of pretty. But she was certainly shapely in her one-piece bathing suit.

Judith showed us another snapshot. "And this here's her Dr. John."

John Sykes was sandy haired and considerably older than Martine, although he looked plenty fit in his swim trunks. He had a kindly face. He seemed happy.

"The two of them were together for weeks in that tropical island paradise," Judith recalled. "Dr. John's wife and kids were back home in New York. I guess something was bound to happen. Marty was like a dreamy schoolgirl when it came to him. Lordy, the stories she told me about them swimming nude in the moonlight and making love under the stars. Why, she practically made it sound like they were Adam and Eve in the Garden of Eden. And it didn't stop when they came back home. They stayed together as a couple, gosh, must have been twelve, thirteen years—right up until he died back in 2003. She went to work for Lenox Hill Hospital after he retired from private practice. But she still spent her vacation with him every year down in Nevis at his clinic. And she entertained him at her apartment in Forest Hills two or three evenings every week without fail. I guess he was devoted to her, too, in his own way. He left her the deed to that two-family house in Jackson Heights when he died. She owned it free and clear. Had a roof over her head and collected a nice income from her tenant. I guess it'll become ours now. I still have to clear out her things and bring them here. I'm just . . . not *ready* yet." Judith's tears started flowing again. "I'm sorry."

"It's okay," I said, patting her hand.

"Thank you, Sergeant. You're very considerate. My Marty was a wreck after Dr. John passed. She just mourned and mourned. After six months or so I said to her, I said, 'Marty, you have got to get on with your life.' She was only forty-four years old. Still real good looking, too, believe me. Steve knew a couple of drivers, real nice fellows, who'd have been thrilled to take her out. But she wasn't interested. When her Dr. John died she was all done with men."

"My mom's the exact same way," I said.

Judith raised her eyebrows at me. "She's a widow?"

"It's been two years now."

"She must have been awful young."

"She still is."

"I'm sorry for her. And for you, Sergeant. A young man needs his father. And I meant to tell you when you walked in just how much I love your friendship bracelet." Judith took hold of my wrist, the better to examine it. Her hand was cold and clammy. "She made it with embroidery thread, didn't she? Yeah, that's awful cute. A whole lot of work went into it, too. She must really like you." Judith released her grip and fetched a diet soda from the refrigerator. Popped open the can and took a sip. "I did wonder, you know. If Marty's death had something to do with *things* she knew about. But Detective Wood was so positive it was a break-in, what with her jewelry and silver being taken. I figured I was just being flighty, like Steve always says."

"You're not being flighty," I said to her. "And we're extremely interested in whatever your sister knew about."

"It's all right there in her letters from Nevis." Judith nodded toward the shoebox. "She didn't just write me about her romance. She had other things to say."

Legs gazed at her anxiously. "Like for instance? . . ."

"Dr. John was down there to see to a messed-up teenaged girl who'd gotten herself pregnant. Poor thing was barely thirteen years old."

"What was this girl's name?" he asked.

"Marty never told me the name of the family. Just the girl's first name—Kathleen. I remember it on account of we had an Aunt Kathleen who used to collect antique cookie jars from the 1940s. She had dozens of them all over her house. That's one of them right there next to the stove." Judith gestured toward a biscuit-colored ceramic figurine of a round chef with a white hat. It was the only object on the kitchen counter that wasn't covered with a cozy. "He's called Pierre the Jolly Chef and he's actually worth a couple of hundred bucks on eBay, last time I looked. Not that I'd ever sell him." She took another sip of her diet soda. "Dr. John and Marty were there to deliver Kathleen's baby when her time came. Her parents owned a huge shorefront estate there. They were hushing the whole thing up the way rich people do. And these were definitely rich people. They flew a Park Avenue doctor and his nurse down there and kept them there for weeks. Can you imagine how much that must have cost?"

"What else did your sister tell you about Kathleen?" Legs asked.

"She was a real handful. An angry, depressed little thing. Didn't want the baby. Didn't even want to be alive. Poor girl tried to take her own life with pills, Marty said. Almost lost the baby. They had to keep watch over her around the clock until she gave birth. It was a boy."

"Do you happen to know when the baby was born?" I asked.

"Absolutely. It was on the twenty-fifth of April. That's our cousin George's birthday."

Which backed up what Paul Weiner had told me. Eleanor Saltonstall Kidd had been quite insistent that Kathleen gave birth at the end of January. The Nevis birth certificate even said so, according to Paul. And yet the baby had been born three months later. Why the discrepancy? I could think of only one reason. But it was a mighty big one. If Kathleen gave birth in April then it meant she hadn't conceived the baby during her previous school year at Barrow. She'd gotten pregnant over the summer—when she was on Nantucket.

"Judith, are you sure about that date?"

"Sergeant, you can read Marty's letters if you don't believe me. Heck, you're welcome to borrow them if you promise to return them. They're all I have of her now."

"We'll take good care of them."

"The worst part of it is . . ." She bit down hard on her lower lip, her eyes avoiding ours. There was more. She was holding on to more.

"The worst part of it is what?" Legs prodded her.

"The poor girl went straight downhill after her baby was born. She was just plain mentally disturbed. Marty felt sorry for her and tried to be a friend to her. But Kathleen was such a messed-up little thing that she had to be placed in an asylum in Switzerland. Marty told me Dr. John wasn't the least bit surprised. I guess he'd, you know, seen it happen before."

"Seen *what* happen before?"

"The way that Kathleen was acting . . ." Judith trailed off, swallowing. "It was pretty typical of *those* sorts of pregnancies.

You know which kind I mean. The kind that decent people
don't talk about."

Legs and I peered at each other before he turned to her and
said. "Are you saying what I think you're saying?"

Judith nodded her head. "It was an 'internal' family matter.
That's what Dr. John told Marty. The father got her pregnant, I
guess. Can you imagine? You hear about such things happening among uneducated, backwoods folks who don't know any
better. But people of wealth and privilege? What kind of horrible bastard would do that to his own sweet little girl?"

"What kind indeed," Legs said hoarsely. The weight of her
words had landed on him like an anvil.

I was plenty staggered myself. I wasn't expecting to find
out that the late Thomas Kidd, the distinguished ambassador,
statesman and philanthropist, had raped his own daughter. So
this was why the whole shitstorm was happening. *This* was the
horrible secret that the Kidds were trying to cover up. Eleanor,
his formidable Fifth Avenue widow, was trying to protect the
family's good name so that her remaining child, Bobby the K,
could continue his march to the governor's mansion in Albany.
Peter Seymour and the Leetes Group were doing the old
lady's dirty work—even if that meant sacrificing Eleanor's
own daughter and biological grandson. Now I understood why
Bobby had shown up at our office to trash his dead sister's repu-
tation. He was doing his mother's bidding, too, no doubt. Keeping us off of the scent. What I didn't understand was why he'd
suggested that his wife's family might be behind it. But I had no
doubt that I'd understand soon enough. Because it was all starting to make sense now.

"Judith, you mentioned that your sister tried to be a friend to Kathleen," Legs said slowly.

"Yes, that's right."

"Do you know if they stayed in touch over the years?"

"Marty didn't hear from her for a long, long time. Kathleen was hospitalized abroad, like I said. But I guess she was finally able to get along better in the world. She returned home to New York and phoned Marty just before Thanksgiving. Marty was surprised as heck to hear from her. She figured that with the holidays coming maybe that explained it."

"Explained what?" I asked her.

"Kathleen wanting to know if Marty remembered the name of the family that had adopted her baby boy. She was anxious to meet him. Mind you, that information was strictly confidential. Marty was never, ever supposed to divulge it to anyone. *Especially* Kathleen." Judith sighed forlornly. "But my Marty had a sentimental streak a mile wide. And she always felt bad for that poor girl. So I think she did give her their name. Heck, she must have."

"Why do you say that?" Legs asked.

Judith's eyes filled with tears again. "Because somebody murdered her, that's why. My Marty's *dead*."

CHAPTER SEVEN

IT WAS NEARLY MIDNIGHT by the time we made it back to the city, which had become shrouded in a chilly fog. A lot of cold, weary cabbies had pulled up in front of Scotty's for hot coffee, hot soup, hot anything. And not just cabs were lined up outside of our building. An unmarked sedan was parked there with two more of my dad's old cronies inside. And so was the same gleaming black Cadillac limo that had delivered Bobby the K to our office that afternoon. Or at least I assumed it was the same limo. It was definitely the same driver. Upstairs, lights were blazing in the windows of Golden Legal Services.

Legs said, "Yo, I think maybe I'm coming up."

"Yo, I think maybe you are."

Lovely Rita was seated at her desk sneaking wide-eyed looks through Mom's half-open office door. I heard voices in there. Female voices.

"Thank God you're here," Rita whispered at me urgently. "She's been pacing around in there like a caged animal for a half hour. And she is *scary!*"

By "she" I assumed Rita meant the indomitable battleship
known as the USS Eleanor Saltonstall Kidd. I was wrong.

It wasn't Bobby the K's mother who was in there with Mom.
It was his wife, Meg, who was pacing back and forth in a long
camel's hair overcoat, pantsuit and low-heeled pumps. She was
pissed. Her cheeks were mottled, her mannish Grayson chin
was stuck out and her eyes were narrow icy slits. She clutched
her BlackBerry in one tight fist like a set of brass knuckles.

Mom was seated at her desk, calmly watching Meg pace back
and forth. "Ah, here he is now, Mrs. Kidd," she said pleasantly.
"Mrs. Kidd has an urgent matter to discuss with us, Benji. I assured her you wouldn't be long. You two already know each
other, don't you?"

"Yes, we met this morning." I hung my duffel coat on the
rack by the door. "Nice to see you again, Mrs. Kidd."

"And I believe you know Lieutenant Diamond as well."
Mom smiled at him. "How art thou, Legs? I keep hoping you'll
stop by to say hello. I must be losing my allure."

"As if." He went around the desk and gave her a kiss on the
cheek. "You look great, Abby."

"That's what good-looking younger men always say to old
broads."

"You're not old, Abby. And you're not a broad."

I sat in one the chairs across from Mom's desk. "I hope you
haven't been waiting long, Mrs. Kidd."

"Not long at all," Mom assured me. "It gave us a chance to
get to know each other. Mrs. Kidd also had a nice chat with our
Mrs. Felcher in the elevator on her way up."

"That *woman*," Meg said tightly, "had just gone out to the

newsstand in her bathrobe to fetch the bulldog edition of the *New York Herald Tribune.* Which, if my memory serves me right, folded at least forty years ago. Does she have someone to look after her?"

"That would be Mr. Felcher," I said. "The more intriguing question is who looks after him."

"Now that we're all here," Mom said, "how may Golden Legal Services help you, Mrs. Kidd?"

Meg stared at Legs. "Lieutenant, was it your intention to stick around for this conversation?"

"If you don't mind."

"In what capacity?"

"As an unofficial observer. But if you have a problem with that I'm out of here. Entirely up to you."

Meg considered this for a moment before she said, "You may as well stay. Maybe we can get this awful business straight once and for all."

Legs took off his leather trench coat and sat down on the sofa.

Meg kept her own coat on even though the furnace was actually behaving that night. I knew this because Gus was dozing on his blanket atop the radiator. She didn't sit down. Just kept pacing, her chin raised, fist wrapped around her BlackBerry. "I understand," she said slowly, "that my husband paid you a visit here today."

I nodded. "You understand right. He told you about it?"

"No, Ralph did. Our driver. *My* driver. He worked for my family for years before he came to work for Bobby and me."

"So he ratted Bobby out?"

"He's a loyal family friend, if that's what you mean."

"It wasn't, but that's okay."

"I'd like to know, word for word, what Bobby came here to tell you."

"Maybe you ought to discuss that with him."

"Maybe you ought to do exactly as I say."

"Maybe you ought to tell us why we should."

She stood there, her jaw clenched tighter than tight. I've been around meth tweakers who grind their teeth. Meg Grayson Kidd was in a different weight class. I swear she could have ground whole raw oats into powder. "You people have no idea what you've gotten yourselves into."

I glanced over at Legs before I said, "I think we realize exactly what we're into. Do *you*, Mrs. Kidd?"

Something in my tone jarred her a bit. She was a tough lady, but she was on shaky ground. Wasn't used to it.

Mom said, "Excuse me for asking, Mrs. Kidd, but does your husband know you're here?"

"He does not," Meg answered shortly. "He thinks I'm meeting with a campaign contributor."

"In that case . . ." Mom reached for her purse, extracted a five-dollar bill and held it out to her.

"What's that?"

"A campaign contribution. Take it, hon. A woman should never have to lie to her husband. It's the undoing of any marriage. Trust me, I know."

Meg allowed herself a faint smile as she snatched the bill from Mom and stuffed it in her coat pocket. "I'm starting to like you a little, Mrs. Golden."

Mom arched an eyebrow at her. "Don't sound so surprised.

I've had my fans over the years." Fans like, say, Bobby the K. But Mom was too much of a lady to mention that. "Now why don't you just tell us what's on your mind?"

Meg resumed pacing. "I don't know what you've been led to believe by the media, but I'm not an evil power broker who sits in a tower somewhere pulling strings."

"That would be your mother-in-law," I suggested.

"Well, yes, as a matter of fact. Eleanor rules this city. I don't. I'm a wife and mother. I love my husband and children. I care about the future. And I genuinely believe Bobby will make a great governor. He knows how to get things done. He's proven that in business time after time. I'm managing his campaign because *I* know how to get things done. I'm responsible for the message that we put out there to the voters and I have to make certain he didn't jump the reservation when he came here. So, I repeat, what did he tell you?"

"That the story his mother fed us this morning about Kathleen was total bullshit," I replied.

Meg took a breath in and out. "*This* is what I was afraid of." She perched at long last on the edge of the sofa. "Did he offer you an alternate version?"

I nodded my head. "That the real reason the Kidds sent Kathleen away to Barrow was that she'd become a stoned-out, wildly promiscuous slut."

"I have no firsthand knowledge of that," Meg responded stiffly. "This is the first I've ever heard of it."

"Bobby said that Kathleen's behavior came as a real shock to him when he came home from Cambridge," I went on. "The last time he'd seen her she'd been a smiling, happy kid who was enjoying every last drop of her summer on Nantucket. Your husband has real fond memories of that summer, Mrs. Kidd. He said it was when he first fell in love with you. Made a special point of mentioning it, didn't he, Mom?"

"Yes, he did," Mom affirmed. "A fond glow came over his face."

Meg's own face remained drawn tight. "He's mentioned that to me many times. To be perfectly honest, I didn't care much for Bobby that summer. I was a serious girl. Bobby was one of those laughing boys who thought everything was one big joke. Plus he was going away to Harvard and was *so* full of himself— not to mention beer, Jack Daniel's and whatever else he and his friends were into. He'd drag me to a different bonfire party practically every night and proceed to get falling-down drunk. I thought he still had a lot of growing up to do."

I said, "He also told us that his father donated two million dollars to Barrow—which hardly makes it sound as if the Kidds held the administrators responsible for what happened to Kathleen."

Meg's penetrating stare bored in on me. "Did you believe what he said?"

"Not entirely, no."

"May I ask why?"

"Because it still doesn't account for the nagging little matter regarding the baby's date of birth."

"What about it?" she demanded.

I glanced at Legs Diamond. "Some of what I know is police business. Are you cool with this?"

"Be my guest," said Legs, who was just as anxious as I was to hear what Meg Grayson Kidd had to say.

"According to your mother-in-law," I said to her, "Kathleen

gave birth to a baby boy in Nevis late in January of 1990. And I was told by someone who saw the baby's Nevis birth certificate—which *does* exist—that it listed his date of birth as January 24, 1990."

Meg continued to stare at me. "So? . . ."

"So we've spoken with two different people who insist that the baby was actually born three months later than that. One of those people had personal contact with the baby soon after it was brought to New York in May of 1990. The other is in possession of a written statement from someone who was there in Nevis when the baby was born. Can you shed any light on this discrepancy, Mrs. Kidd?"

Meg didn't answer me right away. She pulled inward, her sharp mind working every angle. "No, I can't," she said finally. "And I fail to grasp the significance of this. What difference does it make whether Kathleen's baby was born in January or in April?"

Mom's eyes glinted at her. "You're going to play dumb on us?"

Meg bristled. "I'm not *playing* at anything, Mrs. Golden."

"Do the math, hon. If Kathleen's baby was born in January, then that means he was conceived while she was at Barrow. But if he was born three months later it means . . ."

"He was conceived in July," Meg said, her voice almost a whisper.

I nodded. "During that idyllic summer on Nantucket, when your husband fell madly in love with you."

Meg sank deeper into the sofa. "Please, go on. . . ."

"Bobby mentioned that the Kidds and Graysons used to have neighboring beach compounds or cottages or whatever it is you people call them. And that your father and his father spent many an afternoon together that summer on the Kidds' veranda, playing cribbage and drinking gin and tonics."

Now Meg shook her head. "That does *not* jibe with my memory. Bobby's father, the Ambassador, was away for practically that entire summer. I remember that my father missed his company. And Mrs. Kidd was terribly lonely. She kept telling me, 'Such is the life of a political wife, my dear.'" Actually, Meg did a pretty fair imitation of the old dowager. "Mind you, I was already well aware of this. My father was a US senator. When he wasn't in Washington he was out on the campaign trail. The only real chance I had to be with him was when we were together on Nantucket. But that particular summer, the summer of '89, Ambassador Kidd wasn't there to keep him company. He was in Moscow. The Soviet Union was in economic chaos and the first President Bush asked him to broker talks over there because the international business community trusted him." She smiled bleakly. "The two political parties used to work together back in those days. Seems kind of quaint now, doesn't it?"

"Are you sure about this, Mrs. Kidd?" I asked.

"Quite sure. Have your girl out there—the one who's eavesdropping on our conversation—run an online search of *The New York Times* archives. There was a good deal of coverage."

"Rita!? . . ." Mom called out.

"On it, Abby!"

"Why is this of any importance?" Meg wanted to know. "If some teenaged boy got Kathleen pregnant that summer, what difference does it make whether Bobby's father was or wasn't around?"

"It matters," I replied, "because we have information that

suggests it wasn't a teenaged boy. I'm sorry to have to tell you this, Mrs. Kidd, but our source believes Kathleen was sexually abused by a member of her own family."

Meg's eyes widened. "Are you suggesting that Kathleen was molested by her father? That's absurd! The Ambassador adored her. Whoever told you that is a malicious liar who's trying to slime the family and destroy Bobby's candidacy. That never happened. Never."

Rita tapped on Mom's half-open door and said, "Ambassador Kidd was in Moscow for all of July, 1989, and most of August. He returned to DC on the twenty-first of August to brief the president."

"There, you see?" Meg said. "You've been lied to."

"Well, now I'm completely puzzled," I confessed. "Because your husband definitely told us that his father and your father played cribbage together every afternoon that summer. Didn't he, Mom?"

Mom nodded her head. "Yes, he did."

Meg glared at me angrily. "Please tell me you're not suggesting that *my* father molested Kathleen."

"Senator Grayson *was* a member of Kathleen's family, wasn't he? His brother's wife and your mother-in-law are cousins, correct?"

"Correct," she acknowledged, biting off the word. "But my father couldn't have done anything like that to Kathleen."

Mom smiled at her gently. "I understand how hard this must be for you to—"

"No, you *don't* understand. By that summer my father had already been operated on twice for prostate cancer and was, according to my mother, no longer able to perform sexually. It was . . . a difficult time for both of them. My mother needed someone to confide in and she confided in me. We were best friends. Still are. I can produce my father's medical records if you don't believe me. It was a fast-moving cancer that killed him less than three years later, as you may recall."

"Exactly how much of this is your husband aware of?" Legs Diamond asked her.

Meg peered at him curiously. "What are you asking me?"

"If Bobby knows that your father was impotent in the summer of '89."

"It was a private, personal health matter. Bobby was never privy to it. Why would he be?"

"Maybe your father told him about it," Mom suggested.

"Not a chance. My father didn't discuss those things with even his closest friends. And, trust me, he and Bobby were not friends."

Mom tried again: "Surely *you've* told Bobby about it. You two have been married for quite a few years. No secrets, right?"

"Wrong, Mrs. Golden. My father valued his privacy and I've always respected that. I'm quite certain I've never told Bobby about this."

And yet she'd just told the three of us. Why had she? Because she was scared to death? Or because she was playing us?

"If that's the case," I said slowly, "then your husband made a big mistake this afternoon. Putting that out there, I mean."

"He actually hinted to you that my father raped Kathleen?"

"Not in so many words, no."

"Well, what *did* he say?"

"That your family might be behind Kathleen's death, Bruce Weiner's death, all of it—up to and including the murder of Charles Willingham."

Meg frowned at me. "What does Charles Willingham have to do with this?"

"He and Bruce Weiner were close friends. You didn't know that?"

"Of course not. Why would I? *None* of this makes the slightest bit of . . ." Meg got up and went over to the window. Stood there in her long camel's hair coat, staring out at the street with her back toward us. She was struggling to regain her composure. Then she turned back around to face us, her chest rising and falling. "Exactly what did Bobby say?" she asked me in a controlled voice.

"That you're the most ruthless person he's ever met—with the possible exception of your father. That there's nothing you won't do to win an election, up to and including murder. Preventive damage control, I think he called it."

"He said no such thing," she gasped. "You're lying."

"Why would we lie to you?" Mom asked her.

"To throw me off balance."

"And what would be the point of that?"

"I-I don't understand. . . ."

"You understand everything, hon. You're no fool."

Meg shook her head. "What are you telling me?"

"Your husband showing up here like he did was strictly a panic move," I said. "I guarantee you his mother didn't sign off on it. No, he spitballed it all on his own. Trashing his late sister, tossing your father into the mix—it reeks of panic. The man's lost control of this situation."

"I still don't see what you're . . ." Meg's eyes widened in horror. "No, you can't be thinking *that*. His own sister? He couldn't have. It's not possible."

"A simple DNA test would prove it one way or the other," Legs offered. "We have Bruce Weiner's blood sample."

"Fine. We'll have Bobby take one."

"Trust me, Mrs. Kidd, he'll never consent to it," he said. "Not in a million years."

Meg fell silent for a long moment. "If that is what happened then it was my fault."

Mom tilted her head at her curiously. "How was it your fault?"

"He drank too much and h-he wanted sex *all* of the time," Meg recalled in a flat, toneless voice. "Kept trying to go all the way with me on the beach, night after night. He was incredibly insistent. But I wasn't ready yet. I was a sixteen-year-old virgin. I wasn't sure if he genuinely cared about me or just wanted to get in my pants. Which means I sent him home, night after night, feeling sexually frustrated. If he did that to poor Kathleen, it's because I held out. It's my fault."

"No, it's not!" Mom barked at her. "And don't you say that again or I'm going to slap your face. Don't even *think* it."

Meg looked at her, startled, then lowered her gaze. "Eleanor sat me down last year when Bobby decided to run for governor. It was just the two of us, and she was very emotional, which is not like her, believe me. She told me to be sure we made enough time for our children so we wouldn't be sorry later in life. When I asked Eleanor what she meant she said, 'They both got away from me.' She had tears in her eyes," Meg recalled, her own eyes growing shiny. "And then . . . she started telling me about the summer of '89, when the Ambassador was away in Moscow. Kathleen stopped speaking to her that summer. Got terribly quiet and withdrawn. And Bobby became impossible to control. He'd come in at all hours, high as a kite. She actually found a naked girl in bed with him one morning—the daughter of a prominent conservative columnist. Bobby told her he'd been so drunk that he didn't remember bringing the girl home. He experienced blackouts, apparently. Eleanor told him he had to stop drinking so much or he'd do something he'd truly regret. He just laughed at her and said, 'Being a Kidd means never having to regret a thing.'" Meg stood there by the window in shaken silence. "Bobby got so drunk one night that he raped his own sister, didn't he? *He* got her pregnant. And Eleanor knew. She's always known. So has Peter Seymour. They've all known. The only person who didn't know was me. I've been married to that man for all of these years. I've shared his bed. I've given him two children and I've never, ever . . ." Meg's chest heaved suddenly and she clamped a hand over her mouth.

Mom pointed to her bathroom. Meg ran in there, slamming the door behind her.

The three of us sat there in Mom's office listening to Meg throw up. I didn't know what Legs Diamond or Mom was thinking. I was feeling sorry for someone who I never thought I'd feel sorry for.

When she came out, Meg looked extremely pale. "I used some of your mouthwash, Mrs. Golden. I hope you don't mind."

"Not at all, hon. That's what it's for." Mom turned the combination lock on the big old Wells Fargo safe, yanked open the door and removed our bottle of good cognac. She found four glasses in the credenza next to her desk and poured each of us a generous slug. "You've had a shock," she said, holding a glass out to Meg. "This'll put some color back in your cheeks."

Meg took it from her and drank it down in one gulp. Then she sat back down on the sofa. "It makes for a nice story," she said calmly. "You actually had me going there for a second."

Mom frowned at her. "What are you talking about?"

"The four of us are going to do something, okay?" Meg was all business now. Bare-knuckles business. "You're going to forget what I said. And I'm going to forget what you said. We never had this conversation. Is that understood?"

"But we did have it, Mrs. Kidd," Legs pointed out. "You can try to forget, but you won't. And neither will we. Your husband was Bruce Weiner's biological father. That's what he was afraid Kathleen would expose when she established contact with Bruce. That's why Bruce had to die, she had to die, all of these people had to die. Because Bobby's afraid the ugly truth will torpedo his political career. I can't prove it. They're too smart for that. But I know it. And so do you. Your husband signed off on these murders. He and the old lady both. Peter Seymour reached out to Jake Leetes for them, and one of Jake's people took care of it."

Meg let his words soak in before she said, "If what you say is true, Lieutenant, then the only person who has been out of the loop all along is me. I'm still not buying that. But I'll convene an emergency meeting at Eleanor's apartment right away. I'll make certain that Mr. Seymour and Mr. Leetes are both there. And I'll get to the bottom of this one way or the other."

"They'll deny everything," Legs told her.

"I'm quite sure they will. And when Bobby insists he's innocent I'll insist that he take a paternity test."

"That's something he'll never do," he reiterated.

"Oh, he'll take it," she said with total certainty. "If he refuses I have the power to destroy his candidacy."

"How?" I asked her.

"By leaving him. I'll take the children and go. It'll set off such a huge tabloid firestorm that he'll be forced to withdraw from the race. But I don't think it will come to that. You see, I happen to believe you're wrong."

"You *want* to believe we're wrong," I said. "I don't blame you one bit. But you know we're not. And you know he'll never take that DNA test."

"We'll just see about that." Meg stuck her Grayson chin out at me. "I'll find out the truth. And, believe me, if I'm not one hundred percent satisfied that Bobby's telling me the truth I'll leave him—tonight."

"Where will you go?" Mom asked her.

"My mother has a house in Boston. I'll go there."

"Maybe I ought to come to this meeting with you," Legs said.

"This is a private matter, Lieutenant."

"Still, I think I should come."

"No."

"Mrs. Kidd, I'm concerned about your safety. If you confront them over this and then threaten to walk out they're liable to . . ."

"Have *me* killed? Never. They wouldn't dare."

"Tell that to Kathleen," he said. "Oh, wait, you can't. Someone threw her off of her balcony."

"I'll be fine," Meg insisted. "I have Ralph."

"Your driver?" Legs said doubtfully.

"Ralph was a Green Beret before he came to work for the Grayson family. He's armed twenty-four hours a day and he won't allow anything to happen to me or to my children. I'll be safe, Lieutenant. Don't you worry. It's Bobby who has to worry now." Meg took a deep breath and let it out slowly. "I don't know whether to thank you people or curse you. I feel as if I ought to be thanking you, except I hardly feel grateful right now. I don't know what I feel. I don't think I'm going to feel anything for a long, long time."

IT WASN'T GOOD ENOUGH.

Meg Grayson Kidd had brought us as close to the truth as we were ever going to get. And, damn it, it wasn't good enough. I didn't care whether she derailed her husband's bid for the governor's mansion. I cared about real justice, the kind where the bad guys go to jail and stay there. But the ugly reality was that five people were dead and there'd be no such justice. We were up against the wealthiest, most powerful family in New York City and we couldn't prove a thing. The supremely smooth Peter Seymour was too smart for that. The supremely smarmy Jake Leetes was too smart for that. They were all too smart for that. Even Legs had admitted so. And, trust me, Legs Diamond never backs down from a fight.

He took off right after Meg did. I could see the two of them through Mom's office window, talking on the sidewalk next to her limo. Legs was still trying to convince her to let him come with her, I imagined. Meg was shaking her head no.

Mom poured both of us another slug of cognac before she tucked the bottle away and closed the safe. "I'm sorry, Bunny."

"For what?"

"For the way you feel right now."

I drank down my cognac. "How do you know what I'm feeling?"

"I can see it in your face. I used to see that same look in your dad's face. You're dissatisfied. You're frustrated. And you're a little bit angry."

"No, I'm not. I'm a lot angry."

"It's part of the job. Sometimes we get the closure we're hoping for. But a lot of the time we don't. Me, I have faith in that woman. I believe she's going to leave Bobby the K. He *won't* be our next governor. He tried to engineer a massive cover-up and he failed—because of you. You can be proud of that."

"I don't feel real proud."

"I know you don't."

"How did Dad deal with it?"

"Instead of focusing on what he couldn't do, he focused on what he could. Tomorrow, you can go to Bruce Weiner's funeral and be a comfort to that nice girl. Sara needs you to be there for her."

"And the day after that?"

"You move on to the next case." She took a sip of her cognac. "It does help if you have someone to come home to. So that the job isn't all there is."

"I'm working on that part, Mom."

"Sure, you are. Now give me a kiss and go on up to bed. You look exhausted."

"How about you?"

"I'll be up in a minute."

I kissed her on the cheek and grabbed my duffel coat. Rita was still working at her computer, looking grim-faced. "G'night, Rita."

"G'night, little lamb. Wait, come here. . . ." She got up from her desk and gave me a big hug. In her high-heeled boots, Rita's an honest six inches taller than me. My face found its way to her neck, where I got a strong whiff of her intoxicating perfume. "Don't beat yourself up over this, okay? Promise me."

"I promise you, Rita."

I coaxed the elevator up to the fifth floor. My apartment was chilly. My shoulder and knee ached from that headfirst dive I'd made into those trash cans. I was thinking a nice hot shower would feel pretty good if our furnace was in the mood. I hung my duffel coat on the rack by the door, went in my bedroom and took off my Harris Tweed sports jacket. I was hanging it up in the closet when my hand found a folded sheet of paper in the inside breast pocket. It was the list of names that Legs had slipped me— the visitors who'd signed in with the doorman of Kathleen Kidd's building on Riverside Drive in the hours leading up to her so-called suicide. I'd forgotten to look at it. I looked at it now.

And when I saw one of the names on that list I gulped at it in disbelief.

And stared at it. And stared some more—until I had trouble reading it because my hands were shaking so badly.

I put my jacket back on, got my duffel coat and headed back downstairs to the office.

Mom had gone up to her place for the night. Rita was getting ready to lock up.

She looked at me in surprise. "What brings you back?"

"I need you to run a DMV trace for me. Right now, I'm afraid."

"No problem," she said, sitting back down in front of her computer. "Beats going home to a dark, empty apartment. What's going on?"

"We may get some closure after all—unless I'm wrong."

It took her a couple of minutes to run the trace. While she was doing that I unlocked the safe in Mom's office and removed one of our voice-activated microrecorders. I tucked it in the outside breast pocket of my jacket and closed the safe. By then Rita had done her thing.

And I wasn't wrong. I knew I wouldn't be.

I said good night for the second time, dashing for the door.

"Where are you going now?" Rita asked me.

"To finish this thing."

"I DON'T *BELIEVE* IT!" she cried with delight as I stood there on her doorstep. "Is this an honest to God booty call?"

"I really needed to see you."

"Cookie, I can't tell you how happy this makes me." Sonya threw her arms around me and kissed me, her body plastered against mine. She was wearing a silk robe with not a stitch under it. Her hair was gathered up in a bun. She pulled herself away, gasping. "Okay, that's a gun in your pocket *and* you're happy to see me, am I right?"

"I can't fool you one bit, can I?"

"Don't even try. Come in before we both freeze."

She led me inside her town house. The living room and dining room were in darkness. The stairs leading up to the master bedroom suite were lit. "I was just about to climb into bed. Let's go down to the kitchen. I'll make us some hot cocoa first. How does that sound?"

"It sounds great." As I followed her down the stairs I unbuttoned my coat and flicked on the microrecorder in the breast pocket of my jacket. "Sonya, there's something I need to ask you. It's kind of awkward and personal."

"You can ask me anything." She flicked on the lights in her restaurant kitchen. Put a copper saucepan on the Viking stove. Got milk out of the refrigerator, then found a tin of really expensive-looking cocoa in the cupboard. "And you know you can get me to *do* just about anything—except for a threesome. I won't share you with another girl. I'm super old-fashioned."

I stood there with my coat on, hands buried deep in my pockets. "Actually, this isn't about us. Well, it is but it isn't. I was wondering whether you're a kindergarten teacher at all. Or was that total bullshit, too?"

"Of course I'm a kindergarten teacher. Why would you ask me something like that?"

"Because your name's on the list. You were in Kathleen Kidd's building at the time of her murder."

Sonya stuck out her lower lip, frowning. "They said on the news she committed suicide."

"She was pushed by someone. A professional killer employed by the Leetes Group. A professional killer who drives a dark-green Jeep Grand Cherokee—judging by the tire tread pattern they found in the snow outside of the Candlewood Lake house. *You* drive a dark-green Grand Cherokee."

Sonya fired up the burner under the saucepan of milk. Spooned in the cocoa powder and stirred it gently, calm as can be. "Sure, I do. Me and a gazillion other people. I garage it right around the corner. And, you're right, I was in Kathleen Kidd's building that afternoon. One of my kids, Brittany Levine, lives there. Her mom asked me to walk her home that day because Brittany's two-year-old brother had the sniffles and Mrs. Levine didn't want to shlep him around in his stroller in the freezing cold. That happens to me a lot. Half of those West End Avenue moms think I'm their au pair." Sonya continued to stir the cocoa, looking down into the saucepan. "I don't mean to get in your face, Benji, but have you been out drinking with the boys? Because I smelled alcohol on your breath and it's late and you're not making a lot of sense."

"Okay, then let me put it to you this way: Why didn't you finish me off last night?"

She gazed at me those incredible pale green eyes of hers. "Well, I tried my best."

"I mean when you fired those shots at me, Sonya. You threw on some clothes after I left here, followed me down the block and shot at me three times with the same Glock 17 that you used to kill Bruce and Martine. It was you, Sonya. It's been you all along. I can't believe it never occurred to me. I guess I was besotted by your talents."

"I'm a great lay," she acknowledged easily. "Not to brag on myself."

"In your case it's not bragging. Why didn't you kill me?"

"Because I was trying to scare you off of the case." Her voice sounded a bit deeper now, more mature than I was used to. The semi-ditsy Sonya I knew had been something of a put-on.

"You've become someone special to me, Benji. I didn't want you getting in over your head. And the answer is yes, I really am a kindergarten teacher. I like kids. Plus it provides me with a legit cover."

"You work for the Leetes Group?"

"Sometimes." She studied me curiously. "We're not that different, you know. I perform a professional service on a freelance basis and get paid for it. I'm just like you."

"You're nothing like me. I help people."

Sonya let out a laugh. "Is that right? Who have you helped on this case?" On my silence she said, "Besides, I need my freelance career to pay for the upkeep on this place. It's positively criminal how little they pay kindergarten teachers."

The milk was hot. She poured our cocoa into a pair of big mugs, sprinkled some cinnamon on top and pushed one of the mugs toward me.

I left it where it was. "So you don't have a rich father?"

"Afraid not. Sorry to disappoint you."

"I'll get over it. Tell me, how many people have you rubbed out?"

She sampled her cocoa. "I don't keep count."

"Sure, you do. You're a pro. A damned good one, too. And so unlikely that no one would ever suspect you. I sure didn't. But you've been playing me from the get-go. You worked your Uncle Al for that intro at shul. Then you . . . wait, what am I saying? Are you and Al Posner even related?"

Sonya wavered her hand in the air. "By marriage."

"So you're married?"

"Married twice, divorced twice. And, since we're being

completely honest, I fibbed about my age. I'm not twenty-seven. I'm thirty-four."

"Then you dropped by with those cupcakes under the guise of being a smitten kitten. The real reason you were there was to bug our office, wasn't it?"

"I bugged your car, too," she said with trace of pride. "I parked my Cherokee in your garage that day and installed it all by my little self."

"We keep the car locked. And it has an alarm system."

"I can get past any alarm system in ten seconds."

"You used me to get at Bruce."

"It's true, I did. I tailed you out to Willoughby when you went to see the Weiners. And I was on you when you drove to the Warfield place on Candlewood Lake. You stopped for coffee on the way. I didn't. I knocked on Bruce's door and told him I'd gotten lost in the dark. He was so friendly and helpful, the poor dope."

I looked down at her slender bare feet. "Your shoeprints in the snow . . ."

"I wore a pair of size-eight men's clodhoppers. They fit just fine with gel insoles and two pairs of heavy socks. And I stuffed two ten-pound barbell plates in my jacket pockets to add weight."

"If I'd shown up while you were still there you'd have killed me, too, wouldn't you?"

"I'm afraid so, Benji. I didn't know you yet. Not like . . ." Sonya's voice caught. "Not like I do now."

"Did you drive your Grand Cherokee back to the city that night? Because if you did, you'll show up on one of the tollbooth cams."

"I parked in a residential neighborhood in Danbury and spent the night in my car. I came in during the morning rush hour. Me and tens of thousands of others."

"You'd already killed someone else who was connected to this case—a nurse in Jackson Heights named Martine Price. How did you know she was Kathleen's source?"

"The Leetes people listened in on all of Kathleen's phone calls. As soon as Martine gave her Bruce's name, she was a dead woman. I made it look like a break-in. Took some crap jewelry and stuff. Her neighbors heard the shots but I left by the front door and strolled right down the street. I know how to disappear in public. No one sees me. And they for damned sure don't fear me."

God, she was right. We *were* a lot alike—except for the part where Sonya was a hired killer with no conscience.

She nudged my cocoa mug toward me. "Drink up, it's good."

"No, thanks."

"What, you think I *poisoned* yours? Don't be silly. You're the first genuinely nice guy I've met in ages."

"Thank you, I think." I still didn't touch that cocoa. "Sonya, how did you end up doing what you do? Hold on, is Sonya even your real name?"

"Yes, it's my real name. I went into the family business, same as you did. We go back five generations, ever since my great-great-grandfather, Velvel, first came through Ellis Island. He was a hit man for Jake Levinsky. My great-grandfather, Moe, was hooked up with Arnold Rothstein. And my grandpa, Harry, worked for Mickey Cohen out in LA after the Second World War. Legend has it that my grandpa was the man who gunned down Bugsy Siegel."

"Did he really?"

"He'd never tell. Not even on his deathbed. Grandpa passed the family trade along to my dad, who was as unlikely looking as me. If you saw him on the street you'd have figured him for a druggist. No one ever made him for a pro. He taught me everything I know. He was thorough, careful and he never got so much as a parking ticket in thirty-two years working freelance for whoever could afford him. He's retired down in Boca now with my mom. You'd love them. They're real sweeties. Me, I'm Generation Now. I went to college. I teach kindergarten. I live the way I want to live."

"And sometimes you kill people."

"It's the family business," she repeated, flaring at me. "Yours is peeking through keyholes at other people getting sweaty. Don't judge me and I won't judge you, okay?"

"Is Al Posner in it? I always thought he was just my dad's bookie."

"Al has nothing to do with any of it, other than that his nephew's son, Lennie, was my first husband for about a minute and a half. Lennie's in the porn trade and is just a really unclean person. Plus he beat me, so I divorced him. I met my second husband, Andy, on the job. He's a pro like me. We were together for six years. Did contract hits together all over the world. A husband and wife blend in real well in the resorts. God, how I loved Andy. But he was a lying snake. Had a girlfriend on the side the whole time we were married. A crack whore who he kept in an apartment in the Bronx. That bastard broke my heart, Benji. I got even with him, though. The next solo job he took, in Atlantic City, I made sure he got caught. He's currently serving twenty to life in Rahway."

"Remind me never to break your heart."

Sonya's eyes shined at me. "You're breaking it right now, don't you know that?" She took a sip of her cocoa, cradling the mug in her slim, pale hands. "I moved out to LA after that and started working for the Leetes Group. The LA office is Jake's biggest earner. There's a ton of bottom-feeders out there who are constantly trying to shake down the big stars. I worked my little fingers to the bone. Jake liked my work. And he took a personal interest in me. When I got homesick for New York he helped me with the down payment on this place."

I felt an involuntary shudder deep inside. "You're . . . his girlfriend?"

"Kind of. He's married, but we have a steady thing going on."

"And, just for fun, you get barfed on by five-year-olds named Shoko Birnbaum."

"I love kids," she said brightly. "They're so open and un-guarded. They allow *me* to be open and unguarded. I need that in my line of work. I need to be able to drop my guard. I dropped it with you last night. You got to me, Benji. You and your bunny-rabbit eyelashes. I want to keep seeing you. It's so hard to de-velop a long-term relationship in my business."

"I should think so. Considering you have to kill pretty much everyone you meet."

"I didn't kill *you*, did I? I could have. Instead, I tried to scare you off."

"Which I still don't get. I do understand why you said yes when I called you up. You'd gone to a lot of trouble with those cupcakes. I might have gotten suspicious if you then turned right around and blew me off. But why didn't you just get rid of me after one glass of wine? Why did you bother to turn it into a real date? Why did? . . ."

"Why did I fall hopelessly in love with you?" She reddened slightly. "I wasn't planning to, believe me. And I really, truly didn't want to. But I couldn't help myself."

"Sonya, are you actually trying to tell me that last night was *real*?"

"Of course it was. Do you think I could fake something like that?"

"Well, yeah."

"I wasn't, Benji. Remember you told me how tired you are of being alone? Well, I am, too. More than you can possibly imagine. So I thought for one night—one crazy, beautiful night—that I'd go ahead and be the girl you thought I was. I could have just sent you packing after one glass of wine, like you said. I should have. But I wanted you. And I wanted to be *that* Sonya for you. I convinced myself that it was a smart play. What better way to find out your next move than by sleeping with you, right? But that was total bullshit. I slept with you because I fell for you, plain and simple. And I took those shots at you because I wanted you far, far away from this business. I was hoping you'd quit the case. I was hoping I could see you again."

"And then what?" I demanded. "What did you think would happen—that I wouldn't find out who you really are?"

"I guess I was hoping you'd understand."

"Guess again. Just to be clear about this, Sonya, did Jake Leetes hire you to murder Bruce, Kathleen and Martine?"

"Well, yeah," she said with a shrug.

"And then Charles Willingham had to be disposed of, too.

He and Bruce were tight. There was a chance Charles knew too much. Did Jake hire you to take him out, too?"

"Sure."

"Do you know why? Were you told what it is they're covering up?"

"Of course not. That's a need-to-know thing—and I don't need to know. I don't even want to know."

"How much have you been paid?"

Sonya peered at me curiously. "You want the dollars and cents?"

"Yes."

"A fucking fortune, Benji. Fifty large to hit the nurse in Jackson Heights, a hundred for Bruce and a quarter-mil to take out Kathleen Kidd."

"How did you pull that off?"

"Who, Kathleen? I rang her bell, told her I was babysitting the kids across the hall and my phone was dead. Asked if I could use hers. She was so stoned and lonely she invited me in. I oohed and aahed over those paintings of hers, which totally sucked, if you ask me. Then I oohed and aahed over the view from her balcony. When we went out there for a better look I threw her off. I'm much stronger than I look."

"And how about Charles?"

"Charles Willingham had police protection, which classified him as a hard target. High risk, high reward. For him I got a half-mil."

"Why did you kill Detective Ayeroff, too?"

"He was about to draw his weapon on me."

"You killed a New York City police detective, Sonya."

"I had to," she said simply. "He made me."

"So you've grossed, let's see, nine hundred thou in the past three weeks?"

Sonya nodded. "It's been a good month to be me."

"How do you hide so much off-the-books income?"

"I get paid through an account in the Cayman Islands. Then I channel most of it into Posner Properties. I own this building and three others that are strictly rental units. A super-smart accountant figured it all out for me. He's Jake's accountant." She sipped her cocoa, studying me over the rim of the mug. "Anything else you want to know?"

"How much would you get paid for killing me?"

"That would depend on the where and when."

"Let's say right here, right now."

"Right here, right now? You'd fall under the category of an unforeseen emergency—terms to be negotiated later."

"How much would you ask for?"

"Benji, we don't want to talk about this."

"How *much*?"

"A hell of a lot, okay? Because I'd have to dispose of your body. That means paying a top-flight cleaner to transport you out to this meat processing plant in Red Hook where they'd put you through a—"

"Okay, that's enough detail."

"I *told* you we didn't want to talk about it."

"Sonya, there's something that I still don't understand. You've been so careful and meticulous and yet you used the same Glock to kill both Martine and Bruce. Also to shoot at me. How come?"

She looked at me surprise. "You dug one of my slugs out of that brownstone?"

I nodded. "How come, Sonya?"

"Martine was New York and Bruce was Connecticut. The states almost never share information with each other. They're like rival gangs, not brothers in arms. Besides, Jake said I didn't have to worry about blowback, and Jake never lies to me. I'm a paid killer. No one lies to me. Plus, honest to God, it never occurred to me you'd stick around long enough to collect one of my slugs. I figured you'd start running and never look back. My bad. You're such a little softie but you've got a real pair of balls on you, haven't you? And if you convinced someone to run that slug then you must have major juice inside of the department, too. I'm impressed, cookie. And I don't impress easily." Her eyes locked on to mine. "Do you keep thinking what I'm thinking?"

"I doubt it. Why, what are you thinking?"

"That if we team up we are *money*. Absolutely nobody will make a nice, cute couple like us for pros. I can guarantee you we'll gross eight figures within two years. We can retire to an island somewhere. We can get married."

"Sonya, are you proposing to me?"

"I guess I am," she acknowledged. "I'd hate to think that last night was just a one-nighter. I'm all in, Benji. I'm yours. What do you think?"

"I think I'd have trouble sleeping at night. I'd keep wondering when you were going to stab me in the eyeball and make quarter-pounders out of me."

"It wouldn't be like that, silly. We'd have fun together."

"It's 'fun' killing people? Seriously, how many have you killed?"

She stuck out her lower lip again. "I told you, I don't keep count."

"Sure you do."

"Twenty-three, not counting you." She whipped a Glock 17 out of the kitchen drawer next to her. That same Glock 17, I imagined. "You'll make twenty-four."

I stared at it, swallowing. "So you *are* going to kill me."

"I can't let you walk out of here, cookie. You know that. Believe me, I'm not happy about this. I'd much rather marry you. Except, hello, you just turned me down flat." Sonya gazed at me fondly. "Give me a kiss first, will you? One last little kiss? Because it's going to be a long, long time before I meet anyone as adorable as you."

That was when her front doorbell rang.

She frowned at me. "Are you expecting company?"

I nodded, my eyes never leaving the Glock. "That'll be Lieutenant Diamond and a back-up team. I phoned him on my way down here. The house is surrounded, Sonya. And I've been taping this entire conversation."

This amused her. "You're wearing a wire? You are *such* a naughty boy! Now I'll have to shoot you *and* flush that thing before I let him in." She let out a sigh of regret. "And maybe you'd better hand over your gun."

"Why don't you hand over yours? You'll never get away with this."

"Of course I will."

"Really? What will you tell him?"

"That you showed up here all drunk and crazy. . . ." Sonya grabbed the shawl collar of her silk robe and tore it from her shoulder, exposing one of her beautiful breasts. "That you tried to attack me . . ." She swept the cocoa mugs to the floor, shattering them. "And that I had to defend myself."

"He'll never buy it."

"Oh, he'll buy it." She took a deep breath and let out the most deafening scream I'd ever heard in my life.

Now I could hear heavy pounding against the front door.

Sonya flung herself into my arms, half naked and silky. "Kiss me, Benji," she whispered.

I kissed her feverishly, my heart hammering in my chest. It didn't matter what she'd done. It didn't matter who she was. At that moment, I wanted Sonya Posner more than I'd ever wanted any woman in my whole life. Truly, she had a sick hold over me.

A thud shook the building. They were taking a ram to the polished hardwood front door.

She drew back from me, breathless, those mesmerizing goddamned eyes of hers gazing at me so fondly again. "I'm sorry, Benji," she said as her finger tightened against the Glock's trigger.

I said, "So am I, Sonya." Then I shot her three times in the heart through the pocket of my duffel coat.

She looked right at me, startled. Then Sonya Posner didn't look at anything. She was dead before she slid to the floor next to our broken cocoa mugs.

I went upstairs and let Legs in.

CHAPTER EIGHT

I HAD TO BE TAKEN IN. After I answered everything that Legs Diamond asked me, we sat in the interview room together, drank bad coffee and listened to the tape I'd made of my conversation with the late Sonya Posner.

When the tape ended with those three shots from my Chief's Special, he turned it off and said, "Go home. Just do me a solid, okay? Don't try bitter on for size. It's not your style."

I wasn't charged with a crime. It was self-defense all of the way. The Glock 17 that Legs had found in Sonya's dead hand was indeed the same Glock 17 that she'd used to take out Bruce Weiner and Martine Price. And he had her confession on tape.

I happen to know he played that tape at One Police Plaza for Commissioner Feldman. But there was a lot more that I didn't know, such as what was going to happen to Jake Leetes and his Leetes Group. High-ranking prosecutors in the Manhattan's DA's office were debating whether my tape of Sonya would be admissible if charges were ever brought against him. And Legs told me that the NYPD's top forensic accountants were trying to find a money trail between the Leetes Group and Sonya

Posner. Me, I wasn't counting on it. You don't become Jake
Leetes by being stupid.

The murders of Bruce and Martine could be quietly put to
bed now. No need to involve the media. But that was the easy
part. Commissioner Feldman still had the page-one murders of
college basketball's brightest star and a heroic police detective
to account for. If he went public with an allegation that Charles
Willingham and Detective Fred Ayeroff had been gunned
down by the same contract killer who'd shot Bruce and Martine
then it would be damned hard to draw a line connecting Bruce,
Martine and Charles that didn't also go through Kathleen Kidd,
whose death the NYPD was officially calling a tragic suicide.
And Commissioner Feldman was no doubt under a huge
amount of pressure from the Kidd family to keep it that way.

The commissioner had his work cut out for him. It wouldn't
be easy to square the Kidd family's demand for secrecy with an
entire city's need for justice. But you don't become Dante Feldman by being stupid either. He'd figure out how to thread the
needle. If I were a betting man I'd have laid odds that my pal
Legs would be told to find himself a nice, handy fall guy. Like,
say, a three-time loser with known gang ties who'd gotten
himself busted for an unrelated shooting in the past twenty-
four hours. Said three-time loser would be persuaded to cop
to the Willingham and Ayeroff shootings in exchange for
special privileges when he was sent away. A deal would be
struck. A deal that would never, ever be made public. That's
just my bet.

But, like I said, I'm not a betting man.

THERE WERE THREE FUNERALS that stopped traffic in New York City in the days ahead. Kathleen Kidd, daughter of Ambassador Thomas Kidd and Eleanor Saltonstall Kidd, was laid to rest. So was Charles "In Charge" Willingham, the greatest basketball player to come out of the city's playgrounds in a generation. So was Detective Fred Ayeroff, who wasn't famous, but when a cop dies in the line of duty everyone from the mayor on down shows to pay their respects.

Sonya Posner was laid to rest, too, I imagine, but I don't know where. Or who took care of it. And I doubt that her funeral stopped any traffic.

Later that week, Bobby the K withdrew as a New York gubernatorial candidate due to "family reasons." Rumors were rampant in the tabloids and on the blogosphere that his wife, Meg Grayson Kidd, had moved out and taken their two kids with her. Apparently, the super couple was no longer a couple, super or otherwise. Apparently, she had caught Bobby cheating on her. Every paparazzi sleazeball in New York, professional and amateur alike, was desperate to snap a picture of Bobby's leggy, sultry girlfriend. As far as I knew, no such leggy, sultry girlfriend actually existed. But that didn't stop them from chasing after Bobby morning, noon and night. Nor did it stop three different bona fide hard-core porn stars from claiming that they'd been having torrid, kinky sex with Bobby. And possessed the explicit text messages to prove it. For all I knew, they did. And would make his life miserable for weeks to come.

Just not miserable enough. Because I had a sick certainty that when it was all over, Bobby the K would get away with what he did to his thirteen-year-old sister. Nobody was going

to lay a glove on him for raping Kathleen. Nobody could. And
Bobby wasn't the only one who was dirty. Nobody came out of
this clean. Not his mother. Not Mr. Classy Guy. Everyone was
dirty, including me. I sure felt dirty. I doubted whether I'd ever
feel clean again.

THE MORNING AFTER I SHOT Sonya Posner to death, I put on
my dark blue suit, got Dad's Brougham out of the garage and
drove out to Willoughby for Bruce Weiner's funeral. It was a
clear, icy-cold morning. I had to stop off at Brooks Brothers on
the way to buy myself a new duffel coat. It wasn't on sale. I had
to pay full retail, which pissed me off. But I didn't have a choice.
My old one had three bullet holes in it.

Bruce was buried at a small Jewish cemetery on the outskirts
of town. It was a traditional graveside service—topcoats,
gloves and yarmulkes required. He was laid to rest in a simple
pine box. Maybe forty people were there to bid Bruce goodbye.
His parents were not happy to see me among them—especially
with Sara glued to my side, her gloved hand clutching mine.
Bruce's roommate, Chris Warfield, was there. So were his high
school basketball teammates. And so was Charles Willingham's
grieving mother, Velma, whom I recognized from her picture
in the newspaper. She stood there, tall, straight and alone with
her grief. Spoke to no one. Only a couple of us knew who she
was and why she was there. But she was there. Velma Willingham was my idea of one classy lady.

After the ceremony Chris came over to me with tears in his
eyes and said how sorry he was about everything. The poor
guy still thought I was Bruce and Sara's cousin. I didn't bother

to set him straight. It wouldn't have made either of us feel any better.

Sara walked me to my car and kissed me softly on the cheek before she asked me that same question again: "Benji, can I come spend the night with you?"

She wore a long gray wool coat that day over a black dress and black stockings. Her hair was pulled back. There were dark smudges under her eyes. She looked extremely pale and serious.

I said, "Look, if you ever want to talk or cry or laugh I'm here for you, day or night. But when it comes to romance I'm someone who needs to take things a bit slower, understand?"

Her big brown eyes searched mine. "Not really."

"I don't want to rush into things. I've made that mistake. I don't want to make it again."

"You mean you've had your heart broken?"

"Smashed to pieces." I put my hands on her shoulders. "Are you going to be okay with this?"

Sara nodded. "Sure, Benji. You're blowing me off and you're trying to be nice about it because my brother's dead. I get it."

"No, you don't get it. I want to be sure, Sara. I want to be friends."

"I already have friends. I *love* you, Benji."

"Maybe you do. But I want you to be sure, too. You'll be going away to college in a few months. Meeting a lot of new guys. Chances are you'll forget all about me."

"I'll *never* forget about you," she protested. "How could I?"

"If you still feel the same a year from now we'll know it was the real thing. And we'll be glad we waited."

"Because it won't just be about boning?"

"Exactly. It'll be about *us*."

Sara thought this over carefully. "If I text you will you text me back?"

"Cross my heart."

"And you *swear* you'll never take off your bunny bracelet?"

"I *swear*."

Reluctantly, Sara gave me one last hug. Then started back toward her parents before she stopped and said, "Benji? . . ."

"Yes, Sara?"

"You're my soul mate, Benji."

"CLOSE THE DOOR, BUNNY." Mom was staring out her office window again, looking preoccupied and troubled. "We need to have a serious talk."

I felt myself tensing up. "Are you folding the agency?"

"Folding the agency?" She gaped at me surprise. "Hell, no. How would we earn a living?"

"We *don't* earn a living."

"Nobody likes a smart aleck. This is more in the line of a personal favor. Sit down, will you?"

"Sure thing, boss."

"And don't call me boss."

I sat down. Gus jumped into my lap and bumped my hand with his hard little head. I stroked him.

"It's a pretty big favor," Mom said uneasily, hands clasped before her on the desk. "Maybe the biggest I'll ever ask of you. If you say no, I'll understand. But I hope you won't."

"What is it, Mom?"

"I want you to wait until Sara Weiner has at least one year of college under her belt before you jump into the hay with her. She's a real cutie but she's only seventeen. And she's an emotional basket case right now."

"All taken care of," I assured her. "I let her down nice and easy. No need to say another word about it. So, listen, did a cash-paying client by any chance wander in while I was at Bruce's funeral? Because I would really like to keep busy."

"I *haven't* asked you for the favor yet," she said to me sternly.

"Sorry, Mom. What is it?"

"I want you to take Rita out to dinner tonight. Somewhere nice. Use the company credit card."

"Didn't we max that out?"

"It's all paid up, courtesy of the Aurora Group. I want the two of you to have a nice time. Drink a good bottle of wine. And then . . ."

"And then what, Mom?"

"I want you to spend the night with her."

I blinked at her in disbelief. "Are you serious?"

"Perfectly."

"Rita and me? That's crazy!"

"No, it's not. It makes a lot of sense, actually. I happen to know she's terribly fond of you."

"I'm fond of her, too. She's like a sister to me."

"Except she's not your sister. She's a healthy, beautiful, forty-two-year-old woman who is going through a hard time right now. I'll admit she's a few years older than you. But it turns out Sonya was, too, don't forget."

I lowered my eyes. "Trust me, I haven't."

"Rita's my best friend, Bunny, and I'm worried about her.

She has no life outside of the office. She's lonely, depressed and she absolutely will not let go of her feelings for that bum Clarence, who is never getting out of Sing Sing. Or at least I hope he isn't. I'm deathly afraid that she's about to do something foolish and self-destructive—like take up with one of his old running buddies. Some thug who'll only use her and hurt her. She needs a decent guy who cares about her. She needs *you*. And you need someone in your life right now, too. It'll be a good fit for both of you. You're already good friends, right?"

"But, Mom, you're talking about *Rita*."

She arched an eyebrow at me. "And your point is? . . ."

"She used to be my babysitter. She doesn't think of me that way."

"Yes, she does."

I peered at her suspiciously. "She actually told you that?"

"She didn't have to. I know her. When Sonya came sniffing around here with those cupcakes, Rita was so jealous she was ready to spit. And I noticed how upset *you* got when Rita was fussing over Bobby the K yesterday. You should have seen your little face. You looked positively savage."

"You're mistaken. That was gas."

"Don't lie to your mother. It's a sin."

"Mom, I don't think this is a good idea."

"Well, I do. Ask your friend Rita out to dinner. Just don't let on that I suggested it, okay?"

"Okay, Mom. Whatever you say."

"That's a good boy. You can go now, Bunny."

I returned to the outer office and slumped into my desk chair, sighing.

Lovely Rita eyed me sympathetically over her computer screen. "This was a bad one, wasn't it?"

"It was my first time, Rita. I never did that before."

"Banged a perp in the middle of a case?"

"Killed someone. Although, yeah, the other thing too."

"You really cared about that ferret, didn't you?"

"I had feelings for her. Strong feelings. And then I had to shoot her. And now it's all kind of bound up together in one humongous wad of emotional goo. I guess it'll take me a while to get over."

"Trust me, little lamb. They all do."

"Do you feel like knocking off early tonight? We could go get dinner somewhere."

"Why not? I'll see if Abby's free."

"I was thinking just the two of us."

Rita narrowed her gaze at me. "You and me?"

"Well, yeah. Is that a problem?"

"Did Abby put you up to this?"

"Put me up to what, Rita?"

"Asking me out."

"Why would she do something like that?"

"Because she thinks I'm a basket case."

"Are you?"

"That, little lamb, happens to be *my* business."

"Then again, it might be something we could talk about— over dinner."

Rita mulled it over long and hard before she said, "I don't think so."

"Okay, no prob. Except, Rita, we've known each other how long?"

"Forever."

"So why can't we go out to dinner together?"

"You mean like two friends?"

"Of course. What did you think I meant?"

"Nothing. Pay no attention to me. You're trying to forget about your troubles and I'm rattling on like a total idiot."

"So does that mean yes?"

"Benji, I don't think so."

I shrugged my shoulders. "Okay, whatever."

"After all, why do we need to go to some restaurant? We could pick up a pizza, head back to my place and . . ." Rita hesitated, glancing me shyly. "I could dance for you. I still have all of my moves. Would you like to see them?"